Dedica[illegible], I can thank everyone I hold dear in my life.

For my daughter, Meera. I hope you read this for I may not always be with you, but through my writing, I can.

"Everyone's story is worth a tell. And our stories unravel as distinctively as the prints on our fingers." - My father

Special mention to Catherine Sameh, my first Writing Professor, who made me feel I could write a book someday. And also to my Honors Program mentor at Rutgers, Steven Walker, who obliged to read my first manuscript many years ago.

Thank you to my husband, Achint, for being so supportive of my writing endeavors. And to family and friends for your endless support.

Cover design by Priyankar Gupta.
First developmental edit by Tara Khandelwal.

eBook ISBN: 978-93-5406-708-2
Paperback ISBN: 978-93-5406-898-0

CONTENTS

Kismat & Karma

By Sakshi Sharma

Section One: The Learnings of a Lifetime

The Number Nine

Kismat was born a month early, as if she was in a hurry to accomplish all the things she had set out to do. Her mother, Sita, was just visiting the clinic for a regular checkup when the nurse told her she was going into labor. The entire delivery took under an hour.

At the time of her birth, baby Kismat was blessed with a thick, black mane; the mark of a lioness. And in a world that was continually intimidated by the happiness of a woman, Kismat would come to find her unique roar - a laugh that was both hearty and loud.

Baby Kismat was underweight and had some yellowness in her skin which wore off as she gained sustenance on her mother's milk.

No matter how hard anyone tried, the mere act of being born meant causing tremendous pain to someone who was inextricably tied to you. But for the rest of her life, Kismat tried to cause as little discomfort to those she loved. The ways in which she would grow up to develop an even temper, a ruminative mind, and a benevolent heart; she was most certainly like her father, Ajay. In fact, she was through and through Ajay's *bitiya.* This is not to say that she did not love her mother or that she didn't imbibe any traits from her; just that Kismat's affinity for Ajay was ineffaceable.

Ajay and Sita Dharma had to quickly come up with a name for the sake of keeping hospital records so for the time being they named her *Minni* as it fit well with her brother's nickname, *Mannu*. The name really had no significance. This was true of her other relatives who were known by *Pappu, Guddi,* and variations of such syllables, till death do them part.

The grandma was fondly known as *Badi ammi* (elder mother). A stout and strong-headed woman, Ammi was never hesitant to speak her mind and told Ajay to feel fortunate that he was already blessed with a son beforehand. She was certain that since her daughter-in-law had picked two red bangles during the post-marriage festivities, she was guaranteed to receive two grandsons.

When Badi ammi held baby Kismat in her arms for the first time, Kismat gave, what appeared to be, a glimpse of a smile. If you try to mask uneasiness with a smile, you might come up with the same constipated look. Though Ammi would always favor her grandson, she planted a kiss on the baby cheeks, accepting one of the few defeats of her devout beliefs with Kismat's arrival in this world.

It was Ammi who named her granddaughter Kismat, meaning 'destiny' for she had an inkling that this little girl would not only change her own fate, but she had the power to change the fates of those around her too.

When Kismat was only three years old, she suffered a slight cut below her right eyebrow from an accident which luckily spared her eyes. Her father mentioned the accident to Kismat once, but she forgot about it and just grew to assume that the cut came as a package with her other birthmarks.

Besides the long mane, Kismat was born with two distinct black spots called *'til'*, one located on her chin and another one near the bottom of her right breast. As Kismat grew older, her aunts used to tell her that having a *'til'* on your face is a symbol of beauty. That theory sounded as comforting as saying that having a *'til'* near your breast makes you kind-hearted. A few years later, another *'til'* formed on the right side of her nose which gave the appearance of a nose-ring.

And then another one, on her back.

And one more on her left leg.

This was turning into a game of connect-the-dots. The same aunts also suggested, in jest, that since she had more *tils* on the left side of her body, she would be blessed with a daughter in her married life.

By the time she was a teenager, there were a total of nine *til-s* on various parts of her body.

The number nine was, coincidentally, very symbolic of her being.

The year of her birth was such that if one added up all the digits up to a single digit, it would produce the number nine.

The day of her birth had the same story.

The number, nine, as Kismat would come to realize, held a powerful significance over the course of her life.

~

Six months after little Kismat's arrival, Karma was born in a maternity clinic in the city of Kochi. After spending a few hours under observation, both mother and baby arrived home without further incident.

Baby Karma was too young to fathom anything at that point in her life but her life held many surprises.

She would be the first in her family to journey to a foreign land. And one day, her parents would arrange her marriage to a complete stranger.

But her decision to agree to the arranged union would be wholly colored by her love for her mother, Lakshmi.

Within a year, Karma gained a healthy weight, while Kismat remained considerably thin. It seemed as if Karma was already taking strength from Kismat that would prove to be instrumental down the road.

On the day of Karma's homecoming, her countenance was one to remember. With both eyebrows arched in intent, and lips pursed, it seemed as if baby Karma was deep in thought. Either that, or she had just smelled something pungent; perhaps it was the aroma of curry leaves and fruit pickles that filled her house.

Her parents lovingly gave her the nickname, *Rama,* for it rhymed with Karma and borrowed all its letters from her name. But more importantly, it paid reverence to the deity Ram.

Baby Rama was loved by all who played with her. Many relatives who graced their home would immediately start pointing out similarities between the baby and her parents; their responses depending greatly on which side of the family they were from. It was a guessing game using subtle clues that were only discernible to the person that made the connection.

"She has your nose Surya!"

"Look at her smile. She will grow up to be just like her mother."

In her first few months, there was this stillness about her that made Surya and Lakshmi worry whether their daughter's faculties were in place. Karma's grandma, Jyotimala, attributed Karma's quiet nature to her husband, Ram Sankara Iyer, who had peacefully passed away in their native village at ripe age of eighty.

The nickname, Rama, was also in fitting memory of Ram Iyer, Jyotimala thought.

"Even he would act like this all the time – very quiet and reserved. I think he has taken a new life in our little Rama. A reincarnation of his spirit."

Although Jyotimala meant well, she was always found to be speaking of a superstition here and there, likely imbibed from a saint she followed in her prime.

She would preach odd beliefs with the intent to maintain peace and rid evil at home but more often than not, they created more worry.

"Surya, why are you clipping your nails today?! It is Tuesday. You know that we do not use any sharp device on Tuesday."

"And make sure you don't wash your hair on Monday, Wednesday and Friday."

"Absolutely no carrots or potatoes to be cooked on Saturday and Sunday! Anything growing under the ground will attract negative spirits to our family."

"No meat on Thursdays!

No day of the week was spared. Initially, Surya and Lakshmi didn't give much thought to Jyotimala's mystical thoughts. But after their youngest daughter, Sati, nearly succumbed to a bout of typhoid at age two, they started adhering to Jyotimala's requests, thinking it was bettering their destiny.

On one occasion, Lakshmi was leaving to run some errands when Jyotimala proclaimed, *"Lakshmi, don't look at the sky today. It's going to be a full moon. A bad omen."*

A friend greeted Lakshmi near a fruit vendor's cart, and Lakshmi, who had pulled the *pallu* of her sari over her head, whispered a hurried response and sprinted home.

Karma's quiet demeanor and beaming face would make other mothers envious of what she was fed that she had such a peaceful aura about her. However, as soon as she commenced school, she changed into a vivacious spirit, dismissing Jyotimala's first supposition about harboring her late husband's spirit.

But this was only a start for Karma who would dispel beliefs and choose a life of reason.

Karma would excel academically; her wit winning her scholarships and admirers down the road. But those successes would not prepare her for a loss, so tremendous, that it would completely puncture her mind.

And in her darkest hour, on the battlefield of her warring thoughts, she would meet the soul who would change everything she knew.

Every moment, there were thousands of other babies being born with their unique fates intact.

But Kismat and Karma would evince that destiny and actions do not supersede one another, but are ever leveled in their power to alter the course of our lives.

Hiccups in a New Land

Surya Iyer could stomach the occasional trip out of town, but his heart would always bring him back to the comfort and serenity of his home in Kochi. He was employed with a government bank while his wife, Lakshmi, worked as a volunteer from time to time, in places like the local school or temple.

The two-job routine helped run the household not from a monetary standpoint because Lakshmi was unpaid, but more so because Lakshmi was busy and if both spouses are occupied, the marriage is likely to work.

Whilst many middle-class South Indians were enamoring themselves with the ideals of the West and wished to settle abroad, the Iyers were content as and how they were.

On this account, Karma did not get the chance to set foot outside of India in her elementary years, but she did befriend a great number of books and envisioned herself as having traveled for miles and miles, being born and reborn in the molds of those characters.

Since her school library was limited in its reserves of fiction, Karma would source her literature from roadside sellers at Kochi's Broadway *bazaar,* a flea market brimming with stalls of clothing, spices and fresh fish.

Some of the book sellers would even go as far as putting multicolored bangles and *bindis* on display to lure the women coming out from a sari or shoe store and then garner their attention with beauty magazines and novels with teasing Mills and Boon covers.

In her teens, Karma enjoyed the mystery of Nancy Drew

and the magic of Hermoine Granger. From the many books she read, the tales enraptured her so much that she was quick to detach herself from the outside world and venture off to new towns and cities. Reading gave her the power to enjoy the peculiar liberties and destinies of folks that she otherwise would have never had the chance to meet.

Over time, she started feeling a bit of disconnect on stories of Western authors essaying their upbringing in suburban neighborhoods with neatly manicured lawns, cul-de-sacs, and round-the-clock tap water.

So she began incorporating more authors of her clan, the likes of Amitav Ghosh and Anita Desai in her literary diet, whose storytelling described the subtlety of growing up with scarcity in India.

Karma would employ quotes to win arguments in the house. Neither Surya nor Lakshmi had such an affinity for literature. So naturally, Surya was stumped when his teenage daughter asked him why famous authors limited their words of wisdom for "man" and "his" needs, as a means to encompass all of humanity, but ignored the female pronouns.

She assured herself that such a default would never become ingrained in her words, written or spoken.

Karma's younger sister, Sati, was the more doted one, and Karma knew that it was one lost battle to begin with. Sati would always ask for new frocks and dolls. Apart from books, Karma seldom sought joy from other means; Surya's collection of old films being the only exception. Her mother would be so busy in chores that she would take for granted how her elder one didn't bother much with material demands.

Karma saw how Lakshmi would tire from her daily routine and helped her in every occasion - from carrying the bags of vegetables, to washing the stainless steel utensils, and even setting the laundered clothes to dry in their open verandah in the heat of Kochi's year long summer.

Lakshmi was entirely devoted to two things - her faith and her family. She had come from a moderately wealthy background and was accustomed to having a full-time help in her maternal home. In her new arrangement after marriage, she managed all the essentials within their limited budget, and never once made her husband feel as if it was not enough. Despite only having a Bachelors qualification, she mastered many aspects of planning and accounting at home.

The Iyer household was frequented by Surya's friends and colleagues. Many of those families brought kids who were studying abroad, or hoped to at some point in their lives. When the young Karma was not busy devouring her mother's delicious *payasam* and chutneys with *appam*, she would go into the living room and start chatting with her father's friends.

"Uncle, why did you leave our country for London? What is there so special about London that you can't find here?"

"Sorry Venky, she is just curious you see," said the slightly embarrassed Surya.

"My dear, London is very developed and there are a lot of opportunities there which are difficult to find in India."

"Why?" asked Karma.

"Because there are too many people here and the smart ones find something better outside," continued Venky.

Karma pestered on.

"But do they have *rasam* and coconut trees over there like we have in Kerala?"

"No, but they have lots of museums. And parks. And big libraries with all the books you can ever find. You can come to London and see them for yourself."

"Really?! Acha, can I go?"

"If you do well in school, you will be able to go anywhere

you want. How does that sound?"
Karma smiled enthusiastically.

Surya went back to discussing Indian politics with his friend when Karma interrupted them again.
"One more thing Acha."
"What is it Rama?"
"Even if I go, I will always come back to you. Do you know why?"
"Why?" asked Surya.
"Because no place will never have the sun and warmth like I find here with you in Kochi."
Uncle Venky smiled uncomfortably.

Moments later, Lakshmi came in to announce that dinner was ready. Surya, who was beaming within much like the namesake sun, would recollect his daughter's wise words on many an occasion when his buddies would talk of settling abroad.

Lakshmi made it a point to take her daughters to the temple every week. They would fold their hands in front of a pair of idols, one of whom had a peacock feather on his hair. Together, they would recite a small chant that Lakshmi taught them.
"Amma, your name is that of a goddess, right?" Karma asked inquisitively.
Lakshmi nodded as she took the vermillion powder from the temple's *thali* and applied it to the middle parting of her hair and then on the forehead of her two daughters.
"So, why must we come to a temple? We can just worship you at home."
Lakshmi smiled.
"Just think of us visiting the temple as our bonding time as mommy and daughter."
Karma nodded her head.

As her two daughters helped Lakshmi distribute home-made coconut ladoos to the less fortunate waiting outside, Lakshmi felt relieved that she didn't have to convince her rational child any further.

~

Kismat's grandfather, Premchand Dharma, was the first man in his family of eight siblings to make the bold move to migrate from his village in Hamirpur to the capital, Delhi.

Consequently, his son, Ajay Dharma, had the opportunities of city life to realize his dreams of becoming a qualified engineer. Premchand's hard work manifested into manifold opportunities for his son. And Ajay's indomitable spirit to rise from the lower middle class and achieve a new foothold meant that his sacrifices multiplied into even more privilege for his own children. Every generation was reaping and sowing for the next.

Premchand was employed as a tax revenue officer in Central Delhi. His family transportation was the one scooter that miraculously fit four people at once. Little Ajay would stand at the front, and Badi ammi would sit in the rear, holding her husband tightly with one arm and Ajay's baby sister in the other.

Each time the scooter needed a jump-start, Premchand would kick the scooter on the side and little Ajay would push from behind. The scooter would wake up with a loud clank and Ajay would come running like a bolt of lightning and set himself in the front, as Ammi would be riding pillion.

In her home in Delhi, there is only one framed picture of Ajay as a young boy. He is seated in the center, Premchand to the left and Badi ammi to the right, who was then pregnant with her second child.

Badi ammi was born in present-day city of Lahore and

moved to India during the partition. Ammi's father fled back to Lahore during the riots to bring back some of his relatives and save his *dukaan*. His wife begged him not to go and received his dead body in return. So Kismat's great grandmother, all of twenty years at the time, raised the three year old Ammi by herself.

Badi ammi's narration of her mother's tribulations made Kismat want to learn more the stories of her female ancestors, who had sacrificed and survived, but seldom made the cut of being known. Her maternal grandmother (*Nani*) also recounted tales of her family hiding in their rooms for shelter, from fear of air-raids during the 1971 war with Pakistan. Her Nani also told her that the partition sowed its seeds from the reign of the monarchs who had weakened India's immunity - her unity. Ammi's and Nani's stories were what Kismat was raised on and her vivid memory of an Independent India to this day, was mostly on account of those narrations.

Each morning, Badi ammi would start off her day with her long line of prayers to the permutations of *devis* and *devtas*. Every nook and corner of the house would be filled with the sound of her voice dovetailing with the ringing of the brass bell. It was a harmonizing sound, Ammi's 'Om' mingling effortlessly with the same vibrations that seemed to be emanating from the bell. Kismat's ears were conditioned to hearing her Ammi sing praises for Ram, Shiva and Hanuman. As a result, she had memorized quite a bit of their holy chants.

The Dharma family's most frequents trips were to their ancestral abode in Hamirpur, nestled in fields of corn and wheat. Kismat had fond memories of napping in the open roof with her cousins, with the clusters of stars serving as their nighttime blanket. Unlike the artifice of alarms to manage their circadian clocks in the City, crowing roosters would succeed in awakening them in the wee hours of the morning.

Her home was one of the few '*pucca*' constructions in the entire village. Most villagers maintained a shed for domesticated cows and goats and used a central hand pump for their water supply. Kismat was delighted by simple sights of hens strolling on semi-paved paths and crows conveniently finding transport on the backs of bullocks, even as house flies hovered over their manure.

With the aid of a local *halwai*, Ajay would organize a 'langar prasad' (holy feast) in their spacious verandah and invite every villager to relish a main course of traditional *khatti dal* (sweet and sour dal), *maahni, boondi khatta, and bhaat* (rice). Whether it was the happy occasion of *janeu* (sacred thread) for her brother, Dhananjay, or the "*chhat*" puja to commemorate Kismat's late grandfather – serving food to others was an integral part of the Dharma family mores.

To reach Himachal, the Dharmas and extended relatives would shuttle in their minivans and embark on a non-stop drive. The journey up the mountains consisted of dizzying roads and daunting turns wherein trucks wouldn't hesitate to overtake other trucks twice their size; like an underdog challenging his hallway bully.

The family would make stops to every shrine, the likes of Chintpurni and Chamunda Devi, along the way. Kismat did not understand all this temple hopping business, as if skipping on any one holy site would somehow diminish their blessings.

But she did enjoy the routine stops for coconut water and tasty apples from roadside vendors. In one such instance, they stopped to buy roasted peanuts. Kismat was in awe of how the seller calmly took their order and remained unperturbed by a fly that had settled near his eye. A tribe of monkeys were in the vicinity of their car, waiting for any morsel to make its way to them. Badi ammi folded her hands in prayer.

"These monkeys are a manifestation of Lord Hanuman. Revere them and they will protect you."

Of course, Badi ammi conveniently forgot the time in Vrindavan, when a mean *langur* stole her glasses as she was making her way up the temple staircase.

Of all the scenic spots in her native state, Kismat's favorite was Dharamshala, home of exiled Tenzin Gyatso, the 14th Dalai Lama. At Naddi point, she had even adorned the traditional Himachali garb and silver plated jewellery, the photo of which was later framed in her room. While hiking up to Triund, Kismat was mesmerized by the sight of the lush Kangra valleys in the embrace of the Dhauladhar mountain range.

The snowcapped mountains made her wonder about the kind of peaks and lows she'd have to traverse in her own life.

Her parents' marriage had been fixed by a brahmin priest, who ironically, was on the verge of a divorce. The *pandit* studied their birth charts and matched their *kundalis*, a system as nebulous as using outer beauty to determine the prowess of a student.

Ammi and Premchand were bent on receiving grandchildren soon after the marriage ties were knot, but this did not deter Sita from continuing her practice at her old clinic. Two months into their marriage, Sita's Homeopathic pills helped Ajay recover from his persistent tonsillitis and avoid expensive tonsil surgery. His recovery was an auspice that even if other aspects of their life were in a bit of a storm, their marriage would remain strong enough to weather it.

Ajay was the Midas of the family, for he had the golden touch to turn anything broken into brand new. He could effortlessly install a new TV, mend the grid during times of a short circuit, and even repair gadgets and leaks. Ajay's biggest satisfaction from spending all that energy to keep the appliances up and running was the money he had saved from not hiring an outsider. Kismat would often joke with her father, “Excuse me sir, we are only paying you a hundred rupees for this job. Deal or no deal?” Ajay would play along just as well.

“Ok deal. But I'll do it for free if you hand me that monkey-wrench over there.”

Ajay had seen Premchand suffer the hardships that came with earning a decent wage in Delhi. After his marriage to Sita and working through two poorly paying jobs, he received a job offer to change the course of not only his own destiny, but that of his family too. In a year, he was promoted and asked to relocate to the States. Kismat was soon going to get a taste of the alluring American dream.

When the Dharmas went on holiday in India, it gave them a temporary change from their routines. But moving abroad meant handing over their life to a new country. Every city and country has its share of upheavals and joys. But when you stay in one place, they become the wins and battles you are willing to choose.

The person who was most overjoyed at hearing the news of the US offer was Ajay himself. Sita was most disappointed as she never fancied settling down in a foreign land to begin with. As for the kids, the move translated to fewer exams, more outdoor pursuits, and replacing their bathroom canister with toilet paper.

Sita was too attached to her Indian home and parents. Her motion to stay in India fell on deaf ears as Ajay knew that this was an opportunity he would seldom see again.

Ajay was right in his own regard, as Sita was in hers. The opportunities that appear enticing today may not always feel as gratifying later in life. However, a luxury that seems ordinary today comes from decades of veiled sacrifices that generations ahead of us may not fully comprehend.

By the time Kismat reached second grade, the Dharmas shifted base to America.

Kismat's history lessons shifted from *Jana Gana Mana* and India's struggles for independence to the Star-Spangled Banner and the Civil War. School holidays would be spent viewing Fourth of July fireworks and Macy's parades and ringing doorbells for candy in animal Halloween costumes.

Back in Delhi, there were gazetted holidays for people of all faiths to celebrate - Diwali, Eid, and Christmas. This is what made India so unique, her mother would tell her.

In their new apartment in the States, Holi and Diwali festivities were quieter and celebrated by applying a simple '*gulal*' (colored powder), lighting brass *diyas* in the prayer room, and feasting within the four walls of their humble apartment. On Sita's insistence, Kismat mailed a small packet of rice, vermillion powder, and *rakhi* threads to her cousins within the first year of moving, but that enthusiasm died quickly thereafter.

Kismat experienced her own hiccups of adjusting in a new land. The first hiccup came when Sita packed her home-cooked bhindi (okra) and chapatti in her lunch box. The hiccup emerged, not so much from eating her food, but from knowing that she was the only Indian at her table and the only kid who wasn't eating pizza, hamburger, or mac & cheese.

There were some less than welcome stares at her.

Perhaps it was the sight of the slimy green vegetable, she thought.

On weekend trips to the local supermarket, Kismat began adding boxes of Go-gurts, Pop-Tarts, and Frozen pizza bites into their shopping cart.

And if that didn't suffice, her love for start-spangled popsicles from ice cream trucks surely paved the way for her assimilation into the American culture. Still, her love for Maggi and the sweet and sour balls of Fatafat candy remained a constant.

Sita, whose only outings consisted of such shopping excursions to Shop-rite and the Indian market in Jersey City, was dismayed by the addition of all the junk food in her home. Despite Ajay's insistence, she refused to have any packets of frozen *paranthas* and microwaveable curries make its way into her kitchen.

The most notable hiccup for Kismat came in third grade when the teacher held a spelling bee competition during the English period that quickly spilled into recess. One by one, all the students lined up for their word to spell and every wrong letter cost them their chance to move forward.

Ultimately, there were only two students left.

Kismat and a boy named Doug.

Doug made a folly.

It was now up to Kismat to win the competition if she answered the last and final word correctly.

The word was 'Connecticut.' The northeastern state is a tricky one to spell for the second "c" is silent.

She assumed she was spelling the word "connect" and added the rest as it sounded. When the teacher handed her a star ribbon for being correct, Doug was irked by her win and made her privy to his anger at recess.

"Go back to your tribe, you Indian."

Ironically, Columbus Day was right around the corner; a national holiday celebrated in the name of a man who terrorized an entire sect of the indigenous people and named them 'Indians' because he was certain his ship had reached India.

Kismat couldn't think of a fitting response to Doug for she was too young and Doug could be forgiven for his own naivety. But years later, she wished she had said something along the lines of, "You have the wrong Indian in mind. And if I really was that kind of an Indian, I should be telling you to go back."

Doug reminded Kismat of her third grade English teacher, Mrs. Dudsak. Kismat was walking to class after recess when she overheard Mrs. Dudsak making fun of her name in the company of another lady teacher.

Kismat found it rather odd that Mrs. Dudsak, having an equally strange name, would mispronounce hers when she could say other difficult surnames like Wachowski and Reichart with ease.

Folks like Doug and Mrs. Dudsak made her feel like she didn't belong; not only in that school, or town, but in that entire country for that matter.

Still, Kismat believed that her elementary school years were quite possibly her favorite years. She won first prize in the school's jump-roping competition, aced quizzes with her Chinese friend/study partner, Josephine Young, and by the end of the year, even braved writing a handwritten, albeit anonymous, letter to her Hispanic school crush, Ernesto.

At Kismat's last summer camp before moving into senior school, there was one nature activity that stood out from the rest. As soon as breakfast was over and all the students had completed their camp chores, a big round bell was rung three times signaling the start of a new challenge. A group of ten students including Kismat were taken to an open ground inside a forest.

A young man with a blue fishing hat introduced himself as the instructor. He told the students that all they had to do was to find a rather odd looking twig in a demarcated area of the forest. The group was allotted ten minutes to complete the task. The first person to find the twig would receive a generous prize.

The instructor showed everyone what the twig looked like. He waited for a few minutes so the students could imprint the image of it on their minds. Immediately thereafter, he flung it somewhere in the area, specially marked by yellow tape, that was filled with hundreds of other twigs.

The exercise was literally like finding a needle in a twig-stack. The students went berserk to get their hands on the twig first. As they stepped into the box, they tried to zoom in to every twig in sight, hoping they wouldn't pop their eyes out in the process.

“Remember kids, it is very important that you listen to me,” whilst pointing to his left ear.

“The twig is in this area somewhere – keep looking -- and the first one to find it will win the prize!” and he repeated this monologue a few times, each time pointing to his ear.

With little time left on hand, the instructor's words felt like an annoying distraction. They kept their focus on the ground to find the missing twig. Some collided into each other, increasing the pace and tension of the challenge. The whole exercise turned into a rat race of who would come first.

Different students employed different tactics, one even went to the extent of sniffing the wood but no one could locate the mystery twig. When the instructor repeated his message a third time, that's when Kismat noticed something she hadn't noticed before. At first, she thought she was mistaken. She stopped searching, took a closer look and confirmed her original suspicion.

The instructor was inside the area with them. He had never thrown that twig on the ground. The bloody twig was hiding behind the flap of his ear all along!

Having solved the mystery, Kismat ran up to him and whispered the answer in his ear. Pleased to see that someone had finally paid attention, he ended the game. The students accepted their mistake by looking at each other with embarrassed smiles.

The instructor finished the activity with a memorable moral.

“It is great that some of you worked really hard to get to the end goal but you will find that in life, it is not enough that you work harder than the rest. You must also work smarter."

A trite moral, but it resonated deeply with Kismat.

Fifth grade was coming to a close. Kismat relished all four years at Lincoln Elementary. She was excited to commence sixth grade at Dhananjay's middle school now, also fittingly named after another American President, Woodrow Wilson.

Dhananjay would often bring his American friends to play rounds of PlayStation. Kismat was only allowed to call him 'Jay' around them, and keep her chatter to a minimum. In between their games, she would microwave Hot Pockets, and serve them supermarket Swiss rolls.

Gradually his friends, all three in total, warmed up to her and let her play Metal Gear Solid and Grand Theft Auto as they gulped their snacks down with colorful, fizzy drinks.

Dhananjay would irk at any instance Sita would wear *salwar kameez* around his friends, or bring samosa and jalebi from Rajbhog Sweets, and worst of all, call him by his full name.

But Sita didn't relent. She didn't want Dhananjay to become too "Americanized" in the fear that he would never return to India.

Both children were a major source of liveliness for Sita in her lonely, rented abode, but Dhananjay would soon become the reason why the Dharmas would decide to move back to India.

While some of the cooler kids were being invited to swimming pool parties and trips to the Jersey shore, Kismat received no such invitation. She made plans for Six Flags with her family and invited Josephine to her house to work on their summer projects.

Just as the two of them had just exchanged their 'byes' for the day, a boy from another class approached her.

A boy she had never spoken to before.

"Hey! I want you to be my girlfriend."

His tone was rather aggressive. It was clear that he didn't care about her choice in the matter.

A nervous sweat formed on her forehead. The boy, on the other hand, didn't budge, his eyes steady on hers.

Finally Kismat said she would think about it, buying some time to escape. At that point, the boy let her go, hoping she would accept the proposal set forth to her.

She had to only avoid him for a few more days till school was over, she thought.

Kismat pretended as if the odd conversation never occurred in the first place, until the same boy asked her again two days later.

This time he was adamant for an answer.

Panicking, she said "No."

The boy, not expecting rejection, asked her to reconsider.

"No" wasn't even an option, it seemed.

Kismat turned around, making sure he wasn't following her. She ran away from his line of sight and felt relieved to having survived the day.

Later that evening, she confided in her friend, Aisha, who stayed in the same neighborhood.

Aisha informed her that this African-American boy had an elder brother from the neighboring school and he was notorious for having a gang of friends who were up to no good. Aisha was certain of this because her own brother went to that school and mentioned about their misdeeds, particularly against those they considered 'outsiders.'

As she lay awake in her bed, she wondered if she should've been so abrupt in her answer to the boy.

It was nearly midnight now and she couldn't fall asleep. Quietly, she paid a visit to the prayer room in her house, a makeshift area adjacent to her parent's room and the main staircase, where an old closet used to be. Every morning before heading out to work, Ajay lit a cotton wick inside the brass diya and took the blessings of the idols by touching their feet.

She saw idols of deities standing in front of her. She couldn't place their names in her head.

Was he Ram? Was she Goddess Durga? Hanuman and Ganesha had distinctive animal avatars that were easy to identify. Kismat folded her hands in Namaste, following the custom of her Indian mores. She made a silent plea to all of them to make everything okay.

Hoping all would ease out itself, Kismat decided to keep hush on the matter.

A day later, Kismat's brother, Dhananjay, came home battered and bruised. He was playing in the neighborhood park with his friends. As he was cycling back home, a group of teenage boys ganged up on him from every corner. Dhananjay was only thirteen years old and much smaller in size compared to those seventeen-year olds. Needless to say, those teenagers were accomplices of the boy Kismat had rejected.

Ajay and Sita failed to understand what could have been the cause of this battery on their son.

That night when Dhananjay was being bandaged in the hospital, Kismat could no longer remain silent.

She walked over to Ajay and pleaded, "Papa, I don't want to go to school here anymore."

"Don't worry dear…you will be joining a new school now."

"No, I meant I don't want to go to school here...in the States."

The memory of her brother standing in the doorstep, bleeding and scared; and his bicycle, broken as badly as him, shattered her perception of falling in love with a man.

The Shadows of the Past

In our darkness and light, we are all connected. Even the shadow, an integral reminder of our physical selves, needs light.

After Kismat's grandfather, Premchand, had passed away from a prolonged bout of throat cancer, Badi ammi did not bother to maintain any relations with her husband's side of the family. Many of her husband's nephews had taken monetary support from Premchand to find a footing in the city, but disappeared when Premchand fell ill.

These nephews used to visit their home for months at a stretch and Badi ammi would prepare their favorite meals from scratch, wash their clothes in the humid heat, and iron their shirts and handkerchiefs without any complaints. Decades later, when she chanced to meet them at a wedding, or a funeral, she cursed them for all the toil that nearly broke her back.

Ammi was always abrupt in her conversations with her daughter-in-law. She said things to her that, in isolation, sounded disparaging. But in context of Ammi's limited schooling, and an early marriage into a home of five brothers and immense household chores; her tone seemed rather rational, given that it was inherited from the strictness of her own mother-in-law.

Badi ammi confided her feelings to her daughter, but never to her daughter-in-law.

Sita did not mind this, for their bond was always a formal one. But Sita did mind when Badi ammi praised her son and exhorted him to remain in the States so he could make more money. On the other hand, she remarked on how her daughter-in-law had practically abandoned her, particularly in front of Sita's kin.

When Sita became aware of this commentary from her sisters, she informed Ajay, who remained unfazed.

Though he did not disclose this to Sita, one of his primary motivations to move to the States was to lessen the friction between his mother and wife. Their dysfunctional relationship affected the entire household, to the extent that even Kismat and Dhananjay would have to serve as messengers between the two ladies, as they refused to speak to each other for days at a stretch.

Kismat would bury her head in her books the moment she would hear them arguing in and around the kitchen. She hated to take sides when the issues were as petty as who left the *ghee* jar in the wrong spot, and who spilled turmeric on the granite tabletop, or added too much salt in the dal.

The Dharma dysfunctionality could not have been one-sided, of this she was sure. But she was certain that some of it was spilling in her veins too.

With all the pedantic fault-finding Badi Ammi would do for every member of the Dharma household, and all the little fights that ensued because of it, Kismat was certain she didn't want to turn out that way. Ammi was stingy in paying tips or compliments to everyone, whether it was the neighborhood sweeper or her own grandchildren. Criticizing others was Ammi's way of getting work done in the house.

Ajay, on the other end, did not inherit his mother's style. He was a man of few words, but he always told Kismat to find the positive in others, as hard as that seemed. His means of getting work done was to ensure his team was paid overtime at work, and completing all his chores at home, so he could set an example for his kids. He wished every single person in his address book on their birthdays and anniversaries, even if he didn't like them that much.

In time, Kismat's personality was more tempered by Ajay's way of dealing with people. And like Ajay, she would try to remind people of their strengths; this easing some of her own family's frictions.

Ajay was extremely proud to school his kids in the States, but after the attack on his son, he requested for a transfer.

Seeing as his firm needed a Director to manage the India business, Ajay was approved for the relocation, albeit a temporary one, to Delhi.

Sita worked the hardest to ensure everything was in order; that their belongings were neatly packed, the schools provided necessary certificates, and the apartment was as spotless as they first entered it, so the landlord would not deduct any security.

She managed all this with ease, for in her heart she knew she was finally getting the chance to return to her homeland.

Four years in a foreign land had made Kismat forget most of her mother tongue. While she enjoyed an occasional Bollywood film and could grasp some of their dialogues, she was keener to watch reruns of Fresh Prince of Bel-air and Full House on TV instead. Josephine Young and Kismat remained penpals for a year before they lost touch.

Badi ammi was disappointed to see that her grandchildren favored boxed cereal from the supermarket over her homemade butter and sweet vermicelli seviyan. And she was even more disappointed that they didn't partake in any of the *aartis* in the morning, a ritual she had sowed before the kids had left for the States.

Ammi squarely blamed her daughter-in-law for all the *phoren-ness* in her grandchildren. But when Dhananjay touched an elder guest's feet or Kismat could recall the entire *Gayatri Mantra*, albeit in an accent, Badi ammi could not help feel embarrassed.

Just a month into their return to India, Ajay enrolled his children in a private school in south Delhi. Kismat assumed it was solely on account of her stellar entrance test results, only to find out that her father was forced to use his contacts to secure the admission.

This was just one of many culture shocks Delhi had welcomed Kismat back with.

The first shock occurred when Kismat took her first auto ride back with her mother. The *autowala* took a sharp U-turn and missed bumping into the buttocks of a security guard. Hapless pedestrians waiting to cross the road simply walked in groups and raised their palms, similar to an elderly's man *aashirwad*. Lanes, as Kismat came to understand, were imaginary concepts in the mind of an Indian driver.

The day Kismat was born in Delhi, a remnant of the city had also seeped into her veins. Delhi had the uncanny ability to make any of her residents fall in and out of love with her at her own whims. Where a foreigner may conflate her diverse savories and cuisines as 'curries', only a local could aptly describe Delhi's cultural subtleties. And Kismat could entail a few of these herself -- her delicious kebab and *chaat* havens, her decorated avatar during Durga Puja and Diwali festivals, her boisterous bazaars, and her kite dotted skies signaling Independence Day, and the same skies that had hints of blue during the monsoons; all these were some of Delhi's prime attractions.

But Delhi also had her share of aversions – it was a city where having access to hot, running water was deemed a luxury; where getting a child admitted into a good school was as burdensome as the weight of textbooks inside that student's backpack; where bargaining was a birthright, and *jogad*, a necessary shortcut to cope with scarcity.

The Dharmas had returned to Delhi's warm embrace, but even in their absence, the traffic horns had continued to toot, the *kabadiwalas* had made their ceremonial rounds to yell for junk, and the crowds relentlessly surged towards DTC buses and metro.

It didn't matter if the folks born on her soil chose to settle like cobwebs in the byroads of Chawdi Bazaar or moved abroad to the suburbs of California's Bay. Like a devoted mother, Delhi would always receive her children with the same nostalgic charm and fondness they would remember her with.

~

Though Karma was an avid reader, she was never a confident speaker. Whatever little she spoke was punctuated with a whole lot of stuttering and stammering.

The stammering was inherited from her father, Surya, who would fumble over a word, every now and then, in particular, the ones beginning with "v" and "w" like water and vow.

Surya put forth a very simple solution to this problem. He would ask Karma to wake up every morning and read aloud any article of her choice in the morning newspaper. Whenever Karma would face difficulty with a word, he would ask her to try again and again until she finally succeeded in pronouncing everything neatly, in one go. This morning ritual sowed its rewards after several years of practice. Karma even participated in a debate competition for the first time in ninth grade. Standing on a podium to speak in front of a large group of people, including one's peers, can be nerve wracking for any adult, let alone a teenager. Though Karma didn't win any award, she battled a deep-seated fear and that was enough.

Over time, Karma had acquired the rare confidence to acquaint herself with any new person, man or woman. And when the time would be right, she was destined to meet a man, whose kind heart and handsomeness would not only momentarily reprise some of her stammering, but make her fall in love with him, one enunciated syllable at a time.

Her grandmother, Jyotimala, had a repository of remedies up her sleeve. It was like opening an ancient book of magic whenever she would introduce a cure, ranging from the common turmeric and black pepper mixture to cope with common colds and stomach ailments to the uncommonly weird, "*rub some of my joint pain oil on your nostrils because it'll cure headaches too.*"

Unlike Lakshmi and Surya, Karma didn't pay heed to any of her grandma's odd beliefs. And though Jyotimala showed minimal, outwardly affection towards Karma, she loved her the most.

The day her bed sheets showed the first streaks of crimson, Karma was certain she was going to die. She didn't tell anyone about her period the whole day, until Jyotimala sensed that something was amiss about her granddaughter. Lakshmi gave her a few pieces of her ordinary napkins, but it was ultimately Jyotimala who gave her a hot water bag to deal with the pain and accompanied her to the chemist where she could purchase her first pack of modern-age napkins, the kind with adhesive and wings.

A few girls in school would tease Karma about her oily, braided hair; a tactic she'd employ to camouflage her dandruff, but Karma continued to follow her *modus operandi* of avoiding the mirror; focusing on her schoolwork instead. Seeing her grand-daughter slowly maturing into a young lady, Jyotimala offered some tips that her own mother once shared with her, continuing the tradition of passing down the treasure trove of the Iyer family.

Despite being in her seventies, Jyotimala never had a single strand of white in her hair. The first thing she prepared for Karma was an orange paste to apply on her skin to balance her oiliness. Next, she whisked together a whitish paste to apply separately on her hair. The orange colored concoction was still tolerable, but Karma was apprehensive of the hair mask smelling of raw onions and egg batter. Jyotimala assured her that the pungent smell would vanish after she took a bath. And she was right.

Jyotimala made the special mixture every weekend. After the first two tries, Karma didn't notice any difference. That is when Jyotimala shared her best secret for last -- the beauty of patience. In time, Karma's dark carmel colored skin started to glow like her grandmother's and her hair had the lustrous shine of her mother, Lakshmi.

In school, economics was Karma's favorite subject and Lila Ma'am, her favorite teacher.

Lila Ma'am was probably in her late thirties, but her orange hair, as a result of years of henna application, made her appear older and even more sagacious. Her hair was always braided, and her saris were always made of silk, but it was her big, red *bindi* that brought back all the attention to her face.

It was Lila Ma'am who had first informed Karma about the reputed Economics program at Darwick University in London. Only ten students from India were accepted to the two year accelerated program each year. While Karma was content in her Bharatanatyam classes and volunteering with her mother, there was a part of her that wanted to be challenged academically.

Seeing Karma's potential, Lila convinced her to at least think about applying to Darwick. Yet, Karma remained firm on her decision to stay in her home state.

Lila Ma'am approached her on a rainy afternoon after school.

"Karma, ask your parents to meet me tomorrow."

They moved under the shelter of the school premises as the drizzle turned into a downpour.

"Sorry Ma'am, I couldn't hear you."

"I would like to meet your parents.... " and when Karma could not fathom a response, she quipped,

"Did I scare you?"

"Uh...yes Ma'am," Karma whispered.

"All this *Yes ma'am* and *Yes Sir* business even after the British left us. And the irony that I want to send you to London for college."

Lila Ma'am laughed heartily for a few moments before continuing.

"You've scored full marks in your final paper. I just want to meet the lovely people who raised you. Would that be ok?"

"Yes, of course!"

"Also, I don't tell this to many of my students but you are going to find many admirers down the road," Ma'am added smilingly.

"I've taught many classes and I can easily tell these kinds of things – who's paying attention to who in class. It's all very noticeable in the corner of a teacher's eyes."

Amidst the humdrum of exams and homework, there were many students in Karma's school who were sharing a unique species of notes - love notes.

Lila Ma'am must have been a psychic because sure enough, Karma was approached by several suitors towards the end of the school year. But Karma didn't let any of this attention get to her head.

Up until ninth grade, Karma's closest friends were members of the opposite sex; particularly those had good grades and had the same taste in books as her.

A year later, her circle changed dramatically.

Not only did she despise the entire notion of befriending a boy, but evaded even the slightest attention from them. Her fear and self-control on the matter didn't just arise from being plain different to boys.

It stemmed from an incident that Karma hoped she could erase from the depths of her memory.

Karma was returning home after finishing her hourly Bharatanatyam class at the *kala kendram* which was several blocks away from her house. It was unusually humid that day. She waited at the Mundamavalli bus stop, as she would usually do after class.

It was ten minutes past six.

Her bus was late again.

There was a fruit seller and an auto rickshaw stand on the other side of the street but pedestrians were few and far in between.

Karma decided to walk the rest of the way home.

Two men, that looked to be in their mid-thirties, appeared to be following her.

They were mumbling something to each other; their words incomprehensible. The first man brushed his shoulder by her side.

"Hello miss, can you tell me what time it is?"

She felt threatened but glanced at her watch, hoping the men would disappear thereafter.

She was now on a deserted street with a line of parked cars on one side and an empty building on the other. In those few seconds, the first man increased his proximity to Kismat and pushed her against the wall, as the second one held a knife close to her neck.

Karma heard the sound of her attacker's pants unzipping. The two men took turns inserting their fingers in her vagina; her screams muffled by their hands.

After a few minutes, one of them rushed to an unmarked van that was parked a few feet away. Just as the other one was about to place a plain handkerchief over her face and throw her into the van, she retaliated by biting his hand. He yelled in excruciating pain, prompting some distant passersby to look their way.

Karma's bus was now approaching and the attackers noticed it too.

They decided to cut their plan short.

Karma's first attacker groped her chest before running away.

She just stood there in shock, never having felt so violated in her life.

When she finally gained the courage to check if they were gone, she saw one of the men pass her a cunning smile before vanishing into the van.

That ruthless man's face was permanently etched in her memory forever.

She never saw her attackers again but that experience culminated into an unsettling fear of never wishing to be too alone, or being too close to any male stranger.

When Karma returned home, she was quieter and more reserved than her usual chirpy self.

There were blood stains on her underwear from the trauma.

Her mother asked her about her day and Karma only had one line to say.

"Ma, I've finished my Bharatanatyam classes. For good."

Karma didn't make mention of that incident to anybody. She was extra cautious in walking alone; avoiding empty streets, rooms, and spaces. She always looked twice behind her, at times, hallucinating, at times, that even her shadow was a stranger following her.

Books, particularly those with resilient female characters, helped her escape reality, albeit momentarily.

Sati noticed that her sister expressed little about her day, and spoke only when prompted.

For most of the day, Karma buried herself inside her books. Surprisingly, Karma was still performing at the top of her class.

Surya and Lakshmi accorded her reserved behavior to some form of teenage angst and didn't question it further.

With only a week left to the University application deadline, Karma set foot inside Lila Ma'am's classroom.

All the students had already dispersed for the day.

Karma set a printed application on Lila Ma'am desk.

"Ma'am, I'm ready to apply to Darwick."

A Time of Many Firsts - High School Edition

The black, white, and greys; the moles and freckles as dots to play; the gentle curvatures of our mighty thighs and hips and the strength they convey.
Perfection is so passé.

From Kismat's very first class in Delhi Public School, she studied every book till it was imprinted on her mind; from the names of India's holy rivers and her veined tributaries to the dates of freedom struggle in her rich history. If you asked her anything specific from a page, she could recall the sentence, word by word.

Her father always stressed that education, as impractical as some of it may seem, never goes to waste. Much like the bees that worked tirelessly to regurgitate nectar on their beehive honeycombs as a source of future sustenance; Kismat, too, regurgitated her detailed notes on her exam sheets to secure her future livelihood.

Her report cards, printed on the school's unique cardstock paper, would merit that her hard work had paid off.

The tidbits of enlightenment from our school years weave into a wonderful quilt, with a pattern unique to every individual. And Kismat's quilt looked something like this-

Tagore's Kabuliwala was her favorite story because Minni, the five year old protagonist, was her namesake. The Dandi March was her favorite historical fact. The irony of marching peacefully, in even temper, to protest the steep tax levied against salt, a commodity known to raise one's blood pressure, humored Kismat. Robert Frost was her favorite poet for she was always pondered about her 'road less taken.'

In her four years of schooling in Jersey, Kismat had acquired an unmistakable American accent. Initially, she felt a bit estranged because of it, but she grew accustomed to humoring her cousins and classmates with her pronunciations.

"How do you say shhedule (schedule) again?"

"Skechule."

"And internet?"

"Innernet," Kismat replied with ease.

Kismat, in turn, was amused by some interesting mispronunciations –

'Loin' for lion, 'oh-ven' for oven, and listening to questions phrased in the syntax of its answer.

You are coming, no?

We are eating out?

Sita hired a Hindi tutor to help her kids master their mother tongue, and by the time Kismat had completed eighth grade, she was able to read and write Hindi at the same level of her peers.

Kismat's frequented American slang of 'what's up?" was swiftly replaced with "Aur batao."

Not only could she partake in the many inside jokes with her cousins, but even make a few of her own, ranging from the primitive "Santa Banta" ones to the evolved *pahelis (riddles).* This was the kind of *time pass* she couldn't purchase in consumerism aisles of the States.

In class eighth, Kismat had her first period and first pimple; both becoming an integral feature of her adult life too. Though she had no say in choosing a life punctuated by period cramps and pains, she did have a different approach to the punctuation bit of it. The actual use of the word 'period', as Kismat reckoned, should have been reserved for menopause.

Her 'period' actually started off as a question mark as she was never really sure which day it would commence. And after it did, it transformed into a full-fledged exclamation mark from the flow! After three days, that 'period' tapered off into a 'comma', so as to pause till the following month of mayhem. Phew!

Her brother, Dhananjay, lost no opportunity to remark on her teenage acne, as if he were settling scores for all the special attention she got from Ajay and Sita.

"Yuck! What's happening to your face? Your nose looks like this strawberry I'm eating!"

Kismat ran back upstairs to her room as Sita passed Dhananjay a disgruntled look.

"What?! I'm only telling her that for her own good. Besides, she always says mean stuff about me too!"

When Sita first walked in to Kismat's room, she didn't see her anywhere. After a few glances, she saw Kismat hiding behind the other side of the bed; tears streaming down.

She wrapped her arms around Kismat.

"Don't worry. Everyone gets pimples at this age."

"But your skin is so clear."

Kismat had her mother's thick, long hair, though she also inherited Sita's early greys. Her father's genes contributed to her bushy eyebrows and acne.

"Dhananjay called you a strawberry right? That fruit is a symbol of love. It's actually a compliment if you think about it."

Kismat turned her face towards Sita, a sign that she was recuperating.

Sita carried on.

"Everyone has their flaws. Just remember that when anyone says anything unpleasant to you, reply with a 'Thank you.' They will be confused and won't bother you again."

Kismat never forgot her mother's advice.

Eighth grade also brought with it another first. It was the first time a boy expressed his feelings to her by means of a game of truth and dare.

It was the last class of the school day.

Ishant made the valiant effort to confess his crush on Kismat, and as she later found out through another classmate, he was infatuated by her accent and 'whiteness.'

It was planned from the beginning.

Ishant's friends would whip the bottle ever so smoothly such that it would ultimately land on him and he would choose "truth".

*Of all the "truthy" things to ask in a game of dare, the questions somehow end up being about young love.

His friends played along.

"So, Ishant, do you like someone in class?"

He pointed towards Kismat.

All Kismat could recall at that moment was the image of her brother, standing on the doorstep, beaten up, and how she would still blame herself for it.

The school bell rang and she fled downstairs.

Ishant followed her halfway down the staircase and simultaneously exclaimed, "Kismat, you are my American dream!"

With puberty came more facial hair.

After starting her menses, she had already lost her goddess privileges during the nine holy nights of Navratri, but after every visit to a Green Park parlor to tweeze her upper lip, she stepped out looking like an avatar of a new God - Hanuman.

That same year, Sita took her daughter for an expedition to the lingerie store to purchase Kismat's first sports bra. Kismat couldn't help became conscious of her 'small' size when another lady, cradling a newborn in her arm, purchased a large size bra for herself. She would eventually graduate to the bras with the fancy laces, wires, and hooks, but never to the 'D' size of that lady.

In the extended Dharma clan, Kismat's impeccable report card, pointed nose, and fair skin made her the cynosure of her aunts' eyes. In her circle of relatives, she became the quintessential face of *"Dharmaji ki beti ko dekho!"*

A year later, she met her first and only school crush.

His name was Ragyan. Finally, Kismat had found someone who could challenge her number one rank in class. There were only two possible outcomes, either she would really dislike him, or she would end up falling for him.

Ragyan was thin, bespectacled, and as tall and as bookish as she was. The very first time Ragyan spoke to Kismat, she fell in love with the way his glasses magnified the size of his eyes. It was true that Ragyan had no interest in Kismat, but that is what drew her even closer to him. The only times he may have initiated conversation with her would be to ask her about her scores in a recent exam, or what books she used to study for a quiz.

There was something about his sense of decency and diligence which was radiating from his being that completely floored Kismat in one go. It was the kind of diligence she would see in her father, a man who would shudder at the thought of taking a vacation day from work, unless it was mandated by the government or he was kidnapped by aliens. Even then, he would find a way to work from home or outer space.

The Physics teacher was handing back graded test papers to the class in an alphabetical order. When the teacher called Ragyan to collect his paper, nobody walked up. Realizing that he was absent, the teacher requested any of his friends to take his paper on his behalf.

Kismat's human antenna started going berserk. It was her one chance to hold something that belonged to her crush. As Kismat was slowly adjusting back to reality, a fellow classmate raised her hand to take the paper.

Jealously swelled up inside Kismat.

She shot her hand up and won by a fraction of a second; almost as close as the deciding factor between Phelps winning the gold or silver at the Olympics.

An ecstatic Kismat received her medal at the podium. She stashed his paper inside her backpack.

Ragyan scored one point higher that her in the Physics final- a 99 out of 100. She smiled because this would mean that he would be even happier to receive his paper back from her. All Kismat could concentrate on was his beautiful handwriting, how all his answers were beautifully captured in the answer box, how his equations were neatly derived, almost as if he didn't need to make use of an eraser.

She felt so close to him by holding his paper in her arms, so close that she saw a reflection of herself in the mirror facing her and immediately felt stupid.

Ragyan didn't show up again the following day and Kismat felt disappointed with each passing period. To her relief, Ragyan was present the day after.

She made her move.

"Yes, I beat you in Physics!" was his only response, in addition to "Why is my paper so crumply?"

Kismat hastily replied, "The teacher gave it to me like that."

She was content by just hearing him speak.

The following year, all sections got moved around and with that ended Kismat's imaginary love affair with the bespectacled boy.

Her school had an innovative strategy to sort students into new sections based on their scores in the recent 10th grade Central Board examinations.

As a result, Kismat was placed into one of the 'superability' sections. She hated the word 'superability', almost as if she was some kind of caped crusader in a silly cartoon series. Wherein Superman's biggest weakness was the green kryptonite, the kids in her section would cite the green 'herbal' concoctions of shankpushpi, ashwangandha and any variety of brain tonics as their biggest strength. And as any comic series would have its share of villains, Kismat's classroom would also have its share of antagonists who would go to great lengths to beat each other on grades, even if it was a matter of a fraction of a point.

There was one student who wore a special emerald ring on the request of an astrologer. He had a habit of borrowing notes from everyone and flatter teachers with his phony compliments. His classmates secretly called him Ghissu. During any exam, Ghissu would baffle his classmates by routinely asking for more sheets and furiously scribble on them, though his grades remained average at best.

A brahmin pandit, at behest of Ammi, even suggested such a ring for Kismat's long life and success.

"Why should I let a ring get all the credit for my grades?" She flatly refused it.

Her father, Ajay, had adorned multiple rings on his fingers, one for his career, one for his health, and one for his wealth, all because of Ammi. The day her husband, Premchand, passed away, the pandit added another ring on Ajay's index finger, warning that tragedy would befall if he didn't wear it.

In the midst of Kismat's senior year of high school, her wisdom tooth began to pain her lower right jaw. An over-the-counter paracetemol and clove gel provided temporary relief. The pain continued to recur and was finally relieved with the help of Spigelia (an indigenous herb used by Native Americans for centuries), one of her mother's chief remedies for left-sided pain.

The wisdom tooth served no meaningful purpose apart from taking extra space in her jaw, much like how Kismat had started to feel about the memorization of endless definitions and chapters in her brain.

After a few months, the impacted tooth had to be removed through surgery. Her mother gave her a dose of *Arnica* to hasten the healing and Kismat was back to school in a few days.

The seven or eight odd warts on Kismat's palms, which made Badi ammi believe that no man would ever put a ring on her finger, were also cured by a remedy called *Thuja*. The strict Ammi, who routinely used Sita's remedies for her gastrointestinal reflux, back pains, and itchy skin, was thankful for her daughter-in-law's prescriptions but seldom praised her for it.

Though Kismat had healed from a wisdom tooth extraction, Sita was still worried about her daughter's growing apathy towards school, which began to reflect in her report card. Amidst her superability peers, scoring became the only criteria towards achievement.

Kismat was now happy being a back bencher. And for the first time in her six years at the Delhi Public School, she scored less than ninety percent in the mid-terms.

"Our Kismat is a bright girl no matter how dull her report card will get," Ajay mollified Sita.

Kismat's apathy wasn't a disorder.

What Kismat was experiencing was perhaps the most normal reaction to a school system that ensured conformity.

For all her school years, she had seen herself turn into another mechanized product on an assembly line of wind-up toys, whose internal springs couldn't spring out of their own helplessness and they continued to bang their monkey cymbals from the motion of an external force.

Many of her graduating peers and even to some extent, Kismat herself, continued as grown-up puppets, their strings ever so subtly controlled by the hands of a societal member, defining their next steps of looking good on a piece of paper.

Kismat assured herself that she would not lose her identity in a crowd of sameness.

~

The Iyers visited Fort Kochi every December to witness the Kochin New Year carnival, a festival started by the Portuguese, with its splendor of games, fireworks, and fresh, local seafood.

A parade of dancers would dress up in costumes of Gods and Goddesses and make their way down the length of the crowd in their attractive floats. As a trained dancer, Karma was enamored by their facial expressions; in particular, their eyes that fluidly conveyed so much that vocabulary could not.

Lakshmi told Karma how she once mimicked these painted performers by lathering her face with the green, gooey mixture called '*chyawanprash*.'

Her younger daughter, Sati, followed suit, except she put the *chyawanprash* in her hair like her mother's henna.

Darwick University acknowledged the receipt of her application on the very last day of their deadline, but Karma hadn't heard from them for months and she had come to reason that they had found more worthy candidates than her.

Karma seldom missed school, so Lakshmi found it unusual that she'd left her backpack at home on a regular school day. She immediately got in touch with the school staff and Lila Ma'am confirmed that Karma was, indeed, marked absent for the day.

It was Sati who finally confessed that Karma had skipped all her classes to visit the Fort Kochi beach.

Karma had visited the beach with friends and family before, but never alone.

In fact, this was the first time she was visiting any place alone since her incident at the bus stop.

She took a handful of the caramel colored sand, a shade lighter than the color of her skin. Karma's skin had the kind of the color that would appear if you heated sugar and butter too long, leaving a tinge of black. And much like the bitterness left behind in the burnt caramel, Karma had dealt with many bitter comments on her dusky shade from some of her fairer peers and relatives. But as Lakshmi had taught her, if warming something so sweet as sugar and something so soft as butter could, together, produce the dark shade, then Karma should take pride in the noble ingredients that formed her spirit and lent her the same color.

She let the smooth sand particles fall between her slender, dusky fingers. Karma felt immense control on her life in that very moment; of picking and dropping the handfuls of sand.

But more than the sand, it the sea that moved her. There was something incredibly soothing about witnessing the waves hurling at the resolute rocks. The fervent energy of the sea, in its turbulence and stillness alike, taught Karma that she, too, had immense power; the kind that her surroundings couldn't diminish.

Karma arrived home a few hours later.

Lakshmi's displeasing face was indicative that Karma was due to receive a long lecture from her.

Instead, her mother pointed towards the living room table.

A bulky package was lying on top of it.

Karma immediately ran in excited anticipation to see what

it could be.

"Ma, is that my....?!"
Karma glanced to see the foreign postage label before ripping it open.

Inside the assortment of folders and papers, was her acceptance letter, awarding her a full scholarship to study at Darwick University.

When Karma first spoke about applying to Darwick to her parents, she intimated them about her rubber band theory -
That no matter how far she would stretch herself away from her parents, she would always return to her homely equilibrium in Kochi.

Lakshmi, Jyotimala, and Sati bid Karma goodbye from home and it was Surya who ultimately accompanied her to the airport.

A nervous Karma hugged her father one last time before the flight was due to takeoff.
"We are so proud of you my Rama."
"But I'm going to be so far away from you and Amma."
She secretly hoped Surya would ask her to stay back.
Instead, he rested his hand on her head.
"You always have our blessings, no matter where you are."

And just like the many protagonists who had traversed continents and paved new roads for themselves in the novels of her home library, Karma, too, was ready to move out of her nest and chart her own unique story.

A Parting Token of Unrequited Love

In twelfth grade, many students were trying to make the most of their precious time within the protected embrace of high school before entering into the real world. Some were completely clueless about their next steps; some had solidified action plans on the entrance exams they wanted to take. Those who were keen to study abroad were trying to fit any extracurricular activity before the application deadline.

The sheer batch size of her graduating class meant there were innumerable students vying for one spot; the Student Council being the most sought after. Even the Poetry Club, a group that accepted almost anybody; put Kismat on its waiting list.

After finishing her last midterm, Kismat came across a poster on the Cricket grounds, the grounds that were seldom trodden by girls.

The poster had noticeable English errors.

"New Playars Needed Far Womans Cricket Team."

This new team would be the first to historically represent her school in the Women's National Cricket Tournament.

A small photo of the team coach was placed inset. The coach looked to be rather young. He had an unusual middle parting, short hair, but no beard or stubble.

The poster underlined that tryouts were being held the following week.

Kismat had played Cricket with her cousins at her uncle's farmhouse over the summer break, and though she was terrible at batting, she was reasonably decent at bowling.

She decided to tryout.

Kismat was surprised to see that the Coach was actually a lady. A stout, yet strong woman, Coach Ma'am may have been poor in English, but she could understand the rhythm of the game in a heartbeat. Her skill was evident in way she focused on minute details, from the positioning of the bat to the angling of shots.

Only a handful of girls showed up to the first tryout; all of them of varying ages and built; but they all shared the same affinity for playing cricket. The next few tryouts helped to secure just enough members to make a full team.

With only six months to the tournament date, Coach Ma'am had no time to spare. The practice sessions took place in boiling heat of Delhi summers. The girls would change into comfortable tees and shorts after school, prompting some of the school boys to stay back and watch the girls playing from afar.

After a few sessions, Badi ammi remarked that Kismat was getting too tanned, a sight unwelcome to her; particularly in the realm of future, marriage prospects. Though Ammi was not fair herself, the fair skin tone that Kismat inherited from her son, Ajay, was one of the few things Ammi prided in her granddaughter.

Coach Ma'am declared Asha as the Captain of the team, as she was the most versatile player, having played *gilli danda* with all the boys in her colony since she was little. Kismat was appointed Vice Captain because, after Asha, she was the only other senior, and had sufficient oratory skills that motivated the team during practice.

The girls learned to gain strengths from each other; with Anamika having the best fielding, Kirti the best bowling, and

Asha, of course, having the best batting skills of all.

In December, ten teams from all over India congregated together in the open auditorium at Pinegrove School in Kasauli district for the opening ceremony of the National Tournament.

All teams were required to wear their uniforms to represent their schools with pride.

Asha inadvertently forgot to pack her blazer and skirt. When all the school captains were asked to come on stage, the Coach asked Kismat to follow suit and within those few moments of a missing uniform, Kismat was made the new Captain.

Asha cared very little about her title and giving speeches. She was more concerned about her game.

In this new arrangement, Kismat managed the onus of being the new Skipper. She learned how to arrange the line-up of her batswomen, how to distribute the fielding, and how to motivate the bowlers; Kismat managed all of this with a steady head and guidance from the team's five feet tall, spirited lady, whom the team lovingly addressed as Coach Ma'am.

Coach ma'am was also dear to them for another very special reason. She would commence every practice session with the same words of encouragement (in Hindi):

"My ladies, today the day has come again. We can win, we will win. Don't let the other team get the better of you. You are born fighters. Go out there and show your true strength...."

The speech would be moving along so well until she ended with one line of English:

*"And always remember- **Do and Die**."*

The girls would hold back their giggles. The team never bothered to correct the Coach, mainly to avoid hurting her feelings and Coach Ma'am continued to use that speech forever.

After gearing up, they would hi-five Coach ma'am, and enter the field together. In their hearts, those last three words became an almost auspicious tradition to start their game.

The National tournament was held at **Chail** - the highest Cricket stadium in the world, coincidentally, in her home state of Himachal Pradesh. Kismat was humored to think that the self-reflection she had at mighty Dhauladhar mountains in Dharamshala, that inspired her to wonder about the kind of heights she would seek, was now a reality today.

To pad up and enter the field with the heavy hopes and expectations of her team, and then to calmly ease herself for the first delivery - those were the times Kismat would think back and find herself all grown up.

Asha had the audience's adulation when she was the only woman in the tournament to score a century, so much so that the ESPN commentator liberally gave her the title of a "Delhi Tigress."

The black and blue bruises, scrapes, and happy faces upon making it within the Top Five rank in their debut tournament, attested to the spirit of their endeavor.

The strength to brave criticism and keep up her team's morale after a loss shaped Kismat into a new woman. Just like the customary coin toss on the pitch, life would throw more tosses at her, the outcomes of which wouldn't always be in her favor.

Ajay had been living away from the family for almost three years now since his firm had requested him to return to Jersey and maintain his old accounts. He decided not to disrupt his children's education and moved alone. Dhananjay, who was nearly two years older than Kismat, had already moved to the States to study at repute State college in Indiana.

Kismat's natural trajectory was to shift to the States too, a respite for her, since she scored less than ninety percent in the twelfth board examinations and would have no future of securing a good college in Delhi. Sita, who had stayed back in India till both her children completed their high school, supported the choices of her children to return to their father, to newer pursuits, though her emotions were bittersweet, at best. She felt guilty to leave her husband alone in a foreign country to fend for himself, to cook and clean for himself, something she had done singlehandedly ever since they wed, no matter which part of the world destiny had taken them to. But at the same time, she had very little motivation to move back to the country she had worked so hard to move away from.

Kismat had applied to four Universities in the States.

In early spring, the letters of acceptance and rejection had begun pouring in at the Dharma residence. With decent SAT scores, Kismat managed acceptances to two, top private universities within the tristate area – Stern and Carnegie Mellon. However, there was one acceptance that caught her eye, one that she wasn't even sure of applying to in the first place.

The acceptance package was from Douglass, a niche all-women's college, housed within the larger St. Regents University. Douglass even offered her a promising scholarship.

The cost of public school was almost free in America yet paying for college, in-state or private, was drastically more expensive. After a thorough analysis using Excel at the request of her computer geek of a father, Kismat truly understood what it meant to be a part of the 'middle class' in America. Kismat was rich enough to take hefty student loans at Stern, but not poor enough to be awarded any financial based scholarships.

With all the acceptances in hand, there was still a ton of doubt in her mind. Should she go for the University with higher rankings or the one putting less debt on her balance sheet?

Ajay helped her in cementing her decision.

"Minni, the older you get, the more you will realize to not run after the name and instead focus on the goals you seek for yourself."

Those goals, exactly nine in number, were to come later in Kismat's life.

And she would fight against all odds to finish them, even if those odds came from the mouth of a doctor.

Kismat had finally set her heart on Douglass.

The cherry blossoms outside her dormitory, the Georgian colonial architecture, and charming bridges and lakes, all made for a gorgeous setting. But it was the women leadership course offerings that drew her to the college.

She was ready to call it home for the next four years.

Little did she know that this decision would transform her life in many ways, including meeting a man who would help her complete her final wish as she faced a battle that would devastate her body and mind, but never her soul.

Kismat was soon to embark for the States, but not before receiving a token of love.

He was a fellow classmate named Purab.

When he first laid eyes on her in tenth grade, his mind and body discovered a mate so contemporaneously; that this is what one may call 'love at first sight.'

She represented to him a timeless companion and beloved, all in those very first moments of seeing her and one can only blame it on the hormones playing games with his heart.

Purab would cast glances in her direction, hoping that she would reciprocate his feelings someday.

All he really wanted was to speak to her once.

He waited and waited until the only chance he had left was at the school's Farewell Party.

Purab imagined that after he would confess his love, she would give him a hug and he would respond by kissing her gently on her cheek.

At the Farewell, the catering staff was busy clearing up their food stalls. The balloons, some moving aimlessly on the grass in the open soccer field and some still tied to their fate on the stage and painted walls, were being taken home by a few attendees as a party souvenir. Students were slowly making their way outside, marking the end of a cherished journey. A few stayed back; finishing their rounds of last minute picture-taking and soaking in the last bits of sweetness, that like wine, would age into bittersweet memories.

Kismat was following her circle of friends, as they made their way outside the Farewell grounds.

He called out her name that instant, as if lightening shocked him from within to regain his senses and capture the moment before it would be too late. Kismat glanced back to see who it was.

He was standing there, amidst his friends, who were smiling out and about.

Purab's eyes were cast down.

As she started walking over, his hands began to tremble.

The sentences he had originally prepared in his head suddenly seemed incoherent.

Finally, she was facing him, evoking a hint of a smile, not sure what was to come of this unexpected meeting.

Purab handed her a small box enclosed in red wrapping.

"For you," he said, his eyes fixed on hers.

Her silver bangles clanged with each other as she reached for it with both her hands. As she held the box, she felt immediately grateful. She chose not to open the wrapping in front of everyone, lest she would make him feel embarrassed.

Her friends called out her name a few times.
She whispered a hurried "Thank you Purab" before joining her friends, unsure of what else to say, what else to convey in those precious moments, as many eyes were fixed on her.

In bated breath, he said, "I love you Kismat" but the words were uttered too late.

Kismat had already left by then. That was the last time he would see her before she left for the States.

Inside the box, there was a set of silver earrings and a small card which read,

"Dear Kismat,
Be happy always.
In memory of my unrequited love,
Purab"

When a man tells a woman he cares for her in a most gentlemanly fashion, he not only leaves an imprint on her mind, but on her heart as well.

Even though it may not have been love at first sight for her, even that inch of respect he carved out for himself in her heart, pure and free, was only waiting to blossom into something more, one day.

Unrequited Love - University Edition

In her first week of orientation at Darwick, Karma was greeted by a handsome man with an impeccable dressing sense. He introduced himself as Konsta, President of the International Students Association. Karma refrained from shaking his hand when he held it out, still wary of making any physical contact with a stranger.

Konsta didn't mind this.

He gave her a pamphlet about the Association; fumbling in English as he spoke in his heavy Greek accent. His fumbling calmed her nerves.

After sharing her name and field of study, she politely excused herself to go to the washroom, even though no such emergency existed.

Karma enjoyed her solitary walks on the cobbled lane leading down to the University's main Library. The lane was illuminated with crowned street lamps on either side, duly preserved in their ancient state. The campus had ample greenery of silver birch, English elm, and walnut trees.

A weeping willow near her dormitory attracted tourists for its mentions in Rowling's Hogwarts, but it wasn't just the tree that was magical; Karma was most fascinated by the Library itself.

The ceiling murals and chandeliers in the main hallway of the Darwick Library added a touch of royal grandeur, and the fountains and statues lining the staircase to the entrance of the library made a remarkable façade.

It was as if Karma was stepping foot inside a century-old palace, except one needn't have royal blood, just an inquisitive mind to enter.

The glass domed auditorium in the main courtyard balanced the sense of the old and the new. This harmony was true for much of London; the beauty of the city having her roots from medieval and Roman times. As soon as Karma would exit the narrow lanes of her campus, she would reach the hustle and bustle of main London, where the architecture changed dramatically; a mixture of the old spires and arches accepting their fate in the penumbra of newer definitions of glass and steel.

Her curriculum started with a mixed bag of four courses of her liking, one from literature and science and two that focused primarily on Economics, her main field of study. Her macroeconomics class was hugely popular, the Professor being a former Nobel Prize Winner. Karma bragged about him to her family back home only to receive in return, a twenty minute lecture from Lakshmi revolving around two burning questions, "What are you eating?" and "Are they feeding you well?"

In the first month of her stay, the Econ department organized a mandatory meet and greet. Karma was open to the meeting aspect; the greeting part was solely dependent on how well the individuals had washed their hands.

Karma was germaphobic. She would catch colds and infections easily, owing to a weak immunity, one of the few things common between her and her little sister, Sati. Karma would get nervous whenever anyone would cough, or even make mention of a sneeze. She would imagine that the virus droplets had entered her nostrils, worked their way in, and slowly engulfed her entire body. Before that compulsive thought became any worse, she would lather her hands with sanitizer and use disinfectant spray on her belongings even if that spray induced more coughing from its irritants.

Over time, as Karma's immunity improved, she had become better at enduring people's proximity and handshakes, so as long as she washed her hands with soap and scalding water right after.

The Econ department's meet-and-greet brought together many students probably owing to the free offering of wine and appetizers. Karma devoured enough cheese, olives, and crackers that night to call it a dinner.

As she turned around to check for the exit, a young, bearded man with olive green eyes, bumped into Karma.

His badge had Rehaan Gujral typed in capital letters.

"Sorry about that. My name's Ryan."

He extended his hand, but withdrew it after she didn't bother extending hers.

"I'm Karma."

He quipped about how he must have such good '*karma*' running into her, but noticing her unchanging expression, he quickly added, "I'm from Mumbai. How about you?"

"Kochi. Your name' s Rehaan, right?"

"I would prefer it if you pronounce it as Ryan."

He spoke in an accent she assumed belonged to a country yet to be created.

"Why?"

"Because it's easier that way. People get it the first time."

"But I'm one of your people."

Rehaan laughed and gave Karma the exceptional authority to say his original name.

Before Rehaan could think of something wittier to prolong their banter, Karma wished him goodnight and made her way to her dormitory.

Rehaan hoped he'd have the good fortune to run into her again.

Surya's old London friend, Venky Uncle, invited Karma to dinner with his family. Though she was initially hesitant to visit them, she was comforted by the taste of Aunty's home-cooked *matthi* curry, dal, and appam at their house.

This was the first thing she missed in London - the taste of her mother's home-cooked food. No matter how many foreign dishes an expat may try, the feeling of being home comes from the taste of the cuisines of one's motherland. She tried her luck to find fresh grated coconut, fragrant curry leaves, and jackfruit jam of her hometown in a local grocery store in Islington, but sufficed with bread, butter and strawberry jam instead.

Venky Uncle recommended a nice Indian place, by the name of Tamarind, near her campus and Karma made plans to try it the following weekend. Two of her friends from the International Students Club tagged along, including Konsta, who had never tried the cuisine before, mostly from the fear of the overwhelming spices.

Cecile, a Moroccan student majoring in Art History, was running late and phoned Karma to get the exact location of the restaurant.

"It's a block away from the intersection of a Starbucks and Pretta MANAGER."

"It's Pret ahh Maugeeee, not Manager. And secondly, there's one of those at every corner."

Karma realized her folly.

She was not accustomed to seeing so many shops of the same franchise back in Kochi. Konsta, who knew London well, helped Cecile with the directions.

The restaurant had mediocre furnishings with miniature elephants, a TV set with a Hindi flick playing in the background, and posters of the latest Bollywood stars donning their bright costumes and pearly teeth, as if to compensate for the dim lighting. There was also an aquarium with more plastic vegetation than actual fish, perhaps, to highlight the fact that the place only served vegetarian food.

That aquarium reminded Karma of her own aquarium back home. Its first residents were a male and female tropical fish. From the naked eye, they looked exactly the same except for a slight difference in color. Karma and Sati were both excited to give their fishes new names.

"The green one is Fido and the red one is Dido."

A month later, Fido and Dido multiplied into fifteen new fishes. Both sisters enjoyed feeding them each day and seeing the school race to the floating, dried shrimp flakes; eating every bit with eagerness. Because the flakes contained meat, Lakshmi made it a point to adhere to Jyotimala's customs and feed them only bread crumbs on Thursdays i.e. the Iyers – 'no meat day'.

"But Ma, they're just fish! How does it matter?"

"Yes, but they're family."

Karma suddenly became very homesick at that thought of her mother.

Celine interrupted her moments of reminiscing.

"Karma, I can't pronounce half the names on the menu. Can you tell me more about this dish?" she asked her, pointing to the description about a Mughlai dish called *malai kofta.*

Karma was struggling how to explain it without using the name of the dish again. There was an English description as follows:

Delectable, sumptuous, mouthwatering, stuffed balls with gravy.

There were enough adjectives to describe five more dishes.

"It's kind of like meatballs, without the meat."

Mid-way during their conversation, Karma got a phone call from an international number. She picked up thinking it was from her mother only to realize it was her cheriyamma, Nandini, asking about her time abroad.

"Hi cheri...I miss you so much....I'll call you when I get home....yes, eating outside...ok bye."

"Sorry, that was my aunt calling from India."

Celine was enamored by Karma's Malayali accent.

"What a beautiful name she has...how do you say it...cherry...?"

"Actually *cheriyamma* is my mother's sister."

Konsta was disappointed to learn that *baingin' masala,* which was an apt name of an Indian rock-band, was really just spiced aubergine.

When the waiter came by, he took everyone's order and asked them how spicy they would like their food on a scale of one to five, one being the least spicy.

Karma asked for three.

Everyone else said something along the lines of a negative integer.

Initially, it was a bit startling for Karma to see strangers greet her on the Tube, or exchange niceties on the street and in the college cafe. But after a month, she, too, began greeting the Tube conductor, the old lady at the library, and fellow dorm-mates in the common lavatory.

Even Sati, who thought her sister to be emotionally distant, more often than not, noticed a subtle change when Karma initiated the phone calls and routinely shared photos of her Darwick campus over email.

Karma had recovered bits of her self-esteem, but she had not fully shed her inhibitions.

London had an undeniable charm. The city wooed her with her neoclassical and Romanesque style churches, Oxford Street shopping junctions, and art and theater havens. Darwick students had the privilege to avail discounts on tickets to West end shows and museums. The University even organized annual parties on a cruise on the Thames.

But Karma was not smitten.

She remained a recluse on most nights and plugged in her headphones during the day so no one would disturb her. Apart from visiting Tamarind once in a while, she rarely ate out, and always walked around with the same pocket knife she had carried in Kochi.

On the days she craved some comfort food, she and roommate, Priya, would boil dal and rice in an electric pot and take turns on who would wash the dishes after. On the weekends, they'd bond on their love for retro movies and music.

Her cheriyamma, Nandini, who had always wanted to visit Europe, asked her about her all the places she had ticked off her list. When Karma confided that she had found her sanctuary in a neat corner of the University Library, Nandini was deeply disappointed. She exhorted Karma to explore new sights, traverse the European continent, and experiment her palate with new cuisines; reminding her that such opportunities seldom come again.

Karma could only think of her mother who toiled all her life. How could she think of enjoyment? She had to concentrate on her studies and earn well so she could make her parents proud.

Karma urged her aunt not to confide any of this to her mother.

Nandini was heartened by Karma's concern but felt that she was burdened by it too. She told her, as matter-of-factly as possible, that her mother had sacrificed so much just so her daughters could afford the kinds of liberties she had now in London, and that it would sadden Lakshmi if her daughter didn't break away from her solitary state.

Karma upheld Nandini's advice. Within a month, Karma and her roommate Priya witnessed The Lion King at Lyceum Theater, admired galleries at the British museum (with Priya noting its remarkable glass and steel roof forming the backdrop of a famous Bollywood number). They bought souvenirs at Portobello market in Notting Hill, some of which made their way to their apartment fridge and some inside Karma's diary.

Konsta and Cecile were surprised to see Karma recommending new dishes at their dinners in Lebanese, Ethiopian, and Mexican cafes.

And when Karma could find no company for food or travel, she had become self-reliant enough to venture alone, whether it be discovering a hidden library in St Paul's Cathedral, or reading on a train to the English countryside, or watching a rendition at Shakespeare's Globe - a reconstruction of the historic Globe that had perished in the London Fire.

London, much like other famous metropolitan cities, had had her share of upheavals from deadly plagues, fires, smog, and even present-day dastardly attacks.

But her spirit never shattered. Karma was learning to hone in London's vibrant energy.

Much like the Globe, a new, resilient Karma was surfacing under the debris of her old self.

Karma had concluded that London was cold and rainy ninety-nine percent of the time. Sati would make her sister jealous about being at home in Kochi, where the weather was sunny and pleasant all year round. But there was one experience which helped Karma win in the weather debate.

It made Karma feel as if heaven had literally touched the ground.

It was her first experience of falling snow.

The first time she saw little flakes falling from the sky, she wondered if some cotton factory had exploded nearby. It was only after she let the snow melt in the palm of her hands that she could realize the wondrous sensation of a snowflake.

One time, it hailed in London and that news reached the Iyer household as well. Karma told her aunt that it appeared as if God was using an ice dispenser in heaven and some of the ice was now making its way through the clouds.

Karma admired how the snow had the power to brighten everything it touched from chalking up the pavements, to blanketing the trees, and decorating the tiled roofs of every home with its powdery flakes, much like how Lakshmi used to pat her face and neck with a fragrant talc after a shower.

She made snow angels by lying flat on her back and spreading her arms out. She slid down hills using the lid of her laundry basket that compensated as a sled; and even built a snowwoman; a snowman being far too mainstream for her.

All that fun in the snow brought Karma down with a nasty cold.

Each time she would have the urge to sneeze, she would reach into her armor of sanitizers and pull out a tissue; faster than a knee-jerk reflex. The first time Karma sneezed in class, a fellow classmate turned around and whispered, “Bless you!”

Karma had to take a look around to confirm that he was, indeed, blessing her. This happened again in the library. These random acts of courtesy were very infectious, for even she started to hold doors and “bless” people around her.

There were instances when Karma could have done without all the extra courtesy. A kind gentleman patiently held the door open for her, while she was still at a distance. Bundled under the weight of three layers of clothing, she ran past the melting slush on the ground, like a marathon runner in super-slow motion just moments before crossing the finish line. When she finally reached the door on the verge of collapsing on the ground, she coughed him a polite “Thank you” and let her lungs rest in peace.

As the mid-terms were approaching, Karma made daily visits to the Women's library, separate from the main one, which was only a ten minute walk from her dormitory. She would bundle up in layers of a thermal, a sweater, an oversized coat, a scarf and matching gloves, only to have to slowly strip away each layer once she entered inside the heated building.

It was a completely pointless exercise to dress up for such a short walk, yet necessary to avoid hypothermia, according to her mother Lakshmi.

As she quietly nestled in her favorite spot in the reading room on the fourth floor, she sneezed.

But this time, there was no one around.

She applied the theory of autarky and said, “Bless me!”

The Darwick Indian Society organized the annual ‘Diwali Dhamaka.” A celebrity singer and DJ were also invited to perform at the event.

Karma put on the one Indian sari that her mother deliberately packed in her suitcase and headed to the Student Center.

Her roommate, Priya, agreed to tag along to the event, but backed out at the last minute.

To Karma’s surprise, there were many Europeans dressed in traditional attire making their way to the same venue.

The hall was completely packed.

Everyone’s eyes were fixed on the enthralling performance of a classical fusion dance troupe on stage.

But Rehaan kept his focus at the entrance.

The moment he saw her enter, his heart raced a little faster. He made his way past the crowds, making sure not to lose sight of her.

Gently, he bumped into her, like the first time they met at

their Econ department's meet and greet event.

His hair was styled with a copious amount of gel and his perfume seemed stronger than usual, as if he had just applied it moments ago.

Though Karma didn't admit this, he was looking dapper in a black kurta pyjama.

"Sorry about that. My name's Rehaan."

A faint smile appeared on Karma's face.

"Finally! A smile from the lady."

He brought two glasses of mango lassi and a plate of samosas to share.

"You look different today Karma – I mean you look good in a sari...with your hair open like that."

"Thanks. You don't look half bad yourself."

"Damn! What's in this lassi?"

"Why? Tastes fine to me."

"No, you're being nice to me," Rehaan added, smiling profusely.

"I saw some of your old photos on FB, dancing and all. You're a pro in Bharatnatyam?!"

"Not really. I stopped once I reached tenth grade."

"Why'd you stop?"

"I wanted to focus more on my studies," Karma lied.

"Well, I still think you should be performing up there. Heck, I'll even join you!" he added encouragingly.

"Thank you, but I'm sure you can find some other girl to dance with."

But he didn't move an inch from Karma's side.

"One day, I will melt your ice-like personality."

"And till then, I'll stay in my freezer."

Rehaan stared at her hair a few seconds.

"Hey, I just realized that we both have something in common!"

"Our indifference towards each other?" she quipped.

He pointed to his own hair.

"No, we both have white hair. It's a sign of good luck!"

"Indians say that about a lot of things – a gap in the front two teeth will bring you wealth, a longer middle toe is a sign of good health, a fat belly is a sign of prosperity – one might as well look like an ogre."

"I'm confused. Do you just hate humans, or are you always this grumpy like an ogre?"

This time, Karma finally laughed.

When Karma came back to her room after the Diwali fest, she found her usually, even-tempered roommate sobbing uncontrollably on her side of the bed.

"What's wrong Priya?"

"I told you about my boyfriend, Karan right? Turns out he's a scumbag!"

Priya started dishing out some more expletives in Hindi that made her calm disposition seem like an illusion.

"Why? What happened?"

Priya started gasping for breath in between her incessant crying.

"NOT only was he seeing another girl, but he is engaged to a third one and all set to marry her in a few months!"

Though inappropriate for the situation, something within Karma made her want to laugh.

"Holy cow! Are you sure about this?"

"A mutual friend told me! I confronted him on the phone today and he casually owned up to everything. I'm such a fool to have trusted him in this long distance relationship."

As Karma tried her best to console Priya for the remainder of the night, her story made Karma further abhor the concept of having a boyfriend in her life.

There were many more places Karma wanted to explore, and so many places that had started to feel like a second home. Even her Darwick library pass and Oyster card seemed like a treasured souvenir.

Rehaan, who was also become a member of the International Club, tagged along on most of the Club's excursions and almost always found a seat near Karma. These actions caught the attention of Priya who hinted that there may be more than meets the eye.

Karma brushed it all off as pure coincidence.

"I don't know why you ignore him so much Kismat. He's actually good-looking. I'd date him now that I'm single."

The group made plans to grab sandwiches and fries at a popular burger joint in Covent Garden.

Everyone had become such good friends that they were willing to share each other's dipping sauces. Karma refrained from such a repulsive act of the possible interchanging of saliva, and therefore, germs.

Rehaan casually dipped his bitten fry in Karma's sauce bowl.

Karma's reaction was exothermic to say the least.

Rehaan smilingly said, *"Bade bade sehron main aisi choti choti baatein toh hoti rehti hain senorita."*

(Translation: These kinds of small instances of romance happen in big cities all the time.)

"Seriously?"

"Oh, c'mon Karma, how can you not like DDLJ?"

"The hero was kind of a stalker. And in that classic train scene in the end, I would've probably ran away to get a new life."

"You must be a feminist," retorted Amyra, who had previously shown interest in Rehaan.

"And you must be a fan of men who play obsessive lovers," Karma responded just as well.

"I'm just saying...feminists always show men in poor light," Amyra added quickly, not to lose any momentum in her stance.

The boys suddenly became intrigued in the fervent debate between the two ladies, particularly since it seemed to be favoring them.

"The misandrists do that. Women have always been raised to compete on beauty as their worth to men. But feminism has changed that now. The movement is really just striving to achieve equality for all."

"Why don't you just call yourself humanists then?" Amyra asked in return.

"It's true that we champion for rights of all of humanity. But to suggest that we are only humanists is to say that our history was non-existent. Why not club the anti-apartheid movement in South Africa, the emancipation of Jews, and the Satyagraha movement in India with human rights too? You can't, because those tipping points of history served specific interests. It's the same case with the movements for gays and transgenders. They are humans too, but with distinct grievances. Women have been systematically denied rights and opportunities. It took hundred and fifty more years after America's independence for women to get the basic right to vote. And fifty more years to do something as basic as run in Marathons. Women have reached the moon and back, but we still need to empower those who are denied their basic rights to freedom."

Karma was surprised at how easily and confidently she spoke, free of any stutters.

A few other girls applauded her speech, until that is, Rehaan, butted into the conversation.

"But I don't think men and women can ever be equal, Karma."

Without any further interruption, he continued his speech.

"You can wear men's clothing and still look sexy, but we can't do the same with your dresses. You have makeup and push-ups to look good, but we have to live with what we have. You have periods, but we get balder faster. You have a biological clock, but we can be fertile longer. And most importantly, we don't have to deal with childbirth and breast-feeding....so, you see, in many respects, we're just not equal."

Amyra and her group of girls hi-fived Rehaan.

Karma simply walked away.

"C'mon Karma. I was just saying we have different problems. Learn to take a joke..."

Rehaan ran over to her.

He gently clasped Karma's hands to make her stay.

She had a flashback of the incident at the bus stop and immediately recoiled from his touch.

"Let go. Please."

Rehaan could sense hurt in her voice that radiated from her eyes.

He immediately let go.

More days passed in the midst of papers and submissions.

Karma had a free day in between her Macroeconomics and English Lit lectures. She was engrossed in the latest Amitav Ghosh book under the shade of the weeping willow. As Ghosh described the setting of the Ibis sailing down the Hooghly, a distributary of the holy Ganges in Kolkata, Karma transported herself to the backwaters in Alappuzha; the soothing waves of Vembanad Lake filling her ears like a sweet lullaby.

Soon after, she fell asleep. The moment she woke up, she made sure that all her belongings were intact.

It was nearly dusk now.

Rehaan was waiting for her at the entrance of the Main library.

"I'm been waiting here since morning to see you."

"Why?"

"Because....I....I love you."

Karma almost dropped her books on accord of his confession.

Surely he must be playing another one of his pranks, she thought.

"Karma, please say something."

"How can you be so sure that you love me? I mean there are so many hot girls on campus for you to choose from – why pick on a studious, unromantic, feminist like me?"

Rehaan knew he had to match Karma's wits to convince her.

"Well, I believe that there are two kinds of people in the world. Those who get lost in the items on display on shelves and those who know exactly what they want and pick it right away because it is their heart's first choice. I belong to the second half."

"So, I am a product on a shelf?" she quipped.

"Yes, no...I meant....."

"Ok, so what kind of a market were you looking at?"

"What do you mean?"

"I mean, did you pick me from a perfectly competitive market where the rest of the girls of your liking were exactly like me, or an oligopoly where there were significant barriers to entry to my heart, or a monopoly where you really had no other option but to pick me?"

"Karma, you are a bluestocking!"

"Did you just call me a piece of hosiery?"

"Why don't you look up the word?" he added smilingly.

Curious as to what the word meant, she did as instructed.

"An intellectual or literary woman."

Like the night of the Diwali party, a faint smile again formed on her lips. She may not have been attracted to him like other girls, but she certainly admired his innovative ways to bring a smile to her face.

"Look Rehaan, you're a nice person but...."

"Karma, before you say anything, tell me one thing.

"What?"

"Don't you think we are destined to meet up, here in London? I think we can create a wonderful story together. What do you say?"

"To be honest Rehaan, forget destiny, I don't even believe in love at this point."

For the first time, she saw a hint of Rehaan's sensitivity. His voice was choking as he spoke.

"It's okay. I would've regretted not telling you anyway."

"I'm sorry Rehaan. I don't feel the same way."

"You know, you didn't let me finish that day. I still believe men and women are not equal."

"Yes, I know that...."

"Because, women are way more powerful. You have the power to create a new life. The power to nurture....And also the power to break our hearts into a million pieces."

He added the last line without inflection.

Karma was lost for words.

"I only have one favor to ask of you Karma."

She looked up and saw a small tear forming in the corner of his eye.

"One day, you will fall in love -- when that day comes, please do remember me."

He didn't ask for anything more, not even a hug, and Karma and Rehaan quietly moved on with their lives, occasionally running into each other to utter a few words of formality.

She felt uneasy the rest of that day.

Underneath the shell of his suave exterior, Rehaan had a guarded, soft spot that was only she was privy to that day.

Section Two: The Spirit of Awakening

Sophia

Kismat's first class at St. Regents was *Calculus I* inside a packed lecture hall. Her Dharma genes of tardiness ensured that she was the last one to reach class. There was only one seat left unoccupied in the front row.

As the semester would progress, the seats would become emptier as the professor did not bother about attendance. The professor, a Caucasian lady in her mid forties, introduced her three page syllabus to the class. She started teaching immediately, much to the dismay of all the freshmen.

First, she started off with some basic logarithms.

Midway during the lecture, she wrote out a question on the board and asked the class, *"What is the log base root 2 of 1 divided by 32?"*

"Minus 5."

The professor, not expecting anyone to revert on the very first day of her lecture, looked around and acknowledged Kismat with a smile.

Not only did Kismat ace all her first semester exams, she even became a partial translator for the Teaching Assistant, a Chinese grad student, who was brilliant in math, but struggled to speak in full English sentences.

Kismat's perfect scores in every subject fetched her plenty attention from her classmates who wanted to have her in all their study groups. Recounting the instances from her Delhi school where the popular girls would photocopy her notes and spend more time chit-chatting than actually studying, she chose to study in peace on her own.

During mid-terms and finals, she would cave inside the

Douglass library. Meals would be eaten in solace like an attentive squirrel focusing on every morsel.

Purchasing textbooks was a costly affair. Half a semester later, Kismat would discover that the latest edition only had a few, new pages for reference. Realizing this was all a sham business, Kismat began renting textbooks from an online platform for a small fee.

Coming from a land where one's profession was decided pre-birth, it was somewhat of a liberating experience for Kismat to wait before deciding on her major.

There were some popular songs she'd listen to as an interlude between her exam preparations, but somehow, she would always trace the lyrics back to Finance.

When she would play Beyonce's 'Halo' on Youtube, she'd connect "*The risk that I'm taking....*" to the "risk-return tradeoff'; when Chris Brown's "*Forever*' would jam on the radio, she immediately thought of a "perpetuity"; and when The Script would be crooning to their hit "*Breakeven*" to lull all the heartbroken lovers, she could only imagine its namesake in financial analysis.

She knew she was meant to be a Finance major.

Like an apt Finance student, she tried to save money where she could. With so many events happening all over the campus at odd hours, it was possible to get 'free' pizza and subway sandwiches every now and then.

However, a quick glance at the tuition bill with lines denoted as "Social Org fee" and "Misc campus maintenance cost" would reinforce the old adage that "*There's no such thing as a free lunch.*"

Kismat would resort to Wal-Mart and dollar stores for clothing and school supplies. She would be proud of herself on the months when her credit card payment would be less than the cost of few Chipotle burritos.

Ajay took it upon himself to entirely fund his kids' education, even though he was almost on the verge of unemployment from the 2008 recession.

It was during this time that Kismat was able to ascertain the difference in the quality of life between the two countries she knew dearly. To make a valid comparison, it didn't make sense to see how two financially stable people were doing. Instead, it was important to see how a poor man survived.

Living in America was not a dream for the faint hearted. It would take one accident or illness without insurance to reach rock-bottom. But Kismat knew that in spite of the prevalent culture of suing, the country also had immense immigrant contributions blending together to create a land of more innovation than she had ever seen before. Living in the United States would only be a dream if Kismat could make ends meet, hopefully beyond paycheck to paycheck.

Kismat considered her father's money like a loan ("without any 'interest' in wanting it back", as her dad would graciously told her) and she was forever in a debt of gratitude to Ajay and Sita. She had just learned about the bond yield curve in her Investments class, and she felt the curve could be loosely applied to describe the bond between her and her parents.

She did this often – trying to merge academic theories with the real world.

This wasn't so much as a mnemonic, as much as her own theory that every formula and theory in the world could be applied to real life scenarios.

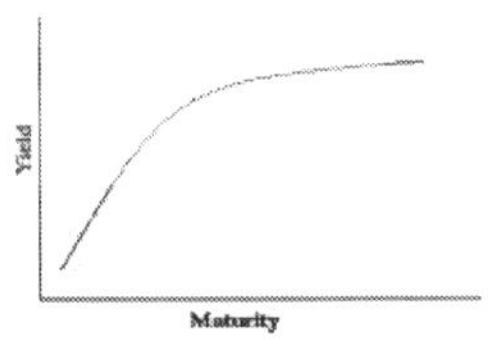

A bond yield curve is a graphical representation of the yield or interest that

a bond delivers on the Y-axis with time to maturity on the X-axis. Since a bond buyer is essentially lending money to the bond issuer with the expectation of receiving it back with due interest, the interest rate should be directly proportional to the maturity. In a stable economy, the yield on the Y-axis will increase as time to maturity increases on the X-axis but the inverse can also happen during a recession.

Assuming the parents or any form of guardians as the bond buyers, they lend their time, energy and savings to their children, or in other words, the bond issuers. The bond buyers live with the expectation that their investment on their kids will pay off with due interest. The interest, here, is interest their kids take in their well-being.

Thus, the happiness of parents can be represented as the yield on the Y-axis and the (mental and physical) maturity of the offspring can be represented on the X-axis. Kismat knew that the bond yield curve was not a perfect analogy as some parents could be absent/abusive, but she still fancied making such applications to the real world .

Like any immigrant adjusting into a new land, Kismat also had her moments of culture shocks, some of which didn't stray too much from the hiccups she had during her elementary school years.

The first shock came when she would have to justify her good English to folks she assumed lived inside a cave. In her head, she thought - I come from a country that probably has more English speakers than any other country in the world. But instead, she would settle with: "Oh, I studied in an English medium school."

Another instance was the sight of her American counterparts wearing shorts and bikinis with near perfect skin at the Jersey shore. Waxing was an expensive affair in the States. Occasionally, she would use store-bought wax strips that gave her about a window of three days of smooth skin and a broken back.

Ultimately, she resorted to shaving which led to her hair growing in every direction of the compass. The parlor ladies that she frequented back in the Green Park salons of Delhi would have fainted seeing the condition of her bumpy legs.

At St. Regents, she would come across couples holding hands on the bus or kissing near the famous Douglass fountain. The legend was that if a couple walked around the fountain three times and kissed at the end, they would be happily married forever.

Out of the many men studying in the larger co-ed campus of St. Regents, Kismat did find a few men to her liking but she never let those feelings progress to love, a word she still continued to dread.

Kismat even made a list of rules to help her stay focused and wait for "Mr. Right" after college. Coupling inspiration from the recession, the pressure from an American dating culture that she didn't want to succumb to, and the Finance theories she learned in class, she put together Five Commandments that every woman should follow.

She promised herself that she would strongly abide by this list no matter what the circumstance may be.

Kismat's Top 5 Commandments for Women Who Mean Business (copyrighted).

1. Attractiveness depreciates over time making it an unreliable measure to ascertain the Present Value of any suitable mate.
2. Be wary because the market is always abundant with high junk yield bonds.
3. Ladies, we are recession-proof.
4. Theory of liquidity- Don't let any mate with a below average credit rating, unwind your assets.
5. On a scale of 1 to 10, you're a certified AAA rated investment.

When Kismat hit her junior year, she enrolled in a one of a kind, living learning community at Bellefir – the "Human Rights House" (HRH).

The HRH consisted of eleven women who were as diverse in their heritage as they were in their ways of thinking that made group discussions on the most taboo topics, such as sexuality and religion, even more enlightening.

Chimama, of Nigerian origin, had volunteered for a year with a Christian missionary in Uganda, even when the terror outfit Lord's Resistance Army was at large. Thandie, of Irish origin, wore sleeveless shirts in the summer and winter alike, baring her toned and heavily tattooed arms. Even when she wasn't in class, she could be found at the University's gay rallies with a LGBTQ pin. Ambar was born to an Egyptian father and a Palestinian mother and though she did not wear a hijab, she enlightened the group on its many merits. These women saw the world through a unique lens, and though Kismat's bio did not have much extraordinary history to add, she was grateful to be amongst them.

Human Rights House's mission was to educate its residents about topical human rights issues plaguing the world at large. Part of the learning experience was visiting the country that experienced the violations and making a difference locally. The theme of that year was "Rights of the Child", with the country of focus being Romania.

The HRH group learned that the plight of Romanian children rose under the oppressive dictatorship of Ceausescu and the passing of his infamous 1966 decree. Under that ruling, all forms of contraception and abortion were made illegal and various measures were put in place to increase the country's population leading to many clandestine abortions, a tremendous rise in abandonment of children, and their subsequent admission in crowded, poorly-run orphanages.

In the late 90s, when his countrymen and women had had enough of his oppression, Ceausescu fled with his wife by helicopter from the majestic Bucharest Palace that he had built to appease his narcissism using the wealth of the Government's treasury. Both husband and wife were lawfully executed a few days later.

Over the winter break, the Human Rights crew made their way to Romania, famously known as the 'Land of Dracul', probably just as well as India was known as the land of Taj Mahal.

On the plane ride, all of eleven women were assigned to sit in three rows while the accompanying professor, Mrs. Rodriguez, took an aisle seat. The group clicked pictures, in happy anticipation, prior to boarding the aircraft.

One seat remained empty next to Kismat. She was secretly hoping it would remain that way so she could use that extra real estate to sleep more comfortably on the flight.

Ten minutes before the flight was to takeoff, a young man in khaki pants and a plain, blue collared shirt hurried his way down the aisle, profusely apologizing to those staring at his delayed presence. He approached the empty seat next to Kismat.

Kismat had placed one of her books on the empty seat to read later, almost as if she had demarcated that space as her own territory.

"Sorry to be the harbinger of bad news, but I'm here to take my seat now."

Kismat looked up and saw the smiling man.

"Oh, I'm sorry."

"No, I'm at fault. I never get anywhere on time."

As he seated himself down, Kismat quickly added, "Don't worry, I have the same problem."

"You too? Well, I feel less embarrassed now."

The flight attendant requested everyone to fasten their seat belts, as the pilot was ready for takeoff.

Half hour later, when the turbulence smoothened and the seatbelt signs were turned off, the man introduced himself properly.

"I'm Jason, by the way."

"I'm Kismat. If you don't mind me asking, are you also visiting Bucharest?"

"Don't mind at all. We're stuck on this plane for another six hours so I appreciate the chit-chat. I have a layover there and then heading to India."

"Really?! That's where I'm from. Are you on a holiday?"

"Kind of. I'm on a sabbatical and wanted to do some exploring on my own."

"That's great! Just so you know, India can startle your senses with unexpected bits of culture shock. I've grown up there, and I still get surprised by some of the things when I go back."

"Really? I can't wait to see what fun things are in store for me....and now that I've said that, I probably sound like some white guy looking for an exotic escapade."

She gave out her distinct laugh, a kind of a guffaw, both hearty and loud.

"So, what are you planning to do in Romania?

"Actually, I'm travelling with a college group. We are focusing on children's rights in Romania. Our plan is to visit some organizations to understand their progress and volunteer some of our time."

"That's amazing! I wish I had done something like that back when I was in school."

"Well, I go to an all-women's college. Our alumni base funds these kinds of projects," Kismat replied confidently.

"Damn! My college used to charge us for extra ketchup in the dining hall," Jason quipped.

Both paused for a few seconds, not knowing who will ask the next question to prolong their banter.

"So, are you majoring in Human Rights?"

"No, Finance actually -- mostly for better chances in the job market. What about you?"

"Physics. Can't say I remember much of what I've learned after finishing my PhD," he humbly added.

"Wow! Should I address you as doctor then?"

"Please don't. I'm nowhere near as brave as a doctor. I actually squirm when I get my blood drawn."

She guffawed again. The other members of her group were startled by her laugh and became curious about the guy whom Kismat was suddenly chatting up with.

Kismat overheard Jacqueline, who was three seats away, whispering to the girl sitting behind her. "Ssssh I can't see him properly...but he looks kind of cute...I wish I was sitting in her seat."

Destiny has its way of working mysteriously to bring people together. Here was Jason, whose attractiveness was suddenly being appreciated by the rest of her women clan. Kismat saw his reflection in the tiny entertainment screen straight in front of her.

Jacqueline was right.

Kismat didn't pay much heed to his looks before but suddenly, his brown eyes, his messy hair and spectacles made him look very intellectually charming. He was probably in his late 20s, she thought.

Kismat's first commandment came flashing across her eyes.

"Attractiveness depreciates over time making it an unreliable measure to ascertain the Present Value of any suitable mate."

"So Jason, which parts of India are you visiting?"

"I'll be staying all over, in the South, the West and the heading North to the hills. Wait, I'll show you."

He got up to open his compartment and took out his backpack.

She glanced over at Jason and noticed how his blue shirt tightly hugged his chest, outlining his well-built physique. Her cheeks flushed even more.

He sat back down and opened his journal. Then he pulled out a small map of India which was dotted with his markings and notations.

"Take a look, if you like..." and handed her the map.

Kismat saw arrows pointing to Jaipur, Ladakh, Amritsar, Pondicherry, Benaras and many more cities in Kerala and

Tamil Nadu.

The map looked like a poster for a domestic carrier showing its interconnectedness of service for India.

"So the question is --- where are you NOT going?"

He chuckled.

"Just so you know, the culture and languages of India change quite dramatically as you move from one direction of the compass to another, so be prepared."

"Yeah, I heard there are over a thousand languages there!" he added with inflection.

He rummaged for something inside his backpack and took out a small notebook.

"Hey, I was wondering...I wanted to get familiar with some common phrases in Hindi...if you can write some down for me, I'd be super grateful."

Kismat happily obliged and started jotting down some phrases for the good-looking stranger sitting beside her.

Jason set his smartphone on the eating tray in front of him. She noticed that his home page was a photo of a famous batsman, whose name she could not recall.

"Hey! You follow cricket?"

"Yes! I was born and raised in Sydney....played a lot when I was in school. Sadly, I don't play anymore."

Kismat was suprised that Jason was Australian as he didn't have any accent. But then, Kismat didn't speak in an Indian accent either, except to her parents. She could easily change between her accents, depending on which fellow she was talking to, like an uncanny brain switch.

"Why did you stop playing Cricket?"

"I tried getting people involved but everybody is loyal to baseball or football."

"You know, I played in a National Women's Tournament when I was in in India," Kismat quickly added, "and I was the Skipper too," hoping it would add for more brownie points to impress him.

"Wow! Guess we have a lot in common. First being late, and now Cricket. You must have played really well to be the Skipper!"

"Not really."

"I'm sure you're just being humble. What was your batting average?"

"Well, I made one run off of 3 balls in the Finals before being caught, so a solid 0.33!"

They both shared a hearty laugh before quieting themselves to be respectful of other passengers.

Kismat continued on about the nonexistent legacy she left for other women in the popular sport.

"Though I did take three wickets in one game!"

"I'm sorry for asking but why in the world did they make you the Skipper?" Jason asked, unable to mask his smile.

"Awesome question. The girl who was supposed to be the Skipper forgot to pack her blazer so the coach made me the Captain at the last minute. But, that's not even the best part."

"I'm all ears."

"Well, in the second game, I was fielding deep mid-wicket and the ball was coming right at me...."

"And?"

"And I was ready to catch it, but it slipped out of my hands and landed over the boundary. The next thing you know, the umpire raised his hand for a six. The rest of my team looked like they were going to eat me alive."

Jason couldn't control his laughter. Fellow passengers passed curious glances at them.

After dinner was served, they spent the next two hours going over the Hindi phrases and talking in detail about their individual itineraries. The plane was about to touch down in less than an hour.

The crew prepared itself for landing.

In spontaneity, Jason ripped a piece of paper from his journal and handed it to Kismat.

"Hey listen, I'll be in India for a full year but if you'd like to keep in touch, I have my email address in that paper for you. Feel free to reach out."

Inwardly, her heart was smiling. She let the hair strand, previously tucked behind her ear, fall on her cheek so he wouldn't catch sight of her blushing.

The attendant asked them to put everything away and put on their seatbelts. The flight landed smoothly at Bucharest Henri Coanda Airport.

Kismat's human rights crew started getting their things together and in the craziness of the moment, she forgot to give him her contact information.

As he got up to take out his luggage from the overhead bin, his right arm lightly grazed her body.

She felt a small electric spark.

Immediately, Kismat thought of her second Commandment.

Be wary because the market is always abundant with high junk yield bonds.

The passengers started making their way down the aisles. As Jason headed out, he said, "Once again, it was a pleasure Kismat. Thanks for all your help. I wish you all the best for your trip."

Kismat had thought of many witty things to say but settled with, "Same to you! Have a great time in my homeland!" Jason waved goodbye to Kismat and the ten other girls staring at him with loving eyes.

Over the course of their two week trip, the HRH crew their accompanying and Professor Rodriguez travelled to four cities of Romania - Bucharest, Brasov, Cluj-Napoca and Sighisoara. Across these cities, the group also made excursions to three, notable landmarks.

The first was the grand Palace of Parliament in Bucharest, the world's largest and most expensive administrative building housing 1,100 rooms, 480 chandeliers, and 2.2 million square feet of carpeting. It was constructed with over 700 thousand tons of steel and 9.7 million square feet of wood. It was the same castle that Dictator Ceausescu had built to appease his greed.

The next spot was the medieval Bran Castle in Brasov, famously known as Dracula's castle. Ironically, it had little connection to Vlad the Impaler, the key figure that inspired Stoker's Dracula character.

The third and last landmark was the Turda salt mines in Cluj-Napoca. The mines had been transformed into a sanatorium for patients with various respiratory ailments, and the underground amusement park was under development. The mines took advantage of the resonating sounds created by the surrounding enclosures of salt walls. Some of the tourists entertained themselves by saying funny words which were echoed back to them.

As part of their HRH mission, the group visited the country's largest university in Cluj, Babes-Bolyai University, and interacted with a panel of students on the available child's rights studies and research they had conducted. In Cluj, the crew also met with social workers at two non-profits to view their efforts to rehabilitate children in need, onsite. Kismat's experience in Romania was incredibly eye-opening, far more than what was originally intended on their three-page itinerary. She knew there was no dearth of human rights violations back in India, and around the globe, but to create parallels between her experiences in South Asia and Eastern Europe was uniquely moving for her.

The best part of her trip was just around the corner.

Sighisoara was housed in the valley of Tarnava Mare River.

The city had preserved its essence of old world charm with winding cobbled alleys, and steep stairways illuminated by medieval lanterns. Relatively untouched by modernization, Sighisoara had its roots in Roman architecture, with its ornate churches and citadels that could rival most picturesque cities and Pinterest towns of Western Europe. Every part of Sighisoara seemed worthy of being framed on a wall.

Sighisoara also housed a non-profit by the name of Meritas that was split up to serve two notable groups of mankind - children (mostly orphaned) and the elderly, who had no family to support them. The Human Rights crew was introduced to the diligent teachers who worked directly with the elementary school children.

For the remainder of their three days at Meritas, Kismat and the rest of the group were given the liberty to spend quality time with kids. The children were at first hesitant to meet such a large group, but their playfulness emerged soon after. They volunteered to play any game their imaginative minds could think of in that instant- from 'musical chairs' to 'statue' and 'follow the leader.'

One girl, about four years of age, with big, black eyes and black tresses, that were held back with a small hairpin, just stayed all by herself in the corner. She refrained from mingling with any of the other kids or Human Rights crew.

Kismat walked over to invite the little girl to play with her own group. The girl saw her approaching and immediately ran to another group, still keeping her eyes fixed on Kismat from time to time. When different groups of HRH crew started switching spots with each other, the same girl ran away to a corner and kept to herself again.

Kismat asked about the little girl from Ms Rosanna, their class teacher.

"Her name is Sophia. She's usually not this reserved but sometimes the kids feel too exhausted and want to stop playing. I would just wait and see if she feels ready."

After waiting for another hour and seeing no change in Sophia's behavior, Kismat decided to try a second time.

The girl was staring down.

"Hi Sophia. My name is Kismat. Do you want to play in my group?"

The girl didn't say anything. She glimpsed at a pink beaded bracelet on Kismat's left wrist that she'd bought in a local market in Delhi.

"Do you want this? Here, it is yours."

The girl looked up, showing a hint of a smile.

"Which side do you want me to tie it on?"

The girl finally responded by pointing to her right wrist.

Kismat tied the bracelet to her wrist.

Sophia hugged her immediately.

"Do you want to play with us?"

She nodded in excitement.

The afternoon of fun and games finally came to an end and the children started saying their goodbyes to the students.

Sophia stayed close to Kismat.

She hugged her several times, not being able to let go.

Kismat promised that she would return again the following day.

"Good night my dear Sophia."

Sophia hugged Kismat and ran away to join her classmates.

The Meritas students and teachers, alongwith HRH crew decided to pay a visit to one of the most loved churches in Sighisoara, and perhaps even all of Translyvania – the Church on the Hills.

Whenever the Human Rights crew would step out on the streets of Romania, they would always garner attention from the locals, if not for the large size of the group but for their unique representation of diversity of Latin, Asian, and African American women. Kismat found this amusing because if any of the Romanian locals were to step foot on the streets of Delhi, they would have been welcomed with the same kind of staring. Such stares were unlikely in New York City which only went to show what a unique melting pot that city really was.

Sophia walked the entirety of the journey hand in hand with Kismat. The church sermon was conducted in the local language but the music and holy vibrations within the church didn't need a translation. They could be easily sensed within every individual seated inside. When the sermon was over, Kismat took a sip of the holy water like everyone else, finding it very similar to her own traditions of drinking the "*Ganga-jal*" as a means to purify one's soul.

Before the entire group headed out, Sophia held Kismat's hand and asked her to come to the front of the church. Sophia kneeled down at the altar and Kismat followed suit, amazed by the devotion shown by this young girl.

Moments later, Sophia dug deep inside the small purse that she wore across her chest. She took out a worn out wallet and squeezed her finger inside one of its pockets to reveal a black and white photograph.

When Kismat looked at the photo, she got goosebumps all over her body.
In the photo was a young woman holding a baby girl, her face showing great contentment in being with her daughter.

Kismat took a closer look of the woman in the photo and fell silent.
This woman looked just like her.

Duality

Barring perhaps the length of the hair and thickness of the eyebrows, everything else was a perfect match.

Sophia noticed the look of bewilderment on Kismat's face and said, "That's my mamma -- God took her away from me," pointing to the photo.

The next thing that Kismat said to Sophia flowed from her deep consciousness.

"Sophia, I have to go back tomorrow but I promise to you, here in this church, in front of God, that I will take care of you. Ok, my dear? I promise."

Kismat hugged her tightly as they both shed tears at the altar. They walked back to the school, hand-in-hand, following the rest of their group.

That same evening, she met with Sophia's teacher again. Ms. Rosanna not only taught English and Math but also held a Senior Adviser role in the Funding Committee at Meritas.

"Sophia joined us a year ago, when she was barely four. Her mother passed away in an accident and she was left on orphan. Luckily a kind old lady brought her here just in time. God knows what would have happened to her if she didn't."

Kismat was speechless.

"Are you okay?"

Kismat took a deep breath and continued where she left off.

"Ms. Rosanna, I wanted to ask you something."

"Yes?"

"Has Sophia ever shown you a photo of her mother?"

"We may have one on record. Why do you ask?"

"Can you please show it to me?"

Ms. Rosanna went to her shelf and starting rummaging through the folders arranged in alphabetical order. She got to Sophia's file and saw a clipping of her mother's photo inset.

"What do you want to know about her? Is there...."

As she set her eyes on the photo and then looked at Kismat, she stopped.

"Oh my god!"

"Yes, I know."

"Did Sophia say anything to you?"

"Nothing in detail but I feel this connection with her. I've made her understand that I need to leave tomorrow. But I have a big favor to ask of you Ms. Rosanna."

Through the look in her eyes, Ms. Rosanna conveyed in ample measure that she was willing to help Kismat.

"Well, I am in no position to take care of Sophia now but I promise, someday, I will --- if possible, can you please send me updates about her so that I can be aware of how she's doing? Please, it would mean a lot to me."

"Absolutely! Just share your contact information and we will send you our monthly newsletter and share her individual progress with you."

Kismat took out five twenty dollar bills that were leftover from her trip. She placed it inside a white envelope and gave it to Ms. Rosanna.

"I'm sorry but this is all that I can donate right now. I'll wire more when I get back to the States."

Ms Rosanna conveyed her gratitude for the donation and wished her safe travels in her journey back to New Jersey.

Now in her third year at St Regents, Kismat settled into a fresh semester of new classes and assignments but the Romania trip still rattled her brains for many days thereafter. The sights of poverty visible on the streets contrasting to the richly magnificent Bucharest palace, the ethereal smiles on the innocent faces of the orphaned children, the natural wonders of Romania's salt caves under the ground and the scenic towns above it, all these memories were thoroughly cemented in her mind.

But what Kismat wanted most of all was to be able to reunite with Sophia.

Ms. Rosanna would share Sophia's drawings, which always had a setting of valleys and trees and sometimes, a woman and a little girl playing with each other. The girl would always have a pink band on her wrist, much like the one Kismat had gifted her. Ms Rosanna also cited that Sophia had an affinity for dancing and reading. Sometimes, she would click pictures of the class and share them in the newsletter and Kismat would be pleased to see Sophia happily smiling in them with her long locks and kind face that could easily vivify anyone's day. Though Kismat could not be there with her, these updates sufficed to help Kismat vicariously live through the sentiments of growing up with her.

After coming back from any long trip, some luggage items tend to magically disappear in the unpleasant activity of unpacking. However, there was one item that Kismat neatly treasured in the zipped pocket of her carry-on purse. It was the pristine piece of paper that held Jason's email address.

His full name was Jason Waugh.

It had been nearly two months since they first met on the plane. All of her Five Commandments failed to make her forget about him. She really wanted to write to him; to know more about him and his traveling adventures in India. In any case, Jason had no means to reach out to her; he didn't even know her last name.

The following Sunday, she finally gathered the courage to shoot him an email.

"Hi Jason,

This is Kismat from the flight.
Hope this email finds you well.

You definitely made the seven hour plane ride very enjoyable for me.

Our crew had a great time in Romania and the locals gave us a very warm welcome. I was humbled by the people who dedicated their lives to helping others.

I even met a girl named Sophia at one of the non-profits and I hope to see her again someday.

Anyway, enough about me. I'd love to hear any interesting stories about your travels in India so far.

Did you try out some new cuisines?...Did you get stared at a lot?...and how is your research coming along?

At first, there was no response. After a week, Kismat was sure that an Indian woman who fancied a handsome foreigner must have befriended him. Jason must have subsequently fallen in love and was probably sitting on a horse to his big fat Indian wedding at that very instant. Either that or there was the more likely probability that he forgot about her.

But a few days later, came a long reply.

"Hi Kismat!

It's great to hear from you.

I apologize for the delayed response. I didn't have any access to internet for over a week now.

To your questions, yes I had the most delicious dosa and chutney at this tiny cafe in Karnataka.

And yes, I get stared at everyday but I have gotten used to it by now.

From Bodh Gaya to Brindavan, I've seen every place of worship full of hagglers trying to perpetuate fear to make more money. I don't know if it is just because I am from outside or if it is common for these guys to do this with locals too. I found that experience to be most interesting of all.

And yes, my research is going well.

*You know, I got pick-pocketed at a train station and I didn't have enough rupees for the fare. Luckily, a college student helped me out. He was really chill and taught me a new phrase - 'Tension na lene ka, na dene ka.'**

*(*Don't take stress, don't give it anyone either.)*

The phrases you taught me are really helping too. India made me realize to never take anything for granted.

I'm already in love with your country!

Glad to hear that your Human Rights trip went well and I hope you get reunited with Sophia.

You know I didn't tell you this - but I really liked your ability to laugh at yourself. Very few people I know have the grace to do that. I'm certain that wherever you go, whatever you do, you will do well. More importantly, you'll be content.

I really hope our paths cross again so we can share our travels in person. I'm heading to Ladakh tomorrow and I'm not sure when I'll have internet again but I just want to wish you best of luck!

Though I know you will not need it.

Your wit and humor will take you places after all.

Warmly,
Jason

Kismat was thoroughly moved by Jason's response.

She was mildly attracted to him before, but she was fully infatuated now; a futile romance, since she was certain he didn't feel the same way. She put together a quick email and sent it the same day.

"Dear Jason,

I'm extremely humbled by your kind words.

I don't think you were aware of this, but half the girls from my crew had a crush on you.

You'll probably be out of connectivity again but I want to wish

you the best in your travels and endeavors.
Hope to catch up with you in person someday.

Love,
Kismat

Weeks had passed and Kismat did not hear a response from Jason after that.

She immersed herself into her University routine, wondering whether that "*someday*" would ever materialize between them.

In addition to her core humanities and business classes, Kismat had made it a point to select one eclectic course each semester in every year of her study at St. Regents. Some of these included the likes of "Behavioral and Abnormal Psychology", "Mythology", "Polynomiography" (which dealt with the science and mathematics of modern day art) and finally, her personal favorite, "The Greek and Latin Roots of English" or better known as "Word Power."

At the end of her sophomore year, she made her first trip to the American Museum of Natural History. The word history, itself, took its roots from Greek word '*historia*' implying 'inquiry' as she learned in her Word Power class. Inside the museum, she came across a cut up tree trunk on display. Instantly, she recalled that the mystery of a tree's age can be told by the number of rings in a cross-section of its trunk as she learned in her Ecology class. At the prehistoric section, she saw the large skeletal structure of T-Rex. (In Latin, Rex meant "king" in Latin, 'tyranno' was tyrant, 'saurus' meant lizard). Sure enough, the T-Rex was the undefeated king of all dinosaurs. In Abnormal Psychology, she came across the term "Oedipus complex" and she recalled the story of Oedipus, king of Thebes who killed his father and married his mother, from her Mythology class. She also discovered that 'Economy' had Greek root of 'ecos' meaning 'house.' As the pattern and/or flow of goods and services and businesses initially began with families in the household, it is no surprise then how the term 'economy' was established the way it was. As a business student, this was a remarkable insight for her.

Thanks to her Word Power class, Kismat would find occasions to suffice as the dictionary herself. She could easily identify sororities and frat houses by their Greek symbols. Of the 24 Greek alphabets, *Pi* and *Phi* stuck with her as her favorites, both being ratios with their own quirks and irrationalities.

Pi, an irrational number, seemed to go on forever, much like how her mother, Sita, would chat at length with her sisters on the phone.

Phi, on the other hand, represented the Golden ratio (1.618). Named after Greek sculptor Phidias, Phi was found in the patterns of Pyramids of Egypt, in Da Vinci's art pieces, and also in the compositions of Mozart. In nature, it was found in the patterns of sea shells, petals, florets, bees and even the golden spirals of the Milky Way.

She was marveled by how *Phi* formed the root of 'philosophy' *('philo' - love, 'sophia' - wisdom)* and was also rooted in nature and many of mankind's creations that inspired that very field of study.

~

Unlike the limited selection of Student Clubs at her school in Delhi, Kismat was paralyzed by all the choices available to her at St. Regents. She saw posters for tens of Campus Clubs, many of whom were rallying for important causes through 5K runs, dance marathons and columns in the college paper. She didn't which one to join.

A feminist club at Douglass had organized a "Take Back the Night" rally, wherein women could roam freely on the campus roads past midnight to protest against the violence against women.

Kismat signed up too.

She had long repressed the incident of the elementary school bully who coerced her to be his girlfriend. As she walked down the poorly lit streets leading to the main road of her dormitory at the feminist rally, holding hands with other women so late in the night, she felt liberated. Every woman in that movement was united by some form of molestation or violence they'd faced.

But this liberation was only temporary. When the roads turned empty and dark again, every woman, no matter how big or brave, felt like they could be another statistic. Repeated headlines of rape, sexual assaults across the world overwhelmed Kismat, and over the course of her remaining years at St Regents, she started having a very cynical view of the world.

She was certain there was no such thing as a God, for a divine being could not allow such suffering and cruel assaults, on any man or woman, to continue.

One day, she decided to address her worldly concerns to her Egyptian professor.

"Hello Professor. My name is Kismat. I'm in your Wars and Politics class."

"Hi Kismat. Tell me, what brings you here?"

"Professor, you've taught us that nations go into war to protect their resources and maintain their power in the global economy. Africa and the Middle East are currently going through such upheaval. I am just young and terrified. The meritorious don't always succeed, the corrupt and ill-willed get away with nonsense, and many innocents are deprived of justice. I mean, is the world really going to hell?"

He didn't open his eyes for a few minutes.

Kismat felt as if he was giving her an opportunity to shoo away.

"Your name means 'destiny', right?"

"Uh, yes sir, it's from Hindi I think."

Just then, he added, "Well, actually it's derived from the

Arabic 'qismah' and was finally adopted as 'kismat' in Urdu."

Suddenly, he shifted the topic.

"Tell me one thing Kismat, can you defend the Hiroshima and Nagasaki bombings?"

"Sorry Professor, I can't. So many innocent lives were lost and there are people who continue to suffer till this day."

"What if I told you that if the bombings didn't take place, WWII wouldn't have ceased, leading to an even greater loss of civilian lives and causalities."

Kismat wasn't sure of what to say. She didn't know how to defend a debate that she didn't side with.

"But Professor, there could have been other ways to make Japan surrender."

"Yes, Japan's defeat remains an area of contention. But I often wonder how something so tiny could have such a titanic effect to end the bloodiest war in human history."

Kismat did not look convinced.

"Look, I'm not advocating for war or weapons. Far from it actually, but it's important to grasp the complexity of the situation. Nuclear energy can do a lot of good and bad, depending on whether the desire for power is for the ego, or for electricity."

Then, with a simple smile, he said the wisest words she would remember all her life.

"What I find really strange Kismat isn't the fact that folks are committing all kinds of wrongdoing, because they are. But, because of all the bad news that fills our heads today, we believe that is the only reality around us.

Kismat, you need not have such a gloomy view of the world. I urge you to think about those who have risked their lives to help others. Think about the amazing roads, highways, and trains connecting millions. When you drive back home, do you think about the intricacy of the red, yellow and green lights that so effortlessly direct traffic?

Do you ever look up in the sky and see any airplanes colliding with each other? No. Because they travel in their designated routes in air, invisible to the eye. Humans, especially those that have challenged the status quo, have made remarkable progress. Sometimes, it is also invisible to our eyes. If we focus on the bad, we will think humans are doomed to act evil. But if we focus on the good, we will do more good."

Like a light bulb, his words illuminated the darkness of her mind.

The professor was right.

Even with acts of terrorism, suicide bombings, wars, wildfires, and pandemics flooding the headlines, there was also news of an eye transplant that helped a blind man to see again, or invention of a simple straw filter that helped villagers get access to clean water in Africa, or development of new vaccines.

And how could Kismat forget Sophia's teachers at Meritas? There were plenty humdingers around her.

Anyone or anything, no matter how tiny, could make a sizeable difference in the world.

Kismat didn't necessarily believe in a divine being just yet. But after hearing her Professor, she did believe in changing her thinking.

And that change was just around the corner.

Happiness without the Pretence

Kismat first got to know about the Gita Club while traveling to her Risks & Investments.

Somebody had opened a window on the bus.

A flyer was now fluttering in the air. After trying its best to stay posted, it flew off and landed on a seat facing Kismat.

She held it up.

A date and venue was mentioned and a brief sentence about the Club's goals to promote yoga and meditation.

Kismat almost set the poster back on the seat until she saw the last line hiding behind her thumb.

"Followed by free Indian dinner."

She saved the date from the flyer onto her phone.

Kismat was at first hesitant to be part of any Indian group or club on campus. She was sure that if she stayed with the same kind of people too long, a certain thought pattern would become customary about her and it would become even harder to break away from them. She witnessed this in the bossy cliques of her school, in the god-fearing habits of her kin, and in the servility of fellow Indians, particularly in the presence of any person in a position of power.
Like a free bird, Kismat did not want to be fixed in any group or place. But Thursday finally came around and for the sake of that one free dinner, Kismat made sure to go hungry to her first meeting in the Gita Club.

When she walked in, she was amazed to see how diverse the group was, yet how they all shared the same language of meditation.

After a half hour of rejoicing to a *kirtan*, the group mingled over delicious, vegetarian food. The stress on vegetarian food was to exemplify '*ahimsa*' or practicing non-violence on animals as well as to achieve the sattvic guna*.

**Guna refers to the quality of the mind and character of a person. Calm, gentle, patient and tolerant (sattvic), Passionate, spontaneous, greedy, materialistic, exploitative and focused on sense gratification (rajasic), or Ignorant, lazy, insensitive and deceitful (tamasic).*

The dinner consisted of eggplant curry, peppers and potato subzi, jeera rice, tomato chutney, followed by sooji ka halwa sweetened with jaggery. The taste was sublime.

After that first meeting, she became a regular attendee of the Club. Different members took turns to prepare the potluck dinner. Every so often, members would bring their own musical instruments and play and sing for the attendees. Some would be so moved by the singing during the *kirtans* that they would get up and start dancing in joy to the percussive rhythms of the drums and the soulful vibrations emerging from keys of the accordion and stringing of the guitar.

At the Gita Club, Kismat felt that every person was a unique drop, by virtue of their heritage, thinking, and personality, yet when pooled together, they created the vast ocean of humanity. If the United States was a melting pot of many different kinds of people, then the Gita Club was a microcosm of that ocean.

In her third meeting at the Club, the members learned about the holy Indian text - the "*Bhagavad Gita*" (translation - the divine song of the Lord). She had heard about the Gita from her parents before, but she only understood as much about it as a preschooler would know about Newton's Laws of Motion.

In addition to applying academic theories to the real world, Kismat also had a habit of making strange acronyms.

She could tune up her unfit body at her college GYM- *Garage (for) Your Mass*.

Post-graduation, her mind could be busied at a new JOB-*Jail Offering Bail.*

However, her dull soul needed a different kind of a repair shop, one that went beyond the body garage or the mind jail. And soon, the Bhagavad Gita would become the answer to that.

The speaker of the evening was Herman Bates. A graduate of St. Regents, he had worked in a securities firm for about ten years, made lots of money, got himself admitted to a rehab center, and eventually lost most of his savings by losing what he realized was his most prized possession - his own self.

Herman began speaking slowly and without inflection.

"For those of you who don't know about the Gita -- It is an ancient text of wisdom that essentially serves as a guide to living by elucidating narratives between Arjuna and Krishna. Arjuna is the warrior at battle with his own kin and he poses most of the questions to his guru Krishna. What is amazing is that the kind of struggles that Arjuna talks about is an allegory to the inner conflicts we face in our lives."

A member started handing out a piece of paper to all the attendees. Herman continued once everyone had a piece of paper in front of them.

"What you see in this paper is a summary of the Gita. It is a refreshing and simplified version of what essentially defines the human existential experience. I am not here to sell you anything, nor am I here to tell you anything new. What I will tell you is common sense, something that we already know, but we easily forget. Even if you don't get time to read the Gita in full, the *Gita Saar* can suffice for the time being. Some grasp the meaning easily, some take many years to grasp it, and others may take many lifetimes to do so."

She looked at the piece of paper in front of her.

This is what it said.

Gita Saar

Whatever happened in the past, happened for the good, whatever is happening in the present is happening for the good and whatever shall happen in the future shall be for the best too.

Do not weep about the past, do not worry about the future and focus on the present.

What did you bring at the time of your birth that you consider as lost?

What did you produce in the present that you consider as having destroyed?

Everything you have, came to you from God.

Everything you give during your time on this planet, you give back to God.

You came empty-handed and you shall leave empty-handed because everything belongs to God.

The speaker sipped some water. He paused for a few minutes to let everyone read the text.

"Everyone can take meaning out of the Gita as and when they consider it valuable in their life ---but, before I continue, does anyone have any questions?"

"Is the Gita related to any specific religion?" asked one curious fellow, who had a big black tattoo of a famous palindrome '*Live not on evil*' painted across his right arm.

"Yes, Hinduism. All religions teach different things but they get to the same point of being good. Personally, I think the Gita transcends the concept of religion because religion can create barriers but such wisdom – it sets you free."

When no one else raised their hand, Herman carried on.

"You are free to replace the word 'God' in the Gita Saar with any understanding of what you consider the ultimate source of life, within us and around us. Some of you may regard this innate belief to be the unknown, the intangible, spiritual being. The atheists or agnostics may attribute all life generation to a purely scientific logic. Some may believe the world revolves around them. Some may believe that their dryer magically eats up their socks and that is why they end up with missing pairs... And some men may believe they are not scared of their wives, when they really are.... And by some, I mean myself."

A few members in the room chuckled at his last line.

He continued where he left off.

"There may even be some who believe in nothing at all and believe it or not, that is also a belief. The point I'm trying to make is that we all believe in something."

Kismat's stomach started to rumble and all she could believe in at that point was that the Indian dinner that would soon be inside her tummy.

"Friends, I used to be a chain smoker and gambler and I did all those things to suppress the hurt I suffered from a few people in my life. But today, I am free of all those addictions. And it was simply because I absorbed the wisdom that everything is a transitory experience – from the people who abandoned me, the failed investments that ruined me, and my fate that took away the things I was most attached to. As the Gita says, what I considered my possession today belonged to someone else in the past and shall belong to someone else in the future because change is the law of the universe."

"But how did you manage to change yourself?" asked Serena, whom Kismat had noticed taking routine cigarette breaks in between the Gita Club events.

"It took me years. This path requires a lot of patience. Every day, I still spend a few minutes asking myself the same questions in the Gita Saar. By doing so, I am able to free myself from unnecessary despair. Some folks choose to let go of all sensory pleasures, but that's just an extreme. By upholding our duties and responsibilities without expectations, treating pleasure and pain alike, we can achieve the same path. The end goal is sweet. It's like nirvana without the drugs. Happiness without the pretence."

Kismat felt like her mind had drowned in the speaker's

words. It seemed all too heavy for her to be able to make her own interpretation about it.
She was at a point in her life when she wanted to make good money and socialize in her new job.

The Gita sounded like a detour that would make people want to quit their jobs, turn into some kind of a detached monk, and potentially become homeless.

She continued on her old path with the same velocity as before, following Newton's First law of Motion, unknowing of the true force of the Gita that would eventually present itself later.

When she came back to her dorm room, she searched the name of the speaker on the internet. Herman Bates was not some vagabond, but a happily married entrepreneur and philanthropist who helped raise capital for small businesses in the Greater New York City area.

Impressed by the man's background, Kismat borrowed an English translation of the Gita from the college library and hoped to finish it before the semester came to an end.

After one month of completing the book in between papers and classes, the words of the Gita had started to soak in. She was mistaken when she thought the Gita would cause her to become so enlightened that she would become lackadaisical about her goals.

Rather than losing the inclination to do any work, the Gita exhorted everyone to uphold the '*dharma*' of selfless action and not stray away from one's duties, no matter how difficult, as evident in the dialogues between Krishna and Arjuna.

Krishna, the omnipresent God, exhorted Prince Arjuna, to complete his warrior duties on the battlefield of Kurukshetra. Krishna served as Arjuna's charioteer and more importantly, as a vital mentor.

Prince Arjuna was one of five Pandava brothers who wished to reclaim the Kuru kingdom that his Kaurava brothers had enthroned by deceit in rigged games of dice. The sight of his erstwhile guru Drona, his grand-uncle Bhishma and even the Kauravas themselves made Arjuna want to withdraw from the battle as he could not bear to kill his own kin.

It became clearer to Kismat that Arjuna's kin represented the inner conflicts she faced in her daily life. *Krishna argued that fighting the enemy is the duty of a warrior and Arjuna must not renounce his responsibilities as a member of Pandava army. The Kauravas waged war for want of victory and power, but Krishna stressed that Arjuna must treat victory and defeat the same.*

Lord Krishna further articulated how death is inevitable. While the body and the relations we attach to it are impermanent, the soul isn't.

Most importantly, Krishna guided Arjuna that no work is ignoble, so as long as you do it without any expectations and your intentions are honest. (In a modern-day setting, this implies that even the work of a sewage cleaner is no less than the work of a major corporate head as both serve important roles to sustain society).

The five Pandavas defeated the hundred Kauravas in a battle that lasted 18 days with 18 akshauhinis in place (spectacular defeat since Pandavas only had seven akshauhinis while the Kauravas had eleven).

(p.s. One akshauhini = 21,870 chariots, 21,870 elephants, 65610 horses, 109350 foot soldiers).

This epic battle was known as the ***Mahabharata****. After the defeat of the Kaurava army, the Pandavas ruled the kingdom of Hastinapur for 36 years. It was evident that the number 'nine' played a significant role in the Gita, for every number quoted above had digits that added up to nine.*

The Gita was divided into three parts.

The first segment dealt with karma yoga which carried the basic premise of reaping good karma by sowing the seeds of good deeds without having any attachment to the fruit of one's actions.

The second segment focused on Krishna's guidance on meditation and spirituality through bhakti yoga.

Last but not least, the final segment was the culmination of Arjuna's entire spiritual journey and the wisdom he imbibed from his mentor, Krishna, through gyaan yoga.

In the Gita, there were no claims about its wisdom making anyone richer or smarter.

There was no fee attached for subscribing to it.

The Gita mainly provided an avenue for a way of living. And most importantly, it was not imposed on her; rather she had the power of exercising her choices.

At the end of her junior year, the Gita Club organized an event at Brooklyn's Hare Krishna temple that hosted a well-traveled *prabhu swami*.

Dressed in a simple beige cloth, yellow shawl, and wooden chappals, the *swami* started with a brief introduction about his childhood, avoiding the microphone.

He was wearing a unique *topi*. The cap was round in shape, but flat on the top and had a band of colorful pattern on the front, each zig-zig line woven intricately on looms. It was a *pahadri topi,* traditional to the native people of Himachal. German by descent and a scientist by profession, the *swami* lost his parents at a young age and was raised by a foster family. After completing his formal education, the *swami* tried his hands at research but felt lost, sitting in his lab, performing experiments on rats to prove one hypothesis, the veracity of which depended on creating other theories to prove the first one for the sake of continued funding.

During his narration, the *swami* shifted his story to his life-changing experiences in Nepal and India. He recalled how he trekked up on the hills of Himalayas and climbed as far as he could on the mighty mountains. The heights that initially jeered him as a coward, eventually absolved him of his own fears. In those mountains, he was amazed by the yogis who were content and unperturbed by everything around them.

In those mountains, he found salvation.

"Dear friends, I made the choice to embark on this path towards attainment of a balanced, selfless being. The world may or may not make sense but we can try our best to make sound decisions that together, will foster peace in the world. Recall that our body is made of the five elements of nature - fire, water, air, earth and sky. The body has to perish one day and return to nature, but our soul, the aatma, as the Gita describes it, is permanent. Just like the elements of our transitory body are naturally recycled through our birth and death, the permanent soul also takes in a new life form with each new cycle."

**The Hindi word for God i.e. 'bhagvan' can be expanded in a similar accord – bhumi (earth), gaggan (sky), vayu (air), aag (fire), neer (water).*

The swami continued, as the audience was still pondering about the elements of their own existence.

"The main point I want to address to all of you today is about our thinking. The Gita stresses that our mind can either be our best friend or our worst foe. It is very easy to dwell on the negative, but if we can focus our mind on the divine and the good, we can befriend our mind. Even today, after all my years of service, I still get hurt by the poisonous words and actions of others. My first reaction might be to retaliate and get hurt again. But when I focus my mind on Krishna, on my inner good, I have better control on my thinking. Remember that meditation doesn't make you numb to the outside world; it makes you more aware of your inner self, so that you don't get carried away by joy or sorrow. I know this may seem easier said than done, but believe me, our fears, our distress, and our liberation from all of them, originates in our thinking."

The audience was desperate to talk to the *swami*, to ask him many questions about his path to attainment of inner peace, and to share their own predicaments.

One man, dressed in business attire, having come straight from work, posed an interesting question that Kismat became privy to by virtue of standing next to him in line.

"Dear *swami*, I am successful in my job, I have a wonderful wife and kid yet I don't feel happy anymore, and I am making it miserable for my family as well. How long will I have to meditate before I can realize happiness in my life?"

"My dear friend, meditation is a personal journey. It is open to self-exploration. How often you meditate is also open to one's level of commitment. I am not here to preach advice about what you should or should not do. Nobody knows that better than you. But I do believe that life has a way of teaching us valuable lessons. Be willing to absorb them. If you keep sheltering away from those lessons, you will continue to live a life that you hate and drift further away from yourself."

Kismat had been moving like a pendulum between India and America her entire youth, for reasons that were, at times, beyond her control.

When anyone asked her which country she loved more, she could never really pick a favorite between the two. The more time she spent in one, the more she missed the other. Torn between the two countries, Kismat couldn't decide where she would be happier eventually.

Her soul belonged equally to both motherlands.

India had given birth to her in her nourishing womb and loved her with all her heart amidst her potholed-prosperity. The States had adopted her into her multicultural family, giving her a new, spirited identity amidst her many colored people.

Kismat was asked to approach the *swami* next.

She had been waiting all evening to ask him just one question. As she came near the swami's presence, she immediately felt at ease.

His expression was simple and his energy was radiant.

“Dear Swami, my heart is torn between India and the America. I think of India and I remember the traditions that bind my family and the soil that I call my own. But then I think of America and I have an unbridled sense of independence and a life that I call my own. Please tell me swami, how can I overcome this tug and pull between my two mothers?”

Even though this man was a complete stranger, she felt a unique sense of calm near him.

“It is not where you live that matters. The less happiness you seek from the outside and the more within, the better you’ll be.”

The swami’s words seemed too generic. She was really hoping he could tell her where to live.

He took off his beaded bracelet and handed it to Kismat.

"What is your name?"

"Kismat."

“These are the beads I used to meditate in the Himalayas. It is yours now Kismat. One day, you will reach the spiritual height you seek.”

His words managed to stay with her. Kismat journeyed on her unpaved path, fully aware that her self-actualization would not happen overnight.

She continued attending the Gita Club events on campus. The members would routinely sing the *mahamantra* in chorus during the *kirtans.*

Mahamantra

Ha-re Krishna Ha-re Krishna
Krishna Krishna Ha-re Hare
Ha-re Rama Ha-re Rama
Rama Rama Ha-re Ha-re

At first, Kismat was quickly bored by repeating the same lines over and over again. She knew that the only way she could gain insight was by first understanding the true meaning of the *mantra.*

After doing some research, she became aware of the significance of every word. The word *Mantra,* itself, carried the basic message of meditation.

Mantra

Man (mind) *tra* (to free)

Krishna and Rama

Kismat discovered that both were Hindu Gods and essentially manifestations of each other. As per the Gita, Krishna is the creator, the destroyer, the preserver, all in one. He is the manifestation of all Gods.

Hare

Kismat found the meaning of Hare to be most unique. Stemming from the word *Hari,* it referenced Radha, who is Krishna's beloved, the feminine power, his *shakti* and some yogis claim to be Krishna's ultimate source of strength. Therefore, chanting Radha's name during meditation is akin to calling out to one's own strength. Without Radha, even mighty Krishna is powerless.

In essence, the *mahamantra* highlights the strength of a woman who creates, destroys, and preserves the world. Without Radha's name, this *mantra* is wholly incomplete.

Different folks had their own versions of connecting to God - some read holy verses aloud from books, some made their own speeches when they desperately wanted something, some knelt down, some sat cross-legged, and some just stood there and folded their hands in *namaste.*

Kismat posed a question to Meera, a regular member at the Club. “Why do we always sing this Krishna *mantra?* Why not just meditate in silence?”

“That's completely up to you. Some days you might want to sing and dance in joy and some days, you might want to pray quietly."

Then Meera asked her a question.

"Do you know why we sing the *mantra* with music?"

"Why?"

"Because music fills up our soul – the organ at a Church, the harmonium at a Gurudwara, the harp, the table, the flute and the sitar – they all create a heavenly confluence of sounds."

Next, Meera asked Kismat to try meditating on "*Om*.' She articulated that many learned yogis considered "*Om*" to be the first sound to emanate from the Universe and chanting it would emanate the same energy and the same vibrations that was present in our environment, our bodies, and even in the very thoughts we generate, sparking Kismat's curiosity about the connection between energy and consciousness.

Kismat employed Meera's advice and meditated on the simple syllable. She sat down in a cross-legged position, her back fully upright. She placed her index finger on either side of her temple while using her middle and ring finger to close her eyes and finally, the thumbs to cover her ears. She took a deep breath and chanted a long "*Om*" in the same exhalation.

Kismat repeated this technique several times. When she finally opened her eyes, she felt fresh as ever.

Initially, it was difficult for her to still sit without multiple, random thoughts traversing her mind.

Thoughts of where she would land her first job. Whether she would be able to make her parents proud. Whether she would ultimately end up as a success or a failure.

But as she meditated on 'Om' every morning, she began to feel a sense of clarity emerging in her mind. Kismat knew she wouldn't become some overnight monk by meditating once or twice, nor would would she achieve long-term happiness by sitting through several sessions like some membership to a yoga club.

As the *swami* had told the businessman, there were no rules or restrictions in how one should meditate for the entire process should be empowering, not caging.

Her favorite time and place to meditate would be near her window, in the morning right after waking up, or the under the shade of a tree near the lawns of her dormitory, or wherever else she could experience peace amidst nature.

The swami's bracelet had twenty-seven beads and she aspired to complete four rounds of the bracelet to reach a total of a hundred and eight, using each bead to chant the mantra, again bringing back relevance to the number nine.

Over the course of these peaceful sittings of tuning into her inner self, Kismat started to get more clarity on the goals that mattered to her.

Some days, she would just be sitting in class, or riding the bus to get to class, or lay awake at 2am in the night, and a new goal would pop up in her head.

Finally, she decided to write it all down on piece of paper as a list of things that she vowed to complete in her lifetime.

Kismat's bucket list:

1. Become financially independent
2. Gift her parents a holiday
3. Move to India after a few years
4. Love and be loved
5. Go scuba-diving
6. Go sky-diving
7. Adopt Sophia

Goal #1: Become financially independent

Walter & Walterson was Kismat's dream, banking firm. Their two year Associate program for young graduates was one of the best in the country. Kismat applied to W&W and even interacted with senior managers at the B-school career fair.

After two phone interviews, Kismat was asked to come to the company headquarters in Manhattan for the final round. Five other aspiring applicants from top schools were also waiting in queue for their grueling rounds of face-to-face interviews. Kismat aced most of the questions on accounting and finance, but fumbled on one important question.

"Where do you see yourself five years from now?"

Kismat was advised to say that she'd be working her way up, holding onto some bar of the corporate ladder for dear life.

Instead she replied with, "I see myself as a mother and as a Manager in this company."

The Senior Manager interviewing her, luckily, was a new mother herself. She pointed out that her own promotion at W&W took much longer than she anticipated but encouraged her to meet her milestone.

Kismat was hired for the position of a Summer Associate. Post her internship, she was thrilled to know that they had offered her a full-time position as well.

Kismat was well on her path to completing her first goal.

Goal #2 : Gift her parents a holiday

Ajay and Sita had dedicated their time, sanity, and money in making sure their children had the best of opportunities. They were so caught up in saving up for their kids that they forgot about their happiness, and quite frankly, themselves.

Her parents' 25th anniversary was coming up next year and she decided to use that special milestone to gift them a holiday abroad.

Goal # 3: Move back to India

One of the primary motivations to move back to India was for the happiness of her mother, Sita, who seldom made her loneliness evident in between her tasty meals, clean rooms, and laundered clothes.

But Kismat was keen to return to Delhi for her own sake too. She was more likely to belch Falguni Pathak hits than any Taylor Swift song in her inebriated state, and would miss the Bollywood hits blaring on the radio in Delhi. Whenever she would find any desi export like herself to practice her rustic Hindi with, she would be overjoyed. In her tiny dorm room at Douglass, tear-blobs would unexpectedly roll down her cheeks when she would listen to "Jahan Piya" from Pardes and the line *"main khush bhi hoon, udaas bhi, nadiyan main jaise pyaas bhi"** would surface. It was almost as if the mellifluous singer Chitra was directly tugging at her heartstrings, prompting her to return.

**I'm happy...but I'm sad too...like the conundrum of a river plagued with thirst.*

In the pendulum motion of shuttling between her two motherlands, the pull from India was steadily growing in her heart.

Goal # 4: Love and be loved

The fifth item related to 'love', that dreaded four letter word she had escaped all throughout college by righteously following her Five Commandments.

Kismat was ready for a relationship with Mr. Right, even if he was Mr. *Partially Wrong but Overall Decent Family Man.*

Goal # 5: Go Scuba Diving

Kismat used the Student Recreation Center at Douglass to swim on her free days. When the world would feel too heavy on her shoulders, she would take a deep breath, dive into the pool, and swim till her lungs permitted. Each time she let herself free in the water and rush back up, gasping for air, she felt like a new person again.

With her breathing measured and controlled and her mind free, swimming felt nothing sort of zen. Kismat had an innate desire to experience the world of nature underwater, in those same measured breaths of taking a swim in the pool. Her adventurous spirit sealed the fourth item on her list.

Goal #6: Go Sky Diving

Following from scuba-diving, Kismat added another adventure sport that would allow her to get a bird's eye view of nature and experience freedom mid-air.

Goal # 7 : Adopt Sophia

Last, but certainly not the least, Kismat had promised a little girl from Romania that she would be back for her.

Whether destiny agreed with this or not, adopting Sophia was a goal she could not abandon, for as long as she lived.

The Dream Job

The W&W office was located in a plush district of Manhattan. It was adjacent to other tall, shiny buildings that could very well serve as full-length mirrors for the giants and beasts that Hollywood so fancied in its blockbusters. The office had everything she could ever dream of:

Feeling out of shape?

Try the fitness center on the 11th floor with trainers, the size of lumberjacks, all waiting to transform your apple, pear, and watermelon shaped bodies into an hourglass.

Feeling tired?

Pamper yourself at the on-site spa and salon on the 9th floor, where the beauty technicians will spoil you silly with an array of avocado and collagen masks and trendy hairstyles. Pets are welcome with a caveat - your pet poodle may come out looking better than you.

Feeling hungry?

Head to the international cafe on the 1st floor where one can gorge on a buffet of exotic and local cuisines – tapas, tandoori, or Thai curry. Then try out the sumptuous dessert options from walnut banana cake, mochi ice cream, and tiramisu. This brings us back to 'Feeling out of shape?'

To sum up, all that was missing was a magical corporate park where W&W employees could glide on water slides during water breaks and wait in line for the scariest ride of all- actually doing work.

Some of her other friends from Business School were lucky if they could grab a free hot coffee in the morning.

After the first month of orientation/honeymoon phase at work, all those aforementioned amenities seemed like an oasis in the lands of the corporate desert. From the dizzying nested formulae and scenario analysis to macro runtime error paralysis, Kismat was in a fully committed relationship with Excel. Six months in, she diligently put in the hours to ace her deliverables for a strong performance evaluation.

Whenever Kismat had trouble finding her car keys, she would think about doing a **Ctrl+F** on her entire house; as she would reach the toll booth, she would think about using a **CountIf** on the number of bills to give to the attendant; the days her room would look like an utter mess, she would think about creating a **Pivot** table with a built in **Macro** that would instantly organize any shoes and clothing lying around.

But real life can't be Macro-fied and finding her keys and cleaning her room would remain universal problems that she would have to figure out on her own.

Kismat took the NJ Transit train to get to the City, just a mere three stops away from her home in North Jersey. On rare occasions, she would drive into the City. As soon as she would enter into the Lincoln Tunnel, she felt like she was in a videogame, hoping to see light at the end of the dimly lit passage. Once she crossed the border into Manhattan, her drive would be punctuated with sneaky delivery boys, aggressive taxi drivers, and jaywalkers. Her heart would skip a few beats when she would have to make space for emergency vehicles on duty. And last but not the least, she had to apply all sensory faculties to read unexpected signage and avoid lanes declaring *"this is reserved... between the hours of ... maximum fine is .... and possibly face imprisonment/other threatening consequences."*

If driving in New York City was akin to getting her eyebrows threaded, then driving in New Delhi was like getting waxed in her private parts. Perhaps that wasn't the best of use of hair removal idioms, but after having driven in both cities, she concluded that they were insane in their own respects.

Kismat had her first taste of luxury in America at W&W's holiday party that was traditionally held at the end of the year. The venue was a historic five-star property at the intersection of Madison and Fifth Avenue, one of the most expensive in the world. To fit in, she requested a glass of Pinot Grigio and was confused to see the waiter only pour a gulp into her glass. The waiter stood aside and simply stared at her. It was only until a colleague nudged her to drink the wine and offer him a perfunctory nod that the waiter proceeded to pour a decent amount in her glass. By the end of the party, she was heady, not just from the multiple glasses of wine and truffle appetizers, but from the excessive socializing she was not accustomed to.

Kismat's lifestyle had changed dramatically from her days of being a Burlington Coat Factory bargain hunter to relishing the many temptations that the city of Manhattan could offer a middle class girl with fabulous income and the freedom to spend it.

The allure of the Big Apple, with all her pleasures, attractions, and captivating billboards intoxicated her too. Her twenties were as good as she was ever going to look and Kismat knew she had to make the most of it; exactly the kind of thinking a city like Manhattan would want all her young adults to have.

Kismat had gathered the self-esteem to set foot inside designer stores on Fifth Ave, dine at restaurants with signature chef specials, and indulge in facials and laser treatments that made her feel like a mini celebrity. This was the same Kismat who would balk at the idea of an expensive wax at a salon and settle for a disposable razor from the dollar store instead.

Friday nights were now reserved for partying with her W&W colleagues in the glory of completing another hectic week of late night assignments and early morning presentations.

Kismat's motto had now become:

EBITDA- Earnings Being Invested Towards Dancing and Alcohol

Kismat could still remember her first sip of alcohol at a friend's basement party in the senior year of college and wondering, "*This tastes terrible! What is this?*"

After almost a year into W&W, that sentiment had changed to "*This tastes delicious! What is this?*"

The City's temptations were plentiful.

Her colleagues decided to hit a swanky, new club that had just opened on the rooftop of a SoHo hotel and Kismat followed suit. A large portion of the crowd consisted of model specimens with their squeaky clean faces and shiny attires. A live DJ enthralled his audience with catchy tunes and laser lights dancing to those same tunes, lending the appeal of a futuristic discotheque.

Kismat made her way to the bar where the bartender informed her about a new concoction that she may find to her liking. Thirteen dollars for one shot was preposterous, but very normal for a city like Manhattan.

A man, standing close by, requested the bartender for another round of shots, his breath reeking of alcohol.

"Hi, I'm Jack."

"I'm Rose," Kismat lied.

"Oh, what do you do for a living, Rose?" he asked, missing the blatant, Titanic reference.

"Well baby, if take you off your silent mode, we can go into vibrator mode on the dance floor."

Kismat's Fourth Commandment kicked in - *Theory of liquidity- Don't let any mate with a below average credit rating, unwind your assets.* She employed her favorite quote from Oscar Wilde, which she used as litmus test to judge whether she should continuing talking to any potential suitor or simply move on.

"You know Jack, I've met many hardboiled eggs in my life, but you're twenty minutes."

"Thank you," came his quick reply.

A few seconds later, he asked, "Wait, I don't get it."

Kismat smiled.

"Eggactly."

In the hope of meeting her fourth goal of finding Mr. Right, Kismat even ventured on a few dates, one arranged by a work colleague and the others by an app called OkCupid. Though she specifically set the criteria for men between the ages of twenty-five and twenty-nine on the App, she often got creepy messages from men who were much older.

Her first kiss, sloppy and forgettable, was with a man who was on a consulting project in the City for a few months. She was won over by his British accent and humor and in between the flow of shots and cocktails; she couldn't even remember his name.

Much like the Five Commandments she had crafted during her time at St Regents, Kismat created a set of career-wise pickup lines, the success rate depending upon the recipient's acceptance of quirky humor.

Financial Analyst

"Damn I'd tap her.....weighted average asset portfolio."

"Your balance sheet looks great. I checked out your assets before walking over."

Lawyer

"We are one kiss away from making an oral cont(r)act."

"I am going to sue you for making me fall.....irrevocably in love with you."

Scientist

"Girl, you brighten my day, your fragrance lingers longer than

radioactive decay."

"Heaven knows you can't be real, you are blissfully $C_4H_{10}O$(ether)-eal."

"Everyday you be calculatin', when are we going carbon dating?"

~

After completing a year at W&W, Kismat had saved enough money to tick off the second item on her list-

#2: Gift her parents a holiday on their 25th wedding anniversary.

Kismat planned a eight day trip in Italy, ironing out all the costs in a neat Excel spreadsheet. Ajay and Sita, who had never been to a new country beyond the States, were adamant that the kids come along with them. Eight days of holiday, only because Ajay didn't want to take any more leave from his office, even though he probably had over a hundred vacation days carrying forward. Kismat even put aside a 'contigency fund' in case of unforeseeable emergencies during their Italian sojourn, an idea she learned when she was preparing a Business plan at St. Regents.

That contingency fund was hidden in different compartments of their travel bags, which came in mighty handy when Dhananjay's wallet got stolen by a pickpocket in Pisa.

Her father was right.

Education, even the minutest of detail, never goes to waste.

Italy was always beautiful, but for years, its burdening debt crisis that was kept private was now starting to seep through the crevices of its stuccoed walls. On the contrary, India's developing woes had always been strikingly public, but the beauty of her resilient spirit was longer veiled like some of her cultural garbs.

During their family *viaggo*, there were some memorable moments and it was not surprising that most of them came from Ajay who, even after living in America for over a decade, proudly retained his Indian accent almost as well as the Europeans had preserved their architecture.

The Dharmas toured inside the breathtaking Vatican, relished spaghetti and mango gelato near Trevi Fountain in Rome, and explored art districts of Florence, the last bit being boring for everyone except for Kismat. On their third day, the Dharmas trekked their way to the top of Michelangelo Square, with a majestic view of Ponte Vecchio, Duomo, and the Arno River. The whole family was famished from all the sightseeing. They found a little café which had limited outdoor seating. Everyone was trying to understand the menu card that was in *la langue francaise* with 'petite' translations for the dishes in Italian. As the waiter came around, he asked everyone to place their order.

Ajay decided to be adventurous and order his dish first. Pointing to the bottom part of the laminated menu, he confidently said, "I will have this piece of crap."

"Excusez sir?!" the waiter exclaimed.

Kismat fumbled with the menu to figure out what her father was actually trying to say.

Putting together whatever little bit of French she learned in tenth grade, she replied, "Oh sorry, mon pere wants la pizza crepe." Exhausted from the trek and all the laughing, everyone eventually ordered the same thing as Ajay.

Out of the seven nights of the trip, not surprisingly, five were spent eating dinners at Indian restaurants. It didn't matter which corner of the globe the Dharmas traveled to, Ajay and Sita could not do without their dal, roti, and chai.

On the sixth day, the Dharmas reached Venice. Kismat wanted Ajay and Sita to ride on a gondola just like the romantic Bollywood song "Do Lafzon Ki" that picturized Amitabh Bachhan and Zeenat Aman. Kismat encouraged them to have their own rendezvous but Sita and Ajay insisted they tag along. Once everyone had settled in, the gondola driver, seated at the edge of the boat, made his presence known.

"Namaste! Kaise ho?"

"You can speak Hindi?!" Ajay exclaimed.

The gondola driver introduced himself as Markus, and he was very fond of Bollywood flicks, particularly from the Raj Kapoor era. He had picked up a couple of words of Hindi from those movies and Indian tourists alike.

If passing under the scenic bridges wasn't enchanting enough, Markus even sang a few lines of Hindi, marking it as the highlight of their trip.

On their last day, Kismat got a call from her boss as they passed by the Trevi in Rome. She was asked to make an important presentation and deliver it the following Monday morning. She spent her day emailing her counterparts for crucial data points. Her family could sense her stress and decided to head back early to the hotel. Once the Dharmas landed back in Jersey, Kismat began working on her slides. She stayed up till 4am to put her final touches on her file and woke up groggily to the sound of the early morning alarm.

With only four hours of sleep, she called for a taxi so she could catch some extra winks in the car.

The cabbie had two distinct scars, one under his left eye and the other near the curvature of his lips that gave him the appearance of a retired soldier who longed for a simple life.

Kismat, meanwhile, dozed off in the back seat, like a recluse.

The cabbie yelled a few expletives at a passing pedestrian who raced in front of his taxi at the very last minute.

"Son of a gun!!! If you wanna kill yourself, don't do it under my cab!" he bellowed out of his window.

Kismat was awakened by his yelling.

"Sorry about that."

Kismat didn't respond at first.

"You know miss, I once came under a car."

Her eyes met with his in the car seat mirror, and he took it as a sign that she was listening.

"I was seventeen years old when my buddies played a prank on me. I ran to the street trying to get away from them and BAM, a car hit me."

"Oh god! I'm glad you're okay now."

"Yeah, broke some bones but the docs sewed me back up. Took me a whole year to start walking normally again. It's like I'm living a second life. You know every time I see these people texting and running around like maniacs, I want to tell them it's not worth it."

Kismat's respect for the man increased tenfold.

"Miss, want to know why we have the temperature gauge on the car's dashboard?"

"To tell us if the engine is heating up?"

"Yeah, that is the main purpose based on the car manual. But it's got another purpose based on the life manual."

"What is that?"

"Well, if you look at the needle, it usually stays put in the middle. If the level of the coolant drops or changes due to outside heat or cold, the needle moves to either side. That's kinda how I see life. You gotta think like that needle and stay balanced. Get too heated up or become cold-hearted to the people around you and you're in big trouble."

The cabbie then went off on a tangent about his early years driving in the City, those long days surviving on dollar pizza slices and soup kitchens and how he finally managed to save up for a second-hand car. Just hearing him talk transformed her mood from a tense, restless feeling to a feeling of gratitude for all that she had. She paid her fare and thanked the cabbie with a generous tip for all his enlightenment.

Once inside the office lobby, she ran to catch the elevator. Another man in a gray suit wanted to jump in but the doors started closing before he could get in.

He asked her to hold it open for her.

"Ctrl Z! Ctrl Z!" she shrieked, much to the amusement of other people standing inside. That MS Office function was ingrained in her brain after much abuse of it on her powerpoint the night before. Kismat pressed the button to hold the door, but it was too late. The man didn't make it.

When Kismat met the Director she had to present her slides to, she turned red. It was the same man she left behind at the lobby as the elevator doors closed on him. Barring the minor embarrassment and her desire to hit "Esc" on the keyboard, her presentation went well.

The rest of the day flew by as her calendar was filled with back-to back meetings. She was exhausted and felt happy at the prospect of getting some sleep at home. But before she could escape, her boss handed her another assignment that she had to complete the following morning.

At about 9pm, she began packing her stuff to go home. As she put her laptop into its bag, she heard some buzzing sound and noticed that the janitor was vacuuming the carpets in an adjacent hallway.

"Sorry for the disturbance miss. I can turn it off," he said apologetically.

"No, that's alright. I was just about to leave."

"You know miss, I'd been struggling to find a job ever since I lost my old one as a garbage pickup guy. I'm thankful this company gave me a contract. My daughter can stay in school now."

Kismat, unsure as to why random people were sharing their life stories with her on a Monday, smiled back at the man.

"She's the smartest in her class, you know!" added the proud father.

"That's wonderful!" Kismat added, sharing his enthusiasm.

He spoke with great pride and joy, almost as if he had been waiting for anyone to acknowledge his daughter's accomplishments.

"I didn't get the chance to study in school. My folks kind of abandoned me. But I won't do that to my daughter. I really hope she grows up and gets a job like you."

Monday blues had failed to meet their inglorious reputation that day, for they had been mitigated by the heartfelt monologues from the cabbie and the janitor; two extremely resourceful people of the world.

Both men reminded her of the Gita again.

Their work was just as noble, if not more, than any other employee in some fancy office. They didn't shy away from their responsibilities. Rather, they were dedicated to their work and to their goals.

Ironically, for Kismat, she was now uncertain about whether she wanted to continue working at W&W. Her lifestyle was paralyzed by late night dates with her laptop, endless meetings, and evening conference calls with international counterparts. Her work meals were mostly takeouts in foam containers from the cafeteria, most of which was eaten in a mindless rush. A good chunk of her vacation days were exhausted in catching up on sleep and doctor appointments who diagnosed her poor appetite and body aches with chronic, adrenal fatigue.

The erstwhile temptations of luxury did not entice her anymore. Rarely did she get a weekend to herself, and even then, her mind was always thinking of the next deliverable that was to come her way.

But this was her dream job.

How could she quit?

She brushed the very thought aside and continued putting in her hours and soul into her W&W tiny cubicle that had become her primary home.

~

When Kismat was still in her senior year at St. Regents, she was itching to graduate so she could start making money.

As always, she would walk in late to her early morning Investments class.

The wrinkly and bright-eyed professor, Mr. Wilkonson, didn't mind, as usual.

He was itching to retire anyway.

In one of his classes, the topic of discussion was the 2009 global recession. He urged his students to share their views on what they had read or heard recently about the black hole of debt created by most of Western world. A guy in the back row, to the relief of all, raised his hand and spoke at great length about how his father lost his job, and how the President should first focus on rebuilding the country before helping any other.

Another girl mentioned a sentence or two about EU's responsibility and need for passing government austerity measures. Professor Wilkonson had a weird habit of chuckling when he was not satisfied with an answer and he would continue to ask his not-so chuckling audience till God had mercy on his soul.

After a brief, awkward silence, he finally said, “To Ireland, Italy, Portugal, Spain and any other country that thinks it is fiscally sound, I have four words for you: That’s what Greece said. Now, all these European countries share something in common that lent to this crisis. Can anyone tell me what it is?” he asked again.

As brilliant as he was, Professor Wilkonson never kept track of the names of any of his students; his age and lack of willingness to remember being the ideal reasons why.

All the students recoiled their heads into their shell like a tortoise. He noticed Kismat pretending to write something, another common tactic applied to avoid the professor from picking on you, the success rate varying upon how huge one's head was.

Pointing to Kismat, he asked, “What do you think, oh-late-one?”

She looked up and realized the professor was looking straight at her.

“Any thoughts?” he asked again.

“Professor, I'm sorry for being late....”

“Not concerned with that. Just tell me what you think Kismat. There is no one right answer.”

Startled to hear her name openly in class, she waited to compose her answer and finally said, “I think that the band-aid of debt has been repeatedly abused to cover the bleeding, infrastructural problems of all these developed countries, stemming from perhaps meeting EU demands, or from government policies to cater to a lifestyle that is popular only to Europe --- But whom am I to say anything? --- I live in the US of AA+.”

A renowned credit agency had downgraded America from its pristine rating a month ago.

Mr. Wilkonson laughed so hard, his teeth seemed to be dangling with his every head movement and the students were contemplating to call an ambulance.

When the class ended ten minutes later, Professor Wilkonson walked up to Kismat and said, “I picked on you because your recent paper on '*What the West can Learn from the Rest*' was a thoroughly unique and refreshing perspective on failures of developed markets leading up to the global financial meltdown. You're a smart lady but remember one thing -- I worked all my life to realize I was not made to be glued inside a cubicle. I know you aren't either. The only difference is that it took me thirty years of that kind of a lifestyle to come back to my senses and it'll probably take you less than three.”

“But professor, I just got a full-time offer from W&W.”

"Yes, I know. Professors keep a tab on those kinds of things from the recruiters. I'll say congratulations to you the day you quit."

Kismat was taken aback by the man who suddenly showed a rare side of himself.

He packed his briefcase and as he walked out of the room, he simply added, "Less than three years, remember that."

Rat Race

Before the sun could make its way over the horizon, Kismat would wake up to her default 7am alarm, put in her usual fifteen minutes to shower, dress up in a simple blouse and trousers, and make her way to the City.

She would return home; mentally fogged, failing to catch a glimpse of the same sun resting behind the clouds as the blue sky turned into a pitch black. The sense of everything being nice and cool that enamored her at the start was now ebbing away.

As she would make her way home amongst the herd of other suited and booted employees exiting the building; running to grab transportation, she felt like one of the Agent Smith clones; her identity demarcated by the corporate badge hanging by her waist.

Many opinions came her way.

"Quitting such a prestigious company will look really bad on your resume."

"It's not easy to find another job."

"You have to stop complaining. Many people would die to work there."

Kismat was going to complete three years at W&W in a month. She was recently promoted to Senior Analyst with a hike in salary. But she wasn't planning to celebrate.

She had become a person consumed with finding happiness in buying things she didn't need, but she could suddenly afford; a person who was following other people who followed other people on the same road of looking good on a piece of paper indented with -- *Objective, GPA, Work Ex, and*

More Stuff that makes you look good.

Kismat recalled the words of Nobel laureate Toni Morrison, who was the Commencement speaker at St Regent's graduation ceremony. Ms. Morrison's speech carried so much truth with such impressive ease that it couldn't be reiterated but just experienced and acted upon.

"I know that happiness has been the real, if covert, goal of your labors here. I know that it informs your choice of companions, the profession you will enter, but I urge you, please don't settle for happiness. It's not good enough. Of course, you deserve it. But if that is all you have in mind—happiness—I want to suggest to you that personal success devoid of meaningfulness, free of a steady commitment to social justice, that's more than a barren life, it's a trivial one. It's looking good instead of doing good."

Much like how she applied Finance theories in real life, she extended Morrison's quote to the formula of Pressure.

Physics teaches us that Pressure is the Force applied per unit Area. Area when spread over a distance 'd' gives us Volume. Force when exerted over a distance 'd' is Work.

Work requires us to expend our Energy. Therefore, if we multiply and divide by the variable 'd', Pressure can also be represented as the Work or Energy per unit Volume. If we apply the right amount of force "F" in the right area/field "A" of our choice, our pressures "P" can help us grow.

Even if we feel pressurized, our hard work "W" can serve as a constructive form of energy "E" to push us to achieve our goals. However, if we are not moving in the same direction as to what we really want to achieve, our work "W" carries no value towards our self-fulfillment. It may help us look good or give us temporary pleasures, but eventually, our life will feel meaningless and empty (W=0).

Kismat felt as if all the energy she was extending on her work and resulting pressures were drifting her further away from herself. It wasn't really the company that she disliked; it was her own self. The job, with all its perks, was wonderfully suited to many other aspirants.

She could look good with the correct use of lighting and photography, but to do good, now that's something that required far more conscious effort. The Gita was relevant even here for it all depended on how Kismat exercised her choices.

Her brother, Dhananjay, was happily settled in sunny California. He visited them during any long weekend that suited him. Seeing as he was already five years into his job, she asked him about his future plans so as to gauge what she should do with her own life.

His first words to her always started with, "Hi loser!"

Ajay, who was standing nearby, quickly interjected, "Minni is not a loser. She's a winner!"

Dhananjay snarled at her. He wouldn't admit to it but he would feel inherently jealous whenever Ajay would take her side.

"So, back again for mom's food, huh?" Kismat quipped.

"Yeah, we all aren't as lucky as you to live rent-free and enjoy her food all the time --- and I probably know how to cook more stuff than you do by now, loser!"

As much as she hated to admit, Dhananjay had become more self-reliant than her. He cooked all his meals from scratch and every nook of his San Francisco apartment was in order. She considered this a miracle given that her brother's teenage years were spent gorging on Kurkure chips and coca-cola and feasting at fast food joints. He was notorious for having piles of dirty clothes on his bed and inside his closet. Kismat, on the other hand, was still on the receiving end of complaints from Ajay to keep her things organized. Her hair ties, glasses, and work files could be found in random drawers. She kept adding new dresses to her wardrobe while keeping old shirts and pants that should've been thrown out a decade ago. So naturally, Ajay and Sita would roll their eyes when she would complain of not having enough closet space.

Kismat went straight for the big question.

"Bro, how's your job going?"

"It's not too bad. I'm expecting to rotate to a new position soon. Hopefully they'll sponsor my MBA in a year."

"Damn! Remember the days when I used to study so much in school and you used to be the one that mom had to run after?"

He laughed.

"And remember that one time when mom came banging on your door because she found out that you almost failed in organic chemistry --- and you hid your exam paper inside the pajama you were wearing!"

That memory was so fresh in her mind, she felt as if it had happened only yesterday. They continued laughing as Dhananjay continued where Kismat left off.

"And she never found that paper -- still cracks me up -- poor mom, she had to suffer so much with me."

"Yeah, but she is really proud of you today. We all are."

Realizing that the moment was too cute to digest for their 'cool' sibling relationship, Kismat asked a more pertinent question.

"So...do you like where you are going with your life right now?"

"Yeah man -- I'm the CEO, Chairman and President of my life. What more?"

That answer was enough for Kismat to know that Dhananjay was not going through the kind of phase that she was reeling with.

"Why do you ask?"

"No, nothing....I was just asking like that," Kismat lied.

"Heard you got a raise too -- congrats! Oh and make sure to deposit some of that money to '*In Dhananjay We Trust*' Foundation."

A sense of despair was growing in her heart, a clash of wanting to change her lifestyle yet not being able to make the leap. She would complete all her work deadlines but her hands and feet would move at the will of an unconscious mind.

Her biweekly salary still kept her going.

As she walked to the train station to get home, she felt no different than Coleridge's 'ancient mariner,' the weight of her work laptop strapped across her chest like proverbial dead albatross around the sailor's neck.

The passersby who rushed to cross the street almost collided into Kismat for no one anticipates such abrupt stops in the City that never sleeps. A New Yorker is expected to keep moving, regardless of whether or not they know where they're headed. Several pedestrians averted her sudden stop and offered less than welcome glares. She took the "A" train to Penn station and stepped inside with the rush of other commuters frantically trying to grab a seat. Her stop was approaching next. Then, Kismat got a hint, as if from the cosmos herself. As the train arrived at Penn, Kismat and three other passengers stepped out. One of them was a guy wearing a plain black T-Shirt, carrying a skateboard in one hand and a can of beer in the other. She chanced to read the back of his shirt.

It had the following words, in bold white letters:

"If you want to know how to keep an idiot busy, look at the front of the shirt."

Intrigued by the unusual statement, she yelled out to the man - "Excuse me!"

A couple of people turned around including the guy.

Kismat caught a peek at the front of his shirt and immediately laughed at herself.

It read,

"If you want to know how to keep an idiot busy, look at the back of this shirt."

Realizing he had made another fool that day, the skater boy gave her a thumbs-up before walking away. Her laughter soon changed into tears. The moral she once learned in a fifth grade summer camp was now reverberating in her mind.

"It is great that some of you worked really hard to get to the end goal but you will find that in life, it is not enough that you work

harder than the rest. You must also work smarter."

As much as her formal education had taught her how to make a living, it would be her self-education that would teach her how to live. Smartness was not relevant here in terms of being well-off, as much as being well.

Kismat spent more and more time introspecting in her basement by dimming the lights and tuning into Mozart's Andante, followed by some melodies from the Indian Mozart, Mr. Rahman. The combination of the two would be strangely soothing.

Finally, she made to move to chalk out the rationale for the next steps in her life. For every fearful thought, she tackled them head-on as they presented themselves.

A fear of seeing her peers get ahead in the rat race.
I'd rather run in a Marathan. And I'd do it for the cause than the competition.

A fear of losing stable income.
I have saved up for the next six months. Once I'm back in Delhi, I'll find a new job.

A fear of being considered a failure by other people
The relevant people (Ajay and Sita) will be supportive in the end. Even if I fail, I will learn and move on.

Kismat had other fears too, like the paralyzing fear of snakes and heights. It was evident that every fear in her mind boiled down to the fear of death. And as the Gita suggested, it was imperative for her to focus on the permanence of her soul. Everything else was a transitory experience.

Ajay was her first and foremost advisor for any of her life's problems. Because his views tremendously mattered to her, she hinted to him about her next steps.

"Papa, there must be so many people who have studied the same course, or have same the job like me...."

He let her continue her flow of thoughts.

"For some reason, I don't feel happy working in this kind of a routine, day after day. Before I joined college, you told me to focus on the goals I sought for myself."

"Okay, tell me what do you want to do now?"

"I want to move back to India."

Initially, he didn't say anything.

"I'll help mummy with her clinic and find a new job. I have my own savings too."

She was speaking quicker than her usual quickness, as if she wanted to convince him before he changed his mind. Kismat knew Ajay wasn't thrilled about her decision to quit such a prestigious firm, but he didn't convey it. Instead he said, "Okay, but don't worry about the savings. I'm still alive for that."

It was settled that Ajay and Dhananjay would remain in the States, while Sita and Kismat would shift to Delhi.

The following day, Kismat stepped outside her W&W building for a brief escape during the lunch hour. Wafts of smoke made its way into her nostrils as she exited from the revolving door occupied by the firm's innumerable, smoking employees. She made her way to Tompkins Square Park that was just a quick subway ride away. She found respite on one of the park's benches. Of the many venerable elm trees that survived the Dutch Elm disease in the park, there was one elm tree, with its enchanting canopy, that was accorded special reverence.

This elm was the 'Krishna tree.'*

**It was under the shade of this tree that that Swami Prabhupada and his disciples first chanted the divine Hare Krishna mantra in the fall of 1966.*

There was a sixteen word chant imprinted on the bark of the tree. It was the Krishna mantra. Kismat recalled the swami's words at the Brooklyn temple who urged her to focus on being happy within. And for her to do that, she needed to focus on the goals that mattered to her.

Kismat put forth her resignation that same day.

She told her W&W team, in the most earnest way she could, that she had decided to move back to India, and agreed to stay a few extra weeks to transition the next hire into her position.

For Kismat, if at least one person chanced to remember her from the office, even if it was just the janitor, she would be content.

Just like every employee in the world, Kismat was replaced by someone new.

When anyone leaves their place in the world, there will be someone else to fill that vacancy. It is up to us to decide the kind of mark we wish to leave on the world.

The words of the Gita reprised itself again: *change is the law of the universe.*

Existential Experiences

Karma's life was at its peak in London.

She had an independent life, a host of new friends, and a choice of many events to attend, the posters of which flooded her Facebook and Darwick campus walls.

Karma had even acquired a bit of flab from all that eating out with her friends but she had the perfect loophole to excuse herself.

If our ellipsoid shaped Earth is allowed to have a bulge at the equator owing to the centrifugal force acting on its rotational movement, then surely, I am allowed to have a bulging tummy owing to my lack of movement.

Unlike some of her friends who wanted to dot their way across the globe, Karma never forgot her rubber band theory - that no matter how far she would stretch herself, she would always return to her family in Kochi.

Even while sitting thousands of miles away, in wintery London, the artifice of imagination transported her to the warmth of her hometown in Kerala.

She would imagine herself basking in the Kochin sun that routinely played hide and seek with the monsoon clouds; or being comforted by the sights of pokkali rice harvesting in saline paddy fields; or even dancing in the open verandah of her home during the autumn downpour; all these thoughts, though figments of her imagination, gave her both joy and bittersweet longing that no dictionary could describe. Imagination was that one free lunch that gave Karma so much for nothing.

After a completing her two year accelerated program in Economics, Karma graduated with the highest honors from Darwick. She was ready to face the world; paper degree in hand, and a resilient spirit in heart.

Surya picked her up from the international airport while Lakshmi greeted her with a plate of sweets at home. Karma noticed that her mother had become a lot thinner since she last saw her. In fact, she was limping on one side. She hugged her little sister and asked her to come to her room.

"Sati, since when has Amma been walking like this?"

"Since the last month now. The doctor gave her some medicines but it is not helping."

"But Amma never told me about this on the phone! Why didn't you tell me?!"

Kismat's tone was drenched in guilt and anger.

"Please don't get angry! Amma told us not to tell you because you might get worried."

When Karma was excited to leave for London, she remembered how Lakshmi had partial numbness in the heel of her left foot and her mother passed it off as some temporary ailment.

A feeling of remorse engulfed Karma's being. Karma waited till dinner was over. She sat down by Lakshmi's side in the open verandah, where some clothes still lay hanging on the clothesline.

"Ma, why did you hide this from me?"

"It's nothing. Don't worry, I'm getting better."

"But Sati said that the medicines have not been helping."

"Everything takes time Rama. I'll be fine."

"Ok, but I'll take you a doctor and get you checked....."

"Forget all that. You tell me -- what do you want to eat for breakfast tomorrow?" Lakshmi interjected.

"Look Ma, I'll find a job and support our expenses. I've already looked into a few companies. I'm not going anywhere now."

She hugged her mother's legs.

"Except when we you get married," Lakshmi added smilingly.

"I'm not leaving until you get better. That's final."

Karma caught her voice getting loud and calmed herself. "I'm going to bed Rama. You sleep too. You've had a long day."

Karma thought she heard a sense of despondency in her mother's voice but changed her stance after looking at her mother's beaming face.

Karma shortlisted three companies that she found to her liking. Two of them required her to be posted in a different city, so she didn't bother with them and applied to the third one.

A fortnight later, she got her first interview meeting from the third company - a big, data analytics firm that was looking to hire a research associate.

The morning of her interview, Lakshmi applied red *tilak* on Karma's forehead. Even on the day of her first exam at Darwick, Karma remembered to apply the vermillion that Lakshmi had packed for her in a small Ziploc bag. This led to some curious stares, followed by questions as to why Indian women wear the red dot on their forehead.

"The red tilak is applied between our brows to mark our Third Eye. It represents the source of our divine energy." "You guys believe in a third eye?" a confused Cecile had asked her.

Karma tried to explain the Indian custom in a language her international friends would be more familiar with. "You guys believe in the red suited Santa, right? Well, we wear the red dot hoping our good actions get rewarded with good presents. Santa does the same thing."

Karma walked into the multi-storey office building, saying

a quick good morning to the security guard on her way in, a simple courtesy she'd adopted from her time in London. A three member panel awaited her on the second floor conference room.

There were a few warm-up questions about Karma's educational experience and her interest in the firm. One of the panelists, a middle-aged man who had been with the firm for seven years, posed two questions to Karma.

"Let's consider a scenario. Two men, Ram and Shyam, decide to feed their dogs some bread crumbs. One dog gets nine bread crumbs and the other, nine raised to the power of two bread crumbs. Tell me, how many bread crumbs did Ram give?"

Kismat took a minute to compose her answer.

"Sir, communication is just as important as calculation. The answer is either nine, eighty-one, or ninety, depending on whether Ram has one dog or both."

The panelist nodded in approval and proceeded with his next question.

"What do you think is the greatest invention of man?"

"Nothing."

"Nothing?" he asked with his eyebrows pulled together.

"Yes, you didn't make any mention of a woman. The question is invalid."

He wasn't expecting such a response. Yet, he smiled in approval.

"Ok, we know you're a Darwick grad. But we also have many great applicants from universities in India. What sets you apart?"

"Sir, I graduated with the highest honors. I'm also familiar with much of the analysis needed to conduct the research here. I'll be honest; I only went to Darwick because of the scholarship. Even then, I'm very grateful to get the opportunity to set foot outside of India because I realized that we need to think the same way - outside the frontiers of our closed minds. The collective world is governed by the actions of all people. We need to help each other and we need each other's help."

Karma successfully cleared her first round. Her next and final round was scheduled a week later.

She was preparing her material the night before the interview, mumbling to herself in front of her bathroom mirror with sample questions she found off the web.

In the morning of her interview, she awaited the auspicious *tilak* from Lakshmi's thali to start her day.

When she went inside her mother's room, she saw that Lakshmi had collapsed on the floor.

Her speech was slurred and she couldn't get up. Surya managed to get Lakshmi into the car as Karma monitored her breathing. He quickly drove them to the nearest hospital. After drawing some blood, and examining her scans, the resident neurologist diagnosed her with early stage *amyolateral sclerosis (ALS).*

Karma held her father's hands as the neurologist spoke in detail about the affliction.

"It's a rare disease. Only a handful in a lakh people get it."

"Why did this happen to her?" Surya asked in despair.

"That is difficult to say because there are really no known risk factors."

"But there is a cure for this, right?" Karma inquired, praying for an affirmation from the doctor.

"I'm sorry, but we don't have a cure right now. But there are a few drugs that we can get Lakshmi started on immediately to prolong her survival. The main problem with ALS is that it's highly degenerative. It can cause more muscles to become impaired as it spreads to other parts of her body. We will do our best to monitor her movement."

For the time being, the doctors moved Lakshmi to a wheelchair. When Karma looked into Lakshmi's eyes at the hospital, they conveyed the same unwavering love for her.

"Ma, I'm so sorry. I should have never left you."

"Why are you saying sorry? I'm still alive and happy."

"But it wouldn't have reached this stage had I stayed with you."

"Rama," she said, as she clasped her daughter's hand, "This is not your fault. We wanted you to follow your dreams so you could learn to stand on your feet even if we couldn't stand on ours. In the end, you can only depend on yourself."

Lakshmi could easily see Karma holding all of that guilt inside her.

"Rama, everything will be fine. Leave it to God."

It was crushing for Karma to see her mother being dependent on a device to move around. She was determined to make her mother recover, and not leave her to her marred fate. Karma fell by Lakshmi's side, burying her face in her mother's sari and fighting the tears that she couldn't release in front of her.

In life, whenever something seems amiss from a well-followed routine, the mind remains entangled to the problem. Karma's sole aim was to avoid people discoursing on her mother's condition as much as possible, so as to achieve normalcy in their house.

Under Jyotimala's and Nandini's guidance, Karma learned to cook many recipes from scratch. She even became an expert in preparing the myriad chutneys her mother was famous for in their circle of family and friends.

Sati and Karma would split the chores during the day, and Surya would take care of Lakshmi at night. The daughters devoted their time to helping their mother with her daily pursuits; not letting her situation handicap her from doing the one thing she loved the most- volunteering at the temple and the school.

The Iyer sisters would serve fresh fruit each morning to the less fortunate devotees who lined up outside the temple grounds. The temple didn't have the facility of a ramp so Karma would walk up the stairs and offer her prayers, pleading to God for a miracle. Without her mother in sight, Karma would kneel down and freely shed her tears in front of the many holy idols, beseeching them to come out of their painted statues and help her mother. There was a part of herself Karma couldn't forgive just yet, not until her mother got better.

In the afternoon, Lakshmi dedicated her time to teaching girls at a *vidya kendram*, which was being funded by the temple's charitable trust. The school girls noticed that Lakshmi was not walking around as her usual self and asked her why she never got up from her chair. Lakshmi smiled at them and said that she had walked one too many miles in her life and God had told her to slow down. Some of her little students took turns sitting on her lap and she would happily whirl them around in her wheelchair.

Karma no longer had any fear of germs that troubled her in her teens. She helped her mother bathe and use the toilet everyday. When her mother would throw up food from the nausea, Karma would change her clothes, and wipe the floor clean.

Lakshmi's conventional treatment plan consisted of a powerful drug that slowed the degeneration of her nerve functions to prolong her life. This drug decreased glutamate, an amino acid that lent to nerve damage as it inhibited the function of neurons that sent messages from the brain to the muscles. The neurologist also prescribed another drug that had some neuroprotective properties and nurses administered it intravenously at the hospital.

Karma was dismayed to see that both drugs came with its bounty of side-effects, the most notable being the loss in appetite, dizziness, and discoloration in various patches of Lakshmi's skin. But the side-effects that bothered Karma the most were the changes in her mood. If Lakshmi was too sad, too anxious, or too numb, a new drug was added to her regimen. These new drugs were prescribed to solve the problem caused by a previous drug, resulting in an endless loop.

Karma wanted Lakshmi to break out of this loop. It was difficult enough to see Lakshmi paralysed from waist below, but it was even more heartbreaking to see her mother's thin built and her rare, yet quiet episodes of grief; episodes that Karma could hear when Lakshmi weeped inside the four walls of her bedroom.

That grief had spread to her primary caregiver too.

Even with her closest family in attendance, Karma felt a profound sense of loneliness. Her tears had become so salty that her eyes burned each time she released them. Still, every morning, she tried to get back up with the same strength as the day before; only for her mother. Karma had lost interest in eating her favorite appams, or reading her favorite authors from her bookshelf. Her family encouraged her to go outside to take her mind off things, but she refused.

Karma spent most of her time searching for any new hospital that could help her mother, but they didn't have anything new to offer. She even had some leftover savings from her Darwick scholarship. Karma had originally reserved the money to do some more traveling, but her priorities had changed.

Karma found the website of a holistic center that specialized in naturopathic treatment; using an array of massages, yoga, acupuncture, and detoxifying herbs to help patients with disability. Karma made an appointment with them the same week.

Dr. Sylvie was the head of the clinic. She was one of the most sought-after holistic practitioners in Karma's paradise state of Kerala, even having won accolades from the State government and had credentials from abroad, the evidence of which was hung as framed certificates on her clinic's pastel colored walls.

Dr. Sylvie was in her early fifties, but appeared to be in her twenties. Tall and fair, she was dressed in a simple flower print kurta and jeans. The holistic clinic was packed with a variety of clientele, several of whom appeared to be from out-of-state and out of the country.

Her clinic was as spotless as her skin. Karma, on the other hand, had blemishes on her cheeks from cycles of hormonal imbalance and bags under her eyes from cumulative nights of sleeplessness. Typically, seeing such a perfectly glowing woman might have lent some insecurity to other impressionable women, but Karma wasn't bothered, possibly because she didn't have the time to worry about anything other than her mother's health.

During Karma's scheduled appointment, Dr. Sylvie outlined the basic "do's" and "don'ts" of her therapy and the kind of organic oils and herbs she used at her center, customized to each client.

"You see Karma, the problem we have nowadays is that everyone wants lots of energy and a fit body. They will go for the energy drink, but they won't exercise or sleep right. They are willing to pop in pills, but they won't eat well. Our in-house treatments of acupuncture, massages, diets, and meditation will help clear your skin and put you in the best of health."

Karma confided that she wasn't seeking treatment for herself, but for her paralyzed mother. She shared some of Lakshmi's reports.

"The doctors don't have a cure. Please help her," Karma's voice was heavy with hurt; the kind of pain no painkiller could reach.

Dr. Sylvie held Karma's hand.

She calmly stated that while they couldn't guarantee a cure for Lakshmi, their team would create a regimen that would try to keep her mother healthy from within, by adding an anti-oxidant rich diet to reduce molecular damage, improving her mother's appetite and immunity, and lastly, maintaining her mental health.

Karma took Lakshmi to the Dr. Sylvie's clinic on the pretext that they would be visiting the temple. When Lakshmi's realized the extent of Karma's plans, she was upset. Karma had already made an advance payment for the treatment, which was hefty as it is. She urged her mother to try the therapy, reminding her that the clinic would refund the money if she didn't show any improvement, even though no such promise was made. Lakshmi eventually conceded to her daughter's wishes.

Only one month into the holistic treatment, Lakshmi noted that she felt more energized and her appetite had improved. After three months, she was able to maintain a healthier weight. Even her face had restored some of the glow that was missing prior to the treatment. With each passing month, Karma hoped for the miracle that her mother would stand up and walk again.

One evening, Karma was home late after purchasing an important medication from the only pharmacy in Kochi that supplied it. Lakshmi scolded her daughter for getting late, citing that her medicines were not nearly as important as her daughter's safety.

This wasn't the first time in her life that Lakshmi had scolded her for being late.

The very first time was when Karma was still in ninth grade. She was returning after working on a project at her friend's house.

"Do you know how late it is Rama?"

It was five minutes past seven.

"Amma, I told you about my plans last week. You don't remember?"

"It is not safe out there. When you have a child of your own, you will understand my concerns."

"Don't worry Amma."

"Do you know what Auntie told me today about some of the girls in your school?"

"What?"

"She said that milk and lemon are kept separate for a reason else it can lead to curdling, and similarly if girls are not kept in their bounds, they may find themselves in some sour situations."

Karma could not help but chuckle. That Auntie could have said, wind when mixed with heat can cause a tornado, and her mother would have quoted that too.

"Auntie must have come over to get some free curd and spices as usual, right? Don't listen to her Ma, she needs to focus on her own kids."

"Rama, be nice. She has a stunt in her heart."

"Stent, Ma."

"I still agree with what she said," and Lakshmi walked away, to show that she had made her point.

"We spend the first half of our lives asking permission from our parents, and the second half from our husbands. When are we ever going to take permission from ourselves?"

Lakshmi could not contest that statement so Karma employed a bit of emotional blackmail to win back her mother's affection.

"I am growing up Amma. One day, you will marry me off and then I will leave the house for good. Will you keep worrying about me then?"

But Lakshmi had an even better answer, blanketed in her undertone of love. "Who said anything about marrying you off? I'm keeping you with me, forever."

One evening, Surya sat down with Karma and to her surprise, he brought up a subject that he hitherto hadn't brought up before - the topic of men and marriage. Surya had given her sufficient freedom such that Karma never felt the need to astray and break his trust. He was the one who convinced the family to let her study abroad. He never questioned her friendships with boys. One could only imagine that for a father to bring up this topic after so many years would constitute awkwardness.

But, it was quite the opposite.

It set the foundation for her soon to be married life.

"Rama, I want you to know something that your grandmother told me when I was young."

"What did she say?"

"She said that people tend to build big dreams out of glass and watch them shatter into pieces when destiny doesn't follow through. She was talking about marriage."

Karma understood where this conversation was going. " Why are we discussing this Acha?"

"I just want you to know that marriage isn't some magical fantasy. It can become rather routine after some time."

"Then, why do people get married if it is going to become so dull?"

"My Rama, you can share happiness with many people. But it's in the dull moments where you really know you're loved. The joy I get in coming home to share my simple day with your mother is something else. That's what makes this commitment so special."

Unexpectedly, he shifted the conversation to her.

"Rama, you are a very mature woman, more mature than me, at times."

Surya spoke to her as frankly as he could.

The Iyers were in talks of her alliance to Bharat Naidu, the son of her aunt's friend who was a software developer based in the Gurgaon area.

Karma immediately expressed her hesitancy about speaking to a guy she had never met before.

"He may have a long history of god-knows-what troubling issues and past affairs – how will I deal with all of that?"

"Rama, everyone has an imperfect past and an imperfect future."

"But Acha, you and mummy were the only people to be with each other. I want something like that with my husband as well!"

Surya smiled at Karma.

"That was just a coincidence my dear. Marriage is a great journey of life. We only ask that you speak to him once. After that, whatever decision you make, we will be happy."

Karma and Bharat had their first call on a Sunday, on a day deemed auspicious by Jyotimala. The conversation flowed naturally from both parties, humor came easy and Bharat was successful in dogging any of Karma's innumerable witty retorts.

She didn't admit it but she felt at ease hearing him stammer initially, because she was equally nervous.

"So Bharat, what are you doing in Gurgaon?"

"Um, right now I was just making some chicken fried rice -- oh wait, you must be referring to my job."

"Yes..."

"Well, the last three years, I have been working as a software engineer. I'm looking to start a venture with my buddies when we have more financing ready from our end. That's been a dream of mine."

"Nice. And, I'm impressed you can cook. Do you launder your own clothes as well?"

"I thought that was going to be your job."

Both were silent for a second.

Realizing that the joke expired sooner than it was delivered, he quickly added, "Yes, I'm pretty self-sufficient and no longer the bachelor pad mess that I used to be. Actually, I have been dying to know one thing."

"What?"

"Why did you agree to talk to me? I mean you're a Darwick grad. And very pretty too. You could have surely found someone on your own. Am I some kind of a last resort option?"

"Well, I did this to make my parents happy. And do looks really matter that much to you?"

"No, not at all. I was just stating a fact."

"So you would be ok if I shaved my eyebrows?"

"Sure, but just let me know when your mood changes. Without your eyebrows, I wouldn't be able to tell."

Karma chuckled ever so softly so that Bharat wouldn't know that he made her laugh.

"So Karma, what are you looking for in a partner?"

"Well, someone who reads. And cares about helping others."

"Well, the function of freedom is to free someone else," he added in an animated tone.

"You read that quote off of my Facebook profile, didn't you?" Karma quipped.

"It's called research Karma. C'mon, I'm sure you Googled my name, didn't you?"

"Twice actually. Nothing relevant came up except a LinkedIn profile of your obvious professional accomplishments. What else have found out about me?"

He waited a few moments to compose his answer.

"I found out that I will have to work with great effort to peel that tough image you've got going on there to reveal the real romantic that you are. Am I right?"

"What rubbish!" Karma exclaimed, though he wasn't too off the radar.

"Well, I'm flying to Kochi next month. Can we meet up once? I know this is rushed but I would love to meet you."

Karma didn't expect a meet-up so quickly after one call. She said she would let him know.

She refused the alliance, keeping Lakshmi's health in mind. It was then that Lakshmi stepped in to counsel her daughter.

"He comes from a good family. I know he will take good care of you."

"Ma, I am not ready for marriage with someone I don't know!"

"My dear, you can know a person for years and still not really know them at all. My mother met her husband on the day of her wedding. I only saw a photo of your father and spoke to him on the phone before agreeing to the proposal. As women, we may have sacrificed more, but we have never been loved any less."

Karma just sat there, not speaking any further.

Her mother knew that she had to pull the final straw to convince Karma.

"If you are worried about me then please understand that I am getting better. I have your father, Sati, and your aunt Nandini to look after me. Please give Bharat a chance -- please for me."

Karma's eyes were about to swell up again.

"Ok, Ma – I'll meet him, but don't be too hopeful that I will accept."

The Iyers was already acquainted with the Naidu's through common friends and functions they had attended together in Kerala. Bharat and Karma mutually agreed to meet in Kochi, keeping the evolution of the Iyer arranged marriage custom going forward.

When Karma was studying abroad, she had only heard of Bharat's name in passing, but never gave it much thought.

Suddenly now, this meeting between them seemed like the most important day that awaited her.

~

A week prior to Bharat's arrival, Karma was preparing dinner for the family. Sati was getting the table ready. Jyotimala and Surya were sitting in the living room when they heard a loud yell from the kitchen.

Jyotimala rushed to Karma. She saw her holding on to the right side of her cheek, while the cooking ladle was lying on the floor, surrounded by drops of oil.
Some hot oil had splashed onto Karma's face and arm.
Jyotimala quickly advised Sati to get some ice and turmeric powder. After several minutes of icing the burnt skin, she applied the yellow paste to her face and arm. Karma was back to resuming her daily chores the very next day and didn't bother much with the incident until Sati reminded her of Bharat's arrival.

She looked at herself in the mirror. She didn't bother about the fresh scar on her arm, but the scar on her face was easily noticeable on her right cheek. It wasn't too big, yet it left a monumental mark on her self-esteem.

But after all that she had seen her mother go through, she was strong enough to accept this in her stride as well. She tried different variations of parting her hair to hide it but nothing worked.

Jyotimala offered to prepare some homemade masks to lessen its appearance. Lakshmi suggested she buy some tinted makeup to hide it. Karma recalled Bharat's words when he said that he didn't place much emphasis on looks. This scar would be test of his words.

"No Amma, I don't want to hide anything from him. He has to see me the way I am."

Lakshmi touched her daughter's head. It was a bittersweet emotion, for she was happy to see her daughters all grown up with such sagacity and yet she was about to bid adieu to one of them very soon. But in her heart, Lakshmi knew this was the right step to take. She wanted to see at least one daughter happily settled in her lifetime.

Bharat's flight was due to arrive in the morning and Lakshmi made sure Karma accompanied Surya to pick him up at the airport.

She wore a light saffron sari. Bharat had recently commented on a picture of her wearing the same, saying, *"You look gorgeous! Hope to see you in this look someday :)"*

Bharat came out with two pieces of luggage, his laptop bag dangling uneasily on his left arm as he carried a big bouquet of roses in his right hand. She recognized him instantly, the flowers helping, of course.

His thick black hair was flowing with Kochi's balmy, summer breeze. His skin was a shade of soft cocoa, just about matching hers. His black rimmed glasses added a touch of elegance to his square face and his tall built, that was not clearly evident in his photos before, now made his handsomeness more palpable in person. As their eyes met again, Karma shyly looked down.

As much as she had prepared herself, she wasn't ready for this meeting with a man who may soon be locked with her for life.

Her mind was racing with many thoughts.
What were his likes or dislikes?
Would he respect her and her choices later in life?
Would he be supportive of her dreams?

There were many more questions fogging her mind and it would take more time to realize the truth than in just one little meeting.

Bharat said a quick hello and handed her the bouquet. She graciously smiled with a word of "Thanks" and helped his luggage onto the trunk of the car.

He caught sight of her scar. In a fit of self-consciousness, Karma quickly sat inside the back seat of the car. In the whole ride back, they didn't utter a single word to each other.

Bharat greeted her family with utmost respect and surprised them with a few presents, which thrilled Sati more than anyone else. She winked at Karma indicating that Bharat had already won her approval.

After lunch, Lakshmi suggested that Karma and Bharat take a stroll around the city if he liked.

Sati excitedly asked if she could tag along with them but Lakshmi gently nudged her youngest to give them some privacy.

Karma took Bharat to a popular district near Fort Kochi. They walked past St. Francis Church. A signage revealed that Vasco da Gama, the most notable explorer to discover the sea route from Europe to India, was once buried there.

"Wow, this place sure has some history! Da Gama and all..."

"Da Gama was not only a horrid colonist, but a perpetrator of genocide," Karma added quickly.

"First time I've heard a lady bring up something so morbid on the first date," Bharat added smilingly, hoping Karma would smile back.

She discreetly covered her scar again with a flap of her hair.

"You don't have to cover it Karma."

"Look Bharat, if you don't want to accept this proposal anymore, I'll understand. I'm happy being at home with my mother."

Bharat didn't respond at first.

He simply moved from his spot beside her. She stopped when she found him directly facing her. He took off his thick rimmed glasses and Karma noticed a deep cut under his right eyebrow and a smaller one on the bridge of his nose. "I got these marks as a teenager. They should really put some warnings on narrow staircases."

Karma almost proceeded to touch his face out of concern but held back.

"I like scars. They show that we made it through a really

tough time."

Bharat gently tucked her hair behind her ear to reveal her mark again. "I know you are worried about your mother. But we can help her together. You don't have to do it all alone."

Tears trickled down her face, and he wiped them gently. He held her hands and continued talking. This time, Karma didn't flinch at his touch like the time she did with Rehaan.

She fulfilled Rehaan's promise of remembering him at a time when she would be the one falling in love and hoped that he had found a wonderful lady who loved him back. Karma let her hands remain clasped with Bharat.

Ok, ask me anything you want," he asked politely.

"Anything?"

Bharat smiled, as he knew what she was thinking.

"To be honest Karma, I only dated one girl before you. We studied in college together but we broke up after a few months."

Karma felt relieved to hear that.

"What about you? How many ex-boyfriends do I need to tackle? Tell me now so I can go to the gym and prepare myself physically."

"I've never been in a romantic relationship."

"Really?"

She let go of his hand.

"Bharat, I wanted to tell you one thing"

"What is it?"

"I would like to work after marriage."

"But in our family, women stay in the kitchen. Men hunt and gather for their wives."

Bharat initially started speaking with a dramatic face, but began chuckling even before he could finish his last sentence.

"No one will stop you from living your life the way you want to. Just know that there'll be days when we'll be irritated the heck out of each other, and might have a tiff or two. But I'll do everything I can to make sure that we are together. I hope you feel the same way."

Bharat wanted to hug Karma that instant but decided to wait for a better occasion.

Karma asked her third and final question for the day.

"What made you want to meet up so quickly without even knowing me?"

"Well, the thing that impressed me the most is your honesty and the love you have for your family. Plus, you're really smart. I've met other girls and believe me, finding someone like you is not easy."

She saw his eyes brimming with affection for her.

"Karma, I have been dying to know. Did I pass, or did I fail?"

Her parents were right about Bharat.

He was a good man, in fact, a very good man. She gave him her nod of approval. It seemed as if the both the Iyers and Naidus were just waiting for them to meet for they had secretly made all the arrangements for an intimate ceremony at their home the following day.

Karma and Bharat put a ring on each other fingers'; sealing the first step of their lifelong union.

And luckily for Bharat, he finally got the hug he had been waiting for.

Six months later, Bharat flew down again for their wedding ceremony.

The guests included Lila Ma'am and two of Karma's closest friends from Darwick. The stage was resplendent with a decorated idol of Krishna, standing lamps, and an assortment of fresh flowers against a pastel colored drape, matching the elegant simplicity of both the bride and groom.

Bharat couldn't keep his eyes off Karma that day.

The black kohl intensified the beauty of her eyes contrasting with the white jasmine flowers that delicately adorned her long tresses. She wore her mother's gold necklace that elegantly matched the golden zari of her *kasavu* sari.

As he tied the *mangalsutra* around her neck, he whispered, "I love you."

The two exchanged garlands and walked around the stage three times. A grand sadya (feast) of khichadi, sambar, aviyal, appam and payasam was served with steaming rice on banana leaves.

The elders took turns to pour rice grains on the bride and the groom, as the newlyweds, in turn, took their blessings.

In the midst of all the picture-taking and religious ceremony, Bharat took her aside where no one could see them. He caught a minute to tell Karma what he had wanted to say when he first met her.

"When I saw you wearing that saffron colored sari for me at the airport, I knew we would be together."

She moved in a little closer, the fragrance of the *mogra* in her tresses emboldening him to kiss her.

They were lost in their own world in that brief moment, their love blossoming even further with their first kiss.

As much as Karma was grateful to have a man like Bharat by her side, she could not restrain her flow of tears after the wedding was over.

The guests were slowly making their way out. She asked Sati to come to her room after the culmination of the ceremony.

"I am leaving Amma in your care. Promise me you will not let anything happen to her in my absence."

Sati's eyes welled up with tears.

"I promise Chechi."

Karma was now a part of Bharat's family just as much as Bharat was of her own.

And just like a migratory bird, she was soon going to leave the nest she once called her one and only home.

Section Three: The Final Enlightenment

Truth, Time, and Love

Moving into Bharat's one bedroom flat in Gurgaon took only one day; settling in would take more time and conscious effort. Karma spent the first week organizing her things in her new bedroom, getting accustomed to having her toothbrush lying close to his, and seeing his undergarments in plain view as he got ready for work; all the little things that came as a part of living with someone new. She used the remainder of her time to research jobs and speak to her mother. Still somewhat of strangers to each other, Karma was hesitant with intimacy and Bharat was very respectful of that.

A week after their nuptial ceremony, the two of them took a weekend trip to Agra, as neither of them had seen the Taj Mahal before.

The way that India had advertised the Mahal was similar to how Karma would showcase her London dorm room to her family over a video call. They could only see the cleanliness based on the positioning of the camera and the rest of the mess was better left hidden under the bed.

The Mahal could awe any visitor from any angle they saw it. Barring the calligraphic inscriptions of verses from the Quoran, every facade of the marble mausoleum was perfectly symmetrical; this being the brilliance of Mughal architecture. And up close, there was more to marvel - from the intricate floral and abstract motifs to the balustrade of exquisitely carved marble. But just as much as the Mahal left everyone breathless with its beauty, it was also suffocating in smog and was flanked by a river that was laced with garbage.

Their tour guide was a young boy who seemed to have

memorized the entire history of the monument in English and he was speaking all of it in one long breath.

Karma interrupted him in between to ask a question about use of sandstone in the construction of the mausoleum. The young guide paused for a minute and began repeating verbatim from the start of his speech. Karma and Bharat didn't bother to ask any more questions.

The small bit about the historic romance that led to creation of the Mahal was better left open to one's interpretation. Karma wasn't sure if any woman would have fancied the idea of her husband marrying multiple women and then making all of them jealous by building a glorious structure dedicated to only one - Mumtaz.

Not only did Shah Jahan father a dozen kids with his beloved Mumtaz; the thirteenth kid lead to her death in childbirth.

"Well, the least Shah Jahan could have done was to have built a Mahal for her," Karma quipped.

Once they exited the mausoleum complex, Karma noticed kids selling key chains with a tiny replica of the iconic Mahal floating inside. Their malnourished faces were smeared in black soot and their white vests, or whatever was left of it from the wear and tear, had now turned into an unsightly brown. She bought a few keychains, paying them far more than what they asked, and kept them inside her purse.

"What a pity that Shah Jahan's own son imprisoned him in a tower facing the very Mahal he built!"

"Rama, are you always this morbid around tourist spots? You brought up genocide on our first date near the Vasco da Gama church. This place is supposed to be romantic!"

She laughed with abandon and planted a full kiss on his lips, much to the disapproval of other families who passed them by.

The newlyweds returned back to their small flat in Gurgaon, old for Bharat but still very new for Karma. Bharat would often surprise Karma by bringing home a garland of jasmine flowers that she could adorn on her braided hair, or tickets to a movie, or doing something as simple as picking up the dishes for the day.

On many occasions, Bharat would goof around by wearing his tie too short or making irregular shaped dosas just so that he could hear her laugh; the laugh that made him feel more accomplished than anything else he'd done at work.

One night, as both of them lay in bed, his hand found its way underneath her pajamas and eventually between her legs. Triggered by the incident in her childhood, she recoiled from his touch on her vulva and got up from the bed.

"Sorry, I thought...maybe we could..." he added in a tone of embarrassment.

She hadn't intimated him about the incident near the bus stop.

"I just have to rush to the bathroom."

"Rama, are you sure you're okay?"

She assured him that she was fine, even though she wasn't.

One day when Bharat was still at work, she desired to see herself fully naked for the first time, a desire she had suppressed for long.

She saw her petite, yet firm breasts in the bathroom mirror. Bharat had undressed in front of her many times, but she hadn't given him that intimacy with her body just yet.

She thought of him, his toned physique, his manly brows, the curly hair on his chest, the way that he intertwined his strong fingers with hers. She began shedding some of her inhibitions and accepting her physical attraction towards him. In the privacy of their bedroom, she began caressing herself; rediscovering her body, bit by bit. One afternoon, she felt a euphoric sensation, thinking only of him.

Bharat's birthday was soon approaching.

From what Karma could gather about her husband, Bharat

wasn't too fond of fancy accessories, but he was particularly fond of desserts. She decided to make something with her own hands - *almond payasam*. After making a quick ride to a food mart a few blocks away, she bought some nutmeg, cardamom powder, and almonds to garnish. On his birthday eve, she set out to prepare the pudding on her own. Once the dessert turned into a rich, creamy mixture, she turned off the gas and let it cool in the fridge.

To Karma's surprise, Bharat was home a little earlier than usual that Friday evening. She matched his unexpected arrival with a warm embrace at the doorstep. Dressed in a simple chiffon sari, she wore a tiny, black *bindi* and silver *jhumkas* to match. He immediately dropped his office briefcase and hugged her as soon as their eyes met. A couple from the apartment above them was walking down the stairs and giggled at the two newlyweds lost in embrace. Karma blushed from all the attention and immediately let go.

In the frenzy of these newly discovered feelings, they forgot to step inside their own apartment.

"I think we should go inside now."

Bharat happily nodded in agreement with Karma.

"Hey Rama, would you like to eat outside tonight? My friends told me about this new Chinese restaurant in Cyber City. I thought we could give it a try."

Bharat had become familiar with Karma's house name and called her Rama since the day they tied the knot. Karma was very happy to hear it, in fact she felt even closer to him, as if he was a part of her now. She was about to say 'yes', when she realized that she had made a special dessert for him and responded with a last minute excuse.

"Can we eat in tonight?....I am a little tired."

"Sure, we can go there another night."

After ordering in, her hands were trembling with excitement to share the dessert. After dinner, he walked away to his sofa and set the channel for a live Cricket game between

India and Sri Lanka. Without revealing the secret beforehand, she set the dessert in the best porcelain bowl they had in the house and served it to him on the living room table. He smelled the aroma of the saffron and almonds and his eyes were filled with immense joy like a small child who just found out that his mother was letting him play outside.

"Did you make this for me? You remembered Rama! It smells so good."

"Yes, of course, I remembered. It's all for you."

Before the spoon reached his mouth, she startled him with a pop-up quiz.

"So, does it taste ok? Is it too sweet? Do you like it?"

He laughed heartily.

"Rama, I haven't even tasted it yet – ask me in another ten seconds."

He teased her further by bringing the spoon ever so slowly to his mouth.

She enjoyed all his little nuances.

The payasam was not as sweet as he wanted it, but he chose to reply with, "It's the tastiest dessert I've ever had!" He ate some more spoonfuls and finished it all with a big smile.

"Thank you Rama. I haven't told you this before but I am really lucky to have you in my life."

Karma's stammering reprised itself again.

Their chemistry was fully acknowledged; as powerful as two fervent waves in a calm blue lagoon.

He put his arms around her and just waited there, not moving back. Karma could feel his heartbeat getting faster through the thin layer of his collared shirt. He proceeded to kiss her on the nape of her neck and then back on her lips. Bharat wanted time to come to a complete stand still so he could treasure every kiss with her. Neither one was bothered with their surroundings anymore.

Initially ticklish by the caressing of his hands on her skin, she tried to tickle him back, thereby inducing some giggling on both ends. She put his one hand on her exposed waist and let him open the pleats of her sari. She moved his other hand upward and he responded just as well by caressing her breasts, first with his hand and then with his lips. They had managed to undress each other completely; their kisses covering every inch of their bodies. He carried her to their room; the ensuing foreplay ensuring that both of them were ready. The penetration was expectedly painful for her, but he made sure not to cross any limit she wasn't comfortable with. That night, neither of them could think of a better place to be than to be loved in each other arms.

The next morning, she tenderly kissed him on his forehead and whispered, "Happy birthday dear."

He was awakened by the touch of her lips and wet hair that carried a lingering fragrance of her perfume. He tried to get a hold of her but she ran away just in time and winked at him in the glory of her escape.

Bharat repeated "I love you Rama" with so much exhilaration that Karma made her way back to the room and into his arms.

"Rama, I am going to make something special today. Get excited to taste the wonderful creation of yours truly, Master Chef Bharat."

He jokingly bowed in front of her.

"But it's your birthday!"

As he put his kurta back on, she saw a few scratch marks on his back from the previous night and immediately turned pink.

"I will make something special today!"

Karma helped cut the veggies and set the table as Bharat hid himself behind the kitchen.

An hour later, he cleaned bowled the fried rice, reverse swept the kimchee salad and stumped the stir-fry veggies spliced with soy and duck sauces that dollied up into a dipper of a delectable delivery.

He served it all very neatly on a plate for Kismat.

As she took her first bite, he nervously asked, "Howzzzzzzat?"

"Not bad for your first innings. In fact, it is the best Chinese food I've ever had."

Their souls had already connected when they first met but after consummating their love, their commitment to each other deepened even further.

~

Whenever the topic of arranged marriage came up in the Dharma household, it would usually be from Badi ammi who would stress on finding a man who fulfilled at least two of the following criteria to match Kismat – her so-called elite Brahmin caste and elite fairness.

Kismat's response would always be, "I'd rather find my own man, regardless of any denominations, and with a lesser return than have my marriage arranged to some man I barely know, posing a higher risk." Badi ammi would crib that all that extra education had gotten to her head and that Kismat had become too 'modern.'

It had been close to five years since Kismat had set foot in India. The first, most palpable difference she experienced was the remarkable taste of Delhi food. The piping hot samosas after an impromptu rain; the crunchy gol gappas that reigned only in India's capital; the chole bhature, the papdi chaat, the malai chawal whose deliciousness multiplied when she ate with her hands; all of this transported her to some place in her heart she called home. Even though Kismat's taste buds were exposed to all kinds of Indian cuisines in America, there was something so extraordinary about the dishes in Delhi that made it nonpareil.

The morning sweepers and the cloud of dust engulfing them, the fatigued bullock pulling a poor man's cart load of green vegetables, the fresh coconut vendors that sold coconut water for a mere thirty rupees, the Mother Dairy and Amul ice-cream carts at every few intersections, the women sitting cross-legged to prepare *bhutta* (roasted maize) on their make-shift bonfires, all of these sights, though unusual to a foreigner, carried hints of Kismat's early days of going to school.

She felt like she was a teenager again, pulling off those classic one-liners with her cousins, as they hosted sleepovers and relished Maggi at midnight. It may have seemed childlike for Kismat to live in this bubble of nostalgia ad nauseam, but she knew that exhibiting maturity need not be mutually exclusive from learning to live in the moment.

One afternoon, her cousins took her to the popular Sarojini Nagar market. Kismat narrowly escaped the paan-spits and overstepping from locals who were clueless about the concept of personal space. The "Made in India" clothing label she would see in the "Forever 21" and 'Gap" clothing chains back in States were now a reality with the hordes of garment shops in every nook and cranny of the marketplace.

Sarojini was famous for bargain shopping. Even though she had visited the marketplace many times with her aunts and cousins, she was completely overwhelmed by all the sounds of humanity all around her. Local sellers would not hesitate to tape their merchandise on her face with, *"Madam, tablecloth? Madam, bedsheet? Madam, hosiery toh le lo?"*

Kismat had missed all this concoction of humdrum back in the quiet pace of her life in the States where no one was concerned about her need for hosiery in full public view.

During the harsh winter months, the only time she could even tell that life existed in her Jersey neighborhood was when the municipal snow blowers would clean the streets, or when her neighbors would turn on the ignition key and drive their car to work.

Her Delhi colony posed a lively contrast; the neighbors would spend their afternoon's chit-chatting in their balconies or sipping tea on their verandahs, though this, too, had diminished over the years.

The overwhelming noise continued further with the sounds of scrap dealers roaming around at odd hours yelling, *"Kabadiyeeee!!"* and the subziwalas starting as early as seven in the morning with their reverberating jingle of, *"Tamatar le lo, bhindi le lo, kela, santra, bhaingannnnnnnn!** in the fastest speed known to mankind.

* *Buy tomato, okra, banana, oranges!*

On some days, Delhi's lagging water supply taught her to suffice with a bucket of hot water and tolerate the ancient inverter that could only support two fans in two rooms when the light would go out. It was appalling for Kismat to see her aunties wait hours for an electrician to do minor fixes like changing a tube light, when she could do it herself. Then there were the new-age service apps; the kind that delivered produce at home, or matched her to a plumber and even a parlor lady who was ready to wax and tweeze at the slightest sprout of hair; all of these being some of the facets of the modern mess that Delhi had become.

Delhi impressed her with its well-connected metro system built under the aegis of E Sreedharan, a brilliant civil engineer, and new stretches of marked flyovers and buildings, albeit scarred with the cracks of corruption from the hosting of the 2010 Commonwealth Games. A cluster of shopping malls had been set up where she remembered nothing but an open land of trees or a buildup of slums occupying those once open lands.

Luxe malls and office spaces with glass exteriors were

under development; build by the hands of diligent laborers, consisting of emaciated men and their wives, who picked up heavy bricks while their infants were sheltered under a tin roof or played alongside dangerous construction material.

Laws for workplace safety were only for the suited employees inside the aforementioned glass enclosures.

The middle and lower classes could be found sprawling on the gardens of flyovers around Delhi, eating their tiffins, or simply resting, but those same, manicured lawns abroad would find no such visitors.

The common thread in Delhi was that having lots of money wasn't nearly as important as having the ability to show it off. But this wasn't just true for Delhi. In the world, there were people who misused their power, connections, and money to sideline the law when they needed to, much like the Kaurava clan in the Gita.

But those who fought terror, served the marginalized, and essentially cleaned up the garbage dumped by their less than moral counterparts; those that upheld their duties and morals were the true heroes, as espoused in the ideals of the Pandavas, and particularly the warrior Arjuna.

Gurgaon's growing skyline of hotels, corporate buildings, and residential towers gave her the impression of what Dubai may have looked like in its days of infancy. New buyers were taking out mortgages to continually keep up with home prices that were skyrocketing as fast the city's skyline, much like the mortgage crisis of the West. The less fortunate were living in congested villages or tents adjacent to some of these high-rises in the hope to seek employment as their servants or drivers. New government schemes were bent on pushing the same class of people out of servitude and towards independence.

One of her distant uncles invited Kismat to his newly built luxury villa that had cropped up in a posh area of Gurgaon, with most of the roads and infrastructure around the gated community still screaming for attention. The villa residents were relaxing in the Club restaurant as their kids were swimming in the pool, each being attended to by their own individual help. The Spanish colonial tile roofing, the stucco white coated walls, brick chimney, and private courtyard of each villa gave her a temporary façade of being in Europe, minus any underpaid maids. This was kind of a strange *deja vu* for her.

Within the six months of her return to Delhi, Kismat found herself sheltered inside her home with Ammi, a relative's house, or her airconditioned car. At home, Sita had hired a part-time maid, ironically named Rani (queen), who cleaned the dishes, wiped the floors, and for some extra bucks, also did some cooking on the side.

Whenever Kismat would halt her car at a red light, there was the most peculiar combination of transport ranging from branded sedans to rickshaws, bullock carts, scootys, and government buses with unruly drivers. There were also the odd sellers, beggars, and transgenders, lightly tapping people's windows for money either out of purchase or pity. Some of those accosting people for money would try to get a peek of the passengers inside the luxury vehicles, chauffeured or not. Instantly, the delineation between the upper and lower class was evident in this exercise.

At times, Kismat would travel around with her cousins who had drivers and full-time maids and lived in multi-storey homes with sprawling lawns. Soon, she became enamored by this illusion of royalty. Her lofty lifestyle came to a halt the day Rani had to take a week's leave and all the dishes piled up at home and the soles of her feet were blackened from all the dust on the unmopped floor. Kismat sorely missed her dishwashing machine and the unpolluted air of Jersey suburbs where every day dusting and *jhadoo-pocha* wasn't a mandatory affair.

Ammi and Sita prohibited her boarding an auto alone, or even take her bicycle out for a spin, from fear of recent headlines about assaults.

This peeved her. The "common" man or woman of India were the ones cleaning another person's dishes, driving another person's car and the rest who dared to peek inside, hoping to be seated inside the cool comfort of a car. No matter how many saris or lehengas she draped or how much Hindi she spoke to assimilate, her life of convenience made her feel like just another foreigner in India. In the States, she was her own cook, her own cleaner, and her own driver.

Two months into her stay in India, Kismat made the leap to do what she had learned to do in the States -- use the metro, ride her bicycle, and complete her own chores with minimal help. She relished Rani's cooking and paid extra money for her daughter's school fees. It was only after reaching this level of independence did she feel like she had assimilated into the fabric of her people.

~

When Kismat uploaded a photo of her eating at a cafe in Delhi, there was one man who was ecstatic with this update, perhaps minor to others but a monumental one for him. He started a school group thread and encouraged his old friends to organize a small class reunion so that he would get the chance to meet her.

Kismat remained in touch with only a few of her classmates and to his despair, none of them responded. After waiting for nearly a month, he finally decided to reach out to Kismat directly with the miniscule hope that she would respond.

Hi Kismat,
It's great to see that you're back in India!

Mustering more courage, he typed further.

"I hope you remember me, we were in the same class. I used to sit in the back."

In his mind he was thinking, *"I remember everything about your smile, the way your hair would gently caress your face in class, the headbands you would wear that would make my heart restless..."*

He had almost typed out, *"I love you..."* but eventually changed it to a safer sounding composition of *"Hope you are doing well."*

Three days later, he received a reply on his Facebook profile from the girl that still made his heart flutter.

"Hi Purab! Of course, I remember you! You were the one that gave me those earrings. What are you up to?"

He responded to Karma's message but this time around, paying close attention to his grammar and vocabulary.

"I am currently working at the Gandhimarg Govt Hospital and completing my residency. You know, I've never traveled abroad. I would vicariously live through your photos when you'd visit a new place. I must add that you looked stunning in all your pictures."

To avoid rambling on further, Purab added a simple one line. *"Let's catch up sometime. Take care."*

Purab hounded his profile everyday for her reply like an eager detective sniffing out a crime scene for any hint of a clue.

Finally, two days later, Kismat wrote back.

"Yes, it would be great to meet up! I stay in South Delhi. I really haven't kept in touch with any of our classmates. Here's my number: 9182736XXX.

If you know any other classmates in our area, feel free to invite them too!

Purab knew fully well where she lived. He would pass by her house when she left for the States, hoping someday she would return and stand on the third floor of her balcony playing with her long hair and find him waiting for her down below. One time, that dream actually came true except when that person turned around, it was a young man with a wet towel on one hand and a turban cloth on the other. Purab realized the Dharmas must have rented out the house again. He laughed and wondered why some idyllic love stories were incomplete without the mention of a lady waiting on a balcony.

Not wanting to waste any more time in cat and mouse threads, Purab called her up that following weekend.

The bell rang a few times and finally, a voice replied, “Hello – who is this?”

“Oh, so sorry, I....I didn't give you my number before. Um... this is Purab...from school.”

“Hi Purab!”

Purab's heart skipped a beat.

“So, how are you doing?” she inquired after the brief pause. Purab adjusted himself back to reality, realizing it was his turn to respond.

“I'm good. The weather is so hot now-a-days, right?”

As soon as he said that, he wanted to slap himself.

“Yes it is. How's work?”

“Not too bad. I work with a team of doctors, and we get new cases every day. Seeing the sick children really gets to me. I think God can be so cruel sometimes.”

“But you're doing a great job treating them.”

“Thanks but it's not always that noble. Doctors can't save everyone and only those with money end up getting good treatment. I think that money makes people evil.”

“I don’t think money is the issue. We could still be trading goats for grains and greed could still get the better of us. It’s all about how the person uses the money.”

He jumped to the main question.

“Kismat, let’s continue this interesting conversation in person! Can I take you out for some coffee?"

"Sure."

"Really?! Does Friday evening work for you?"

"I think that works."

Ecstatic to hear her accept, Purab secretly hoped that all natural calamities would hold off until after Friday.

Luckily, Purab had already thought of an answer to Kismat's next question, "Where should we meet?"

"Oh, there's this new cafe in SDA."

"Okay, pick whatever you like."

"So Friday is confirmed then?"

"Yes. I'll see you then."

Purab may not have set foot in a temple in years but he made sure to pay a visit to the one inside his house, ignoring the look of amazement on his mother's face.

God was giving his dreams a second chance.

Purab was seated in a quiet corner of the cafe when Kismat walked in. She glanced around before she saw him waving at her. As soon as she arrived at the table, he got up from his seat. For a few seconds, he was just standing there, his eyes fixed on hers.

Her face still carried the glow as it did back in school, albeit with few blemishes, like the radiantly flawed moon. And like a potent tide in a Gulzar lyric, he allowed himself to be carried away by her pull.

In anticipation of this meeting and his previous night shifts at the hospital, Purab hadn't had a good night's sleep in days. Yet his eyes compensated for all the energy that his body appeared to lack. He was wearing a strong scent, and his coarse hair looked as if he had just combed it moments ago.

"Gosh, it feels like only yesterday that we had the farewell party in school and you were wearing that orange colored sari --- you looked amazing."

"I'm surprised you even remember the color!"

"You look really nice today too....I mean, you always do."

Purab caught himself blabbering and stopped his flow of thoughts. Kismat was grateful that he was wearing spectacles, for she found his affection too overwhelming to meet him eye to eye. She had always been allergic to flattery with major side-effects including quickly changing topics in conversations.

"So Purab, what are your plans for the future?" she asked hurriedly.

"Well, one thing is for sure. I want to make money and lots of it. I don't want to be married till I'm content with my financial condition."

"But why so keen on making lots of money?"

"Well, I've seen my family go through a lot of tough times, times when we could only afford the bare minimum. I told myself that I would earn so much that I wouldn't have to be in those situations again. Basically, I want to live a comfortable life. I want the big car and fancy home and if my wife wants gold and diamonds, I want to be able to meet her expectations."

"Wow! Don't say these things too loud or some girl might hear you and make a move," Kismat quipped.

"Will you make a move? I mean, do you want those diamonds?" Purab asked with hopeful eyes and seeing Kismat's unchanging face, he quickly said, "Don't worry, I'm only kidding."

A waiter came by, reprieving Purab of some awkwardness. Kismat asked for a mocha latte. As Purab was placing his order, Kismat glanced towards the TV screen. A fairness cream ad surfaced, the model's face painted with dark foundation, as she navigated the jeers of her college peers. The moment the model applied the fairness cream, she turned into an albino Shreya Ghosal.

Kismat began to laugh.

"What's so funny?" Purab asked curiously.

"Sorry, I was just watching a crappy commercial."

Purab had done his fair bit of research to impress the lady in front of her.

"So tell me one thing. Why is the Rupee depreciating against the dollar? Isn't the Indian economy in better shape than the US?"

"You can't compare the two. Right now, rupee is weakening because of inflation. It simply means we have to spend more money for the same basket of goods."

"Well, why isn't our government doing anything to fix this?" Purab asked in turn, his research failing to contend her knowledge.

"They are. The RBI just temporarily increased interest rates to make borrowing expensive. The government is also investing towards alternate sources of energy. And construction and manufacturing sectors show promise too. Just because our Rupee is weakening doesn't mean our people are."

Purab looked as if he was stumped.

"Actually Purab, I wanted to ask you one thing."

"What is it?" he asked, hoping she may deviate to some romantic discourse.

"Do you know a good library around here?"

He began researching some on his phone.

The waiter arrived with their drinks and a chocolate cake that Purab ordered especially for the table.

"Actually Kismat, I wanted to ask you something too."

"Yes?"

"Are you seeing someone right now?"

"Not at the moment," Kismat replied politely, noticing Purab's grin getting wider.

As they shared the slices of cake, he received a call from the hospital. He expressed his displeasure at the person for having disturbed him. The displeasure changed to anger and yelling and he finally hung up.

"I'm sorry but I have to go back to the hospital. So, when can we meet again? Hopefully soon?"

"Sure! I'm traveling with my cousins next week. Can we plan something later?"

"Okay. Would it be ok if I messaged you in between?"

"Yes of course. We'll be in touch."

She waved goodbye before disappearing into a cab to get home.

He had been waiting anxiously for a ping, a hello, anything from her. But those days felt like years and patience felt like a burning fire in the pit of his stomach. When she checked her email chat a few days later, she found that it was flooded with his messages.

Purab suggested another meetup that weekend.

Each second of their chat was precious to him.

She shared a photo from her Jaipur trip; he shared one from his time water rafting in Rishikesh, one where he thought he looked most dapper. His typing on the chat window quickened to the pace of his beating heart.

The love on her part hadn't set in yet; his love was ready to burst out at any instant. Like any Mills and Boon romance would have you imagine, she was the scorching sun, and he, the saturated clouds around her. And to further lend to this saccharine love story, they would color each other's lives like a transient rainbow paints the sky.

They met again. He was standing outside their proposed meeting spot in Vasant Vihar complex, looking in the opposite direction.

Discretely, she got close to him, and asked, "Guess who?" In the frenzy of the surprise, Purab dropped his cigarette.

"Oh, I'm sorry, I didn't know you were...."

Purab intended to discard it before Kismat would arrive. "It's just a temporary habit from college days."

"Can I try it?" Kismat asked calmly.

"This?....Are you sure?"

Kismat nodded.

"This will be my first attempt at smoking."

Purab handed her a newly lighted cigarette.

She blew out two puffs before coughing up.

Purab wanted to hold her in his arms but held back.

"Pretty much all you do is take a deep breath and exhale slowly. You can feel the same relaxation from yoga too. Maybe you can try that to help you quit."

"It's not that easy Kismat -- the nicotine keeps you hooked. And I don't think doing some funky poses will help me quit."

"I know yoga sounds like that but it'll help you focus. If you're sorted from within, you'll never have the craving for a cigarette."

When he didn't say anything, she quickly added, "Sorry for all the excess philosophy."

"You've got to stop apologizing for everything. How's that for a bit of philosophy?" he added with a wink.

"Waah!"

"I have a feeling you wouldn't want to be with a guy who smokes. Am I right?"

She nodded.

"Whatever happened to the concept of unconditional love?" Purab asked her playfully.

"My grandfather passed away nine years ago from throat cancer."

Kismat's voice had suddenly turned stern.

"He was a heavy smoker. After the radiation, he couldn't eat or drink from his throat. They had to feed him through his veins."

Purab felt like he had disappointed Kismat for the first time in his life.

"I promise I'll quit if that makes you happy."

"I got carried away -- look, I was just offering advice as a friend. You can do as you please. It's your own life and I have no right to interfere."

"But you do have a right. I care what you think about me and if my quitting means a lot to you, I will do it."

Kismat turned silent.

"Kismat, I don't know if you could already tell, but I really like you - I had a crush on you in school and nine years have passed since then, but my feelings for you haven't changed."

Kismat wanted to speak up but couldn't formulate the words, as if her jaw was paralyzed from the intensity of her emotions.

"I've dated other girls but with you, it's different. I can't explain what it is that draws me to you....all I know is that...I love you."

Purab felt relieved at finally telling her what he had wanted to say since tenth grade. He didn't feel afraid of rejection anymore. All that mattered was that she finally heard it.

Kismat felt like she had just woken up from a dream.

"You're the first guy to ever say those three words to me, did you know that? --- well except that one drunk guy in college..."

"And all this while, I thought there must have been so many," he replied in awe.

"I've always been a bit scared about love," Kismat softly added, not having shared that reason with anyone else before.

"Why are you scared? I mean, if you looked at yourself from my eyes when we were in school, you would never have thought that way.....you were my dream girl!"

Purab had boosted Kismat's confidence so much that she had reached the moon and was now effortlessly drifting in space. She admitted that she liked him too, but she needed more time.

After two months of his infectious love over dates, Kismat had finally warmed up to Purab's affection.

His work at the hospital was getting increasingly busy, working six days a week on rotational shifts that made his sleep cycle awry. In spite of living in the same city, they had to struggle to meet in person and spontaneity became key to keeping in touch, from the unexpected phone calls to the last minute dates, even if it meant meeting up for just a half hour.

One such night, he landed up outside her house, waiting for her to look down from the third floor of her balcony, just like he always dreamed he would see her someday. He was holding a heart-shaped dark chocolate bar with hazelnuts, the kind that she liked.

She tiptoed out of her room and silently waved back to him, putting a finger on her lips to signal him not to make any noise. He blew her kisses in excitement. She quietly made her way down and ushered him inside to a secluded corner where no one could see them.

They embraced immediately.

"Even the slightest distance is becoming difficult to tolerate Kismat. How am I going to survive?"

"Just don't let go," she said and he hugged her even tighter.

Kismat had never experienced such an emotion before. It was as pure as the earth, grounding her and as the heavens, taking her up to the clouds.

It was exhilarating, these early moments of falling in love. To add to all the mushiness, Purab went down on one knee and presented her with a big heart of chocolate. He uttered the best speech a doctor (-in training) could ever spontaneously fathom close to that hour of the night.

"Kismat, I heart you -- I also liver you, lungs you, and pancreas you -- basically, I love you from every part of my body and my soul."

"Kiss me already."

In the gentle sweetness of their first kiss, they conveyed in ample measure how much they cared for each other.

The first six months of their relationship flew without a trace; their love was so blinding that they couldn't think about anything else but each other.

He would write her handwritten letters filled with dreamy passion, reveling in the happiness of finding his true soulmate in her. He would share these paper treasures with her on the days they would meet so that she would have something to hold onto when they couldn't see each other. They would talk till the wee hours of the night. At times, she would be telling an interesting bit about her day, only to hear his snoring on the other end.

One weekend, Kismat and Purab decided to spend the day away from any cafe, pub, or any other manufactured area of mingling.

They found a quiet spot under the shade of a tree in Rose Garden and made it their provisional sanctuary. Purab put his head down on Kismat's lap and gazed into her eyes.

He couldn't stop looking at her.

"What's the matter?" she asked.

"Nothing....I just can't believe that I'm here...with you. You're really one of kind, you know that?"

"And you're a tube light, you know that? But a really cute one. So tell me, did you start liking me in school just because I looked a certain way?"

"Looks are what initially attracted me towards you but I am past that stage now. I love you more for your wit, your optimism, your maturity, and I can go on and on."

She gently ruffled his hair and kissed him on his forehead.

"Why are you so good to me? I have never met any guy as sweet as you."

He quickly took her hands in his.

"And I will always be good with you in my life."

They leisurely strolled, hand in hand, their love, new and deep, that made them feel more alive that any exhilarating run; and fresh despite the perspiring heat.

As they turned to walk towards the lake in the middle of the vast park, Kismat noticed a family with two children walking up from their picnic spot, leaving behind a trash of orange peels and an emptied bag of chips. Kismat starting walking towards the family before they went too far away from their crime scene.

"Excuse me, I'm sorry for disturbing you but...."

The family was startled to have an unknown woman following them. Thinking she wanted to sell them something useless, the family continued walking but Kismat continued talking anyway.

"If you teach your kids to litter at this age, they will repeat this behavior. Would you want them to grow up and not be responsible for their actions?"

The mother and father stopped in their tracks. They looked at each other, wondering why this stranger was suddenly giving them a combined lecture on parenting and preserving the environment.

"All I'm asking from you is to please go back and pick up your trash --c'mon, it'll teach your kids to be good citizens. I know you want the same....please."

The parents, abashed, finally conceded with Kismat's words. Together they cleaned the mess, taking them less than five minutes of their time.

As the family finally made their way out, they waved back to her a smile. Purab looked amazed and started to mockingly clap for Kismat.

"That was pretty awesome. So, are you going to clean up everyone's litter?"

"Very funny!" Kismat pouted her lips.

"I know you've lived abroad and stuff but over here, it's just the way it is."

Kismat didn't respond at first.

"Look, all I'm saying is that you can't change everyone," Purab replied in a plain and rational tone.

Kismat remembered her failed efforts in making her grandmother understand the irony of bargaining with vegetable vendors and her mother understand the importance of tipping well in the States.

"I'm not trying to change everyone. I can only change myself."

Purab let Kismat continue, feeling even more drawn towards her for unique approach to life.

"I would've gone and picked up the trash myself if they weren't going to do it."

"You really like giving lectures to people, don't you? I wonder how many lectures you're going to give to our kids when we're married," Purab teased.

"What?"

Purab turned red.

"I'm sorry if I scared you. I'll be honest Kismat -- I imagine you as my wife sometimes. And we have this daughter who looks like you. I even mentioned you to my mother...I know this is all too fast for you."

Kismat was usually quick to respond to most situations in her life but this one really threw her off her mental current. Purab had certainly taught her how to open her heart to someone, something she thought she couldn't do since the incident involving her brother in his teens. But the subject of an even bigger commitment made her wary once again.

In her mind, she thought, *"The thought of getting married and having a daughter makes me extremely happy, but what if you fail to live up to your promises?.....I may appear strong from the outside but I have a fragile heart Purab....Sometimes I want to let go because I have never been loved this way before...."*

During her time at W&W, Kismat made a feeble attempt at dating and it allowed her to better ascertain the kind of man she wanted to be with. But none of those dates ever blossomed into a real relationship. In Purab's adamant pursuit of her, she managed to trespass that self-imposed boundary. Purab took a deep breath and said, "You don't have to say anything if you don't want to."

She looked away, feeling too overwhelmed from the love in his eyes. “I love you but I don't know what destiny has in store for us.”

Unlike Kismat, Purab was mentally and emotionally prepared for this conversation. “Kismat, I know we are young and we have a long way ahead of us, but just remember, in the end, I will ensure that we are happy together.”

They shared all their hopes and fears, reaching a level of comfort and closeness she had hitherto experienced before. Purab was a smart and hardworking man; traits that made him more strong and masculine than any cigarette in his hand ever could.

If there was one thing that attracted her the most to him, it was his introverted poetic side which she was privy to in his letters. While Kismat would be turned on by his speed and accuracy in mental math, Purab would be bowled over by her witty charm.

Together, they found great joy in challenging each other's wits.

“Ok Purab, let's start easy. What's 7 divided by 7?”

“Oh, that's a toughie.”

“Just play along.”

“Obviously 1.”

Kismat proceeded to take off her pink headband. She started wearing headbands more often around Purab to remind him of their old school days. Her cascading tresses gently caressed her face and she brushed them aside with her hand. Her petite breasts, which were partially covered by the length of her hair, could be traced over her light cream blouse. She threw the headband towards him and he grabbed it in excitement.

Purab understood the rules of the game.

“Wow! What's my next question?!”

“Divide the last answer by 7. I want the answer to that particular point before the digits start repeating themselves."

Purab was flabbergasted. Curious to know what she would do next, so he tried anyway.

The first six digits were unique before the same number started to repeat itself.

"Ok, 142857."

Kismat opened the first three buttons of her cream blouse increasing the temperature in the room a notch further. Purab's cheeks were a flushing red now.

"Ok, now multiply by 7."

There had to be some trick for he had just divided by 7.

He started speaking out loudly, "..9..9....." and finally ended with, "damn....999999."

She smiled in approval.

"Don't you think I deserve a kiss for doing so well up till now?"

"I promise you will get your kiss after you answer this last and final question ---now take the first three digits and multiply it by the last three. Then, from the product, add the first three to the last three. Tell me what you get. You have thirty seconds."

"What the?!..... That's not fair."

"All's fair in love and math. Twenty-five seconds left."

"Um...ok I got this...the first step is squaring 999....."

Purab tried his best to keep his focus, all the while struggling to avoid the distractions from Kismat who was now wearing just a hugging camisole and jeans. He was intoxicated by the light perfume scent from her hair. She was impressed that he didn't need to use the calculator even once.

"Ok...the product is 998001.."

"Five seconds left. I'll give you a hint. The answer is a Kaprekar number."

"Kaprekar what?!"

Kismat imitated the sound of a buzzer.

"Time's up. You were so close! The answer is amazingly enough, 999. Sorry, no kiss!"

"You are so mean!" he exclaimed.

"Yes, I'm so average na!" she teased him back.

He took her hands in his.

"Yes, you are...you're the average, main sequence star of my life and the reason for my existence."

"Waah! That's still not gonna get you a kiss."

Purab chuckled and remained resilient.

"Ok fine. My turn to ask a question. Your loss is my kiss. Ready?"

"I'm ready."

"Take the word "astronomer" and reshuffle the letters to get two words to fill in the following sentence.

In high school, you were my __and I was your __.

You have thirty seconds."

She took out a piece of paper and started writing out various permutations of the letters.

"Ten seconds."

Finally, she got one word down confirming Purab's incessant ogling of her in school.

Starer.

She was left with the letters -- n,o,m,o.

"Three seconds left."

"Moooooon!"

"Yes! In high school, you were my *moon* and I was your *starer*."

"So I am your moon AND your sun? It's like I have a solar system identity disorder."

He took her in his arms and said, "You are my entire universe. How about that?"

"Well, as long as you don't call me Uranus...." and she finally gave him the kiss he deserved, the passion lingering on their senses much longer than the thirty seconds they allotted to each other.

Every sight and every sound appeared to be magnified in its beauty; the colors more vivid and ordinary sounds turning into intoxicating music for the ears. Eating and sleeping seemed superfluous when Kismat would rather want to be in his embrace. Her generous pecks on the nape of his neck soothed away his exhaustion from the day, and his tender kisses put her into a trance.

He was a gifted kisser, no doubt.

At every date, they stole kisses in some corner of the street, or in their car. In their youthful spontaneity, all the places seemed the same.

Their story seemed straight out of a book. He was her first love. But somewhere in the back of her mind, she wondered if it had blossomed too quickly. On occasion, she would ask him if she was ever coming in the way of his aspirations and Purab lovingly dismissed all of her fears.

"Kismat, you are my entire heart. And I know you have bared your soul to me as well. This is testament to the amazing bond we share."

"Yes...you have my heart but the rest depends on the kind of bond you're talking about," she added smilingly.

"What do you mean?"

"Ok, I mean we could be a government bond because the government rarely defaults. But come to think of it, our love can also be a corporate bond because we took a risk in uniting after so many years and our love has been so rewarding."

"Well, I think our chemistry is brilliant so I will go ahead and say that we have an ionic bond. You are a positive source of ion-spiration in my life and I have always been attracted to you. But alas, you splashed water on my hopes in school and broke our ionic bond," he added with a chuckle.

"Oh, you had me at ion-spiration!"

She gave him a tight hug. If anyone happened to be privy to their conversations, they would've been nauseated by all their geeky references. Kismat revelled in these conversations, finally having found someone who liked mingling concepts the way she did.

"And when the two of us get married, our bond will transform into a strong metallic one."

"How so Purab?"

"Because we will be two special atoms amongst the sea of other couples in the worldly metallic lattice. Our beautiful babies will be the delocalized valence electrons. Our kids may grow up detached from us because of their need for independence. But as much as they'll freely run around, their attraction to our positive core values will hold us together as one big family."*

**Will their cationic state ever cause them to repulse each other in the absence of their delocalized electrons? Only time would tell.*

There were some men who pleased their partner by knowing how to press the right buttons in their complicated female circuits through an input stimulus; some boosted their beloved's mood by showering her with fancy gifts through a monetary stimulus and some just uttered sweet nothings through a psychological stimulus. But of all those stimuli, there was nothing that stimulated Kismat more than the thought of a lifelong bond with Purab.

Their one year dating anniversary was soon approaching. Leaving no stone unturned, Purab made a reservation at one of the nicest restaurants in Greater Kailash and gifted her a small necklace to match the earrings he once gifted her in school.

Kismat had been wearing those earrings ever since she said, "I love you" to him, the first time she said those three words to any man.

At the restaurant, Kismat asked Purab to help her wear the necklace. As he began to tie it behind her back, he whispered in her ear, "Kismat, this is one of the happiest days of my life."

She kissed him lightly on his cheek. Since the beginning of their relationship, Purab had been reeling with anxiety and severe headaches as his insane work schedule had taken a toll on his sleep.

"Let's order something quick."

Purab didn't know Kismat was fasting for his health that day. She had grown up seeing her mother fast for Ajay's long life every year and she couldn't believe that she was following such a trite and skewed custom. But love had its way of making people do crazy things.

“You know what?” Purab interrupted her flow of thoughts. “The day I get to hold you and our baby at the hospital – that day will be the best day of my life. But I am just scared of one thing.”

“What's that Rabji?”

“If our daughter looks like you, I'll have a tough time protecting her from all the boys when she goes out to party.”

Kismat gently clasped his hands.

“Honey, we are at the age to party right now. Plus, there is no guarantee that we’ll have a girl. I mean, what if we have a boy?”

“Oh no, we'll have a daughter for sure – I will tell my Y chromosome to ‘eff off.”

Kismat erupted in laughter whilst Purab continued blabbering as he would always do around her.

“Boy or girl, I can't wait to share our amazing love story with our kids. I'll tell them that their mom used to pursue me quite ardently back in school.....”

Kismat pulled his shirt so close such that their breaths were intermingling.

“Oh, really?”

He took a few moments to reconnect back to reality. Finally, he whispered, “and I will tell them how I thought she was fairly decent so I decided to give her a chance,” and he flashed his usual dimpled smile coupled with loving innocence.

She gave him a kiss on his cheek and Purab did not have the ability to talk any further. He responded just as well, by kissing her full on her lips.

On the heart of the necklace, Purab had the following inscription made out for Kismat.

'Rab Di Kismat.

The inscription signified that not only was Kismat Purab's destiny, he was just as corny as her in the department of love.

For the remainder of their dinner, they happily basked in conversations about what they would name their kids, or the countries they would visit together and more importantly, how Purab would whisk her off her feet every night he would return from work.

Kismat even confided in Purab about little Sophia from her trip to Romania and her hopes to adopt her into their little family. His keenness to make Sophia their own made her feel so complete with him, that it was almost surreal.

A month later, Purab was posted to a new hospital in Mumbai for training. He assured her, as always, that they would talk as often as possible till he returned to Delhi. During his breaks, as rare as they were, the sound of his voice and her kisses helped them cope with being so far apart. They had nothing but technology to make up for distance. Their "air" hugs over video call compensated for the intimacy they couldn't have in person.

Kismat kept herself busy as usual by working at her mother's clinic. The couple weathered more weeks of separation. They managed to talk once or twice over the course of the week. He sounded stressed out on the phone and he assured her that it was just a temporary phase of work life. Kismat would send him encouraging messages and jokes once in a while to lighten his mood.

These days turned into weeks. Though she desperately

wanted to hear his loving words, she maintained her distance to the best she could. She accepted this phase in the hope that he would come back loving her the same way as before.

Their calls became rarer. When he would return her call, it seemed like she was talking to a stranger.

Finally when the gap between them stretched too long and she missed him more than ever, she wrote him a letter expressing her love. Purab messaged her back several days later and in that small message, he added a few words of apology and despair for being so busy and aloof. Those few words felt like a bright ray of hope.

One evening, Kismat started getting a terrible headache during a trip to a local Safal store. As she made her way back home, she felt dizzy on the flight of stairs and lost her stamina to stand straight. Somehow, she managed to climb up till the floor of her house, but dropped the pouch of milk and vegetables on the concrete floor.

She collapsed on the sofa in the living room. Her grandmother saw the milk flowing out and yelled at Kismat for being so irresponsible. She told her to rest in her own room as the sofa covers were recently dry-cleaned.

But there was no response from Kismat.

Her grandmother touched her forehead and it was burning hot. Badi ammi rushed inside the kitchen and came back with a steel container of ice cold water and a handkerchief from her room. She dipped the handkerchief and applied it to Kismat's forehead. She placed a thermometer in Kismat's mouth with one hand and dialed Sita with the other to inform her about Kismat's condition.

Having spent most of her youth in her native village, Badi ammi had plenty experience kneading dough with her fists, sieving the rice, and putting baby Ajay to sleep, all at once. She was a skilled lady who could complete several chores at once. There was no hospital in Badi ammi's village. Whenever a woman gave birth, they would take the help of the mid-wife. Ajay was born the same way. Once a pregnant woman lost consciousness owing to exhaustion and the mid-wife awakened her by bringing the strong odor of a wild plant. Badi ammi splashed a few drops of water on Kismat's face because she knew that Kismat must regain consciousness at an equally serious time like this. After several attempts, Kismat finally opened her eyes.

Sita hurried home and gave Kismat a pill of quick release paracetamol to bring the fever down. Ammi fed her dal and roti with her own hands and after an hour, Kismat was able to sit up and talk normally.

"Minni, how are you feeling now? What happened?"

"I don't know Mummy – I started getting really dizzy and had this terrible headache. I couldn't even keep my my eyes open, but I'm fine now."

The next day, Kismat got a blood test and Sita kept a tab on her fever readings. To Sita's relief, barring some vitamin deficiencies, everything was normal.

Kismat may still have been recovering physically but her thoughts were still array.

She held on to Purab's gifts and read and reread his letters as a means of having him near her. Her favorite letter from him had the most beautiful lines she had ever seen penned by a man.

"Dear Kismat,

This is the first time in my life I am writing a letter to someone. But with you, there are many firsts. The first time I fell in love was with you. The first time I met a girl who was the perfect combination of beauty and intellect was you. The first time a girl inspired such romantic feelings in me that I felt like marrying her as soon as possible, was you.

I experience all these emotions and never before have I been so strong and so vulnerable at the same time. These letters are not just words, but a piece of my heart, so handle it with care.

You know, your heart will always, always remain safe with me. I just want you to remember that come what may, there will be someone, somewhere who will be there for you, in the good times and bad, always wanting to see a smile on your face. That one smile will light up his day."

Just as the artifice of vocabulary can romanticize, it can very well deceive too.

One evening, a popular song chimed on the radio, a song they had once dedicated to each other. It was a song that Purab would sing to her in the days of their blissful romance in his less than perfect voice and that song acted as a perfect catalyst to reach out to him.

Using her remaining straws of hope, she messaged him for a final chance to talk. She tried to keep strong and manage the pretense that things were okay, fighting her intuition that everything had changed.

But he couldn't abandon her, she assured herself; surely not after all the promises he made.

Finally, when the frustration was exploding in her veins and she could pretend no longer, she confronted him on the phone; her voice tired and drowsy owing to her bed rest.

"Purab, I know you're busy but please, I just have to know – do you still want to be with me? Please be honest."

Sounding more irritated than usual, he finally said, "I told you, I'm going through this phase."

Love has a way of making us feel helplessly vulnerable and yet giving us immeasurable strength, just as the words of his letter indicated, but his actions no longer seemed to merit her love.

He taught her that it was not possible to open the heart to someone without taking the risk of getting it torn apart.

Kismat had never felt more vulnerable than in that one phone call.

She asked him again, softly, on the verge of breaking out in tears, "But do you still love me?"

He spoke in a tone that she had never heard him speak before. It was an emotion of confusion and anger blending in different wavelengths of his voice.

"Relax, nothing's changed. I have to go now."

"I'm sorry if I bothered you -- you always tell me I apologize too much. It's just that I wasn't feeling well and I really wanted to hear your voice but I promise, I won't disturb you like this again."

Unexpectedly, his tone changed to one that was cynical and cold.

"You always wear such little clothing for fashion. If you stopped wearing revealing dresses, you wouldn't have fallen sick in the first place."

His words hit her like a bullet in her heart.

She chose to end the call, in what would be the final time they would hear each other's voices on the other end of the line.

Forgiveness

Three months into her marriage, Karma started work at an analytics firm in a commercial sector of Gurgaon, which was nearby but still took her forty minutes to get to. Her company provided her with a pickup and drop-off van as the city, progressive enough to have high-rises and high waged executives, was still coping to provide safety for many of its working women.

Karma used her daily commute in the van to talk to Lakshmi and sought her best recipes, including idiyappam and parippu curries to make over the weekend. Though Lakshmi had less stamina physically, she didn't convey any of this to her daughter on the phone.

Karma needed the money from her job to help pay for her mother's costly treatment and frequent hospitalizations that couldn't be managed with her father's pension. Though Bharat would not hesitate to help her, she didn't want to be dependent on him just yet.

Nandini and Jyotimala would occasionally call her to ask about any good news regarding the possibility of a little bundle of joy. Karma would resist the topic. The truth was that she couldn't conceive. She'd routinely skip many months of her cycle. After moving to Gurgaon, Karma consulted a gynecologist who diagnosed her with severe PCOD. The gynecologist put her on a regimen of birth control pills to regularize her menses which made her gain stubborn weight around her belly. Motherhood, at this point, was a distant dream for her.

Within a year of their marriage, Bharat received a promotion that made him a Senior Manager in his department. That evening, he casually brought up the topic of adding some more entertainment to their humble abode.

"But dear, we already have such a nice TV and speakers. It would be a waste to spend on another item."

"Rama, I meant the kind of entertainment that will crawl and poop and grow up to become an integral part of our family."

"But who will take care of the dog when we are both working?"

Bharat started laughing.

"Oh God, I mean the kind that will call us Mamma and Papa."

Her heart was heavy with guilt.

"Are you sure? Didn't you want to start your new venture with your friends?"

"I have my whole life to keep making money Rama, but I would love to see our child growing up with us as we make more strides in our life. I see some of my friends with their little ones and I imagine what great parents we can become."

"Bharat, I need to build on my career. I hope you understand." He supported her decision, upholding his promise to her when they first met.

While Karma compensated for her distance by connecting over the phone, it didn't provide the same solace of being in her mother's presence. When Sati spoke to her the following week, she had some heartbreaking news to share.

"Please come here as soon as possible, Chechi. I really need you."

"What's wrong Sati?"

"Ma is slowly losing sensation in her arms. And her breathing has become more difficult. The doctors can't do anything."

The same morning, Karma requested her manager for leave. Noting her extreme anguish on the phone, he approved it the same day. She packed any essentials she could see lying around and hurried to the airport. Bharat assured her that he would be flying down as soon as she would get more clarity on the situation.

Oblivious to the noise and frenzy of humanity around her at the airport, she rushed straight out of the plane and into her mother's arms at home.

But Lakshmi did not hug her back.

Her smiling face was overshadowed by her droopy eyes and thin built.

“Amma?! How are you feeling? Please talk to me.”

“My dear Rama....you're finally here. How is Bharat? Does he like your cooking? Are you hungry?”

As always, Karma put forth a happy countenance and spoke about how Bharat loved her so much and how happy she was in her new life.

Karma spoke with her family in private.

"What happened Acha? She was stable when we talked last week.”

Surya took her aside, and wept, for the first time in his life. “I’m so sorry Rama. I spoke to every doctor I could find. Venky Uncle referred me to a neurologist in London, but they don’t have any new options.”

Surya, Jyotimala and Nandini, all had the same look of sorrow swept over their faces, a look of lost hope and shattered expectations from God.

Karma stormed into Dr. Sylvie's clinic the next day.

“I will give you all the money you need but please save my mother! Please, I beg of you.”

“Karma, we have tried everything but hers is a very unique case that has no cure,” Dr. Sylvie replied as calmly as she could.

“But you said that you could help!”

“I'm terribly sorry.”

Karma lost the ability to comprehend the world around her. Two weeks passed by her mother's side and each day seemed to dampen her hopes further. She had resigned from her company and stayed put in Kochi.

In a month, Lakshmi lost the ability to talk and move her facial muscles, barring the movement of her eyelids. Karma and Sati tried to cheer her up by impersonating her favorite heroines, pantomiming movie names in a game of charades, and playing her favorite melodies on their phones.

Bharat flew down the same week.

Lakshmi blinked once to convey "yes" and twice to convey "no" for basic requests. The Iyers did their best to give her peaceful memories as time was ticking away.

Lakshmi was admitted to an ICU when her lungs collapsed, and they prolonged her breathing artificially with an emergency ventilator.

Lakshmi's eyes were wide open for a full day as the variety of machines made their customary noise to pump medicines, check her vitals, dialyze her blood, and push oxygen into her lungs. Karma did not want to cause any more pain than what the disease had already claimed.

Lakshmi's hands jerked a few times. Seeing this, Jyotimala chanted every *mantra* she could fathom, hoping her daughter-in-law would return to normalcy.

It ached Karma's heart to know that her mother had deeply wanted to live, but could not be afforded such a grace; as if her register of good deeds was insufficient to afford such a miracle. The sanguine chants that Jyotimala sang to praise the many Hindu Gods were full of rampant lies, she thought.

The monitors recording her vitals confirmed that her mother had little chance of survival.

Her organs were failing.

The doctor removed the ventilator at Karma's insistence and kept her on a drip of pain medication.

The nurses intimated her that although Lakshmi could not express herself, she could still hear them. Karma humored her with some anecdotes from her childhood and gently hummed her mother's prayer in her ear. In those final moments, Karma kept her mother's hands in hers.

As Lakshmi breathed her last, Karma affectionately kissed her mother's cheek and gently closed her eyes.

The Iyers observed a week's worth of Hindu rituals. Lakshmi's ashes were preserved on an erect platform in the southernmost courtyard of their house. A lamp was lit daily at dusk and a *tulsi* (holy basil) plant was potted near the platform.

The seven days was a means to vent their grief, and accept that Lakshmi was no longer with them. This acceptance was especially important for Karma, who shouldered the guilt of her mother's passing entirely on herself.

Jyotimala knew of this, which is why she requested her granddaughter, and not her son, Surya, to complete the cow feeding ritual.

Every morning, Karma prepared balls of kneaded *atta* (wheat), ladled with ghee, and rolled it in jowar and bajra seeds. She fed the atta mix to a handful of cows at a cowshed in a village a few kilometers away. Jyotimala suggested that the cow's nourishment was akin to feeding the soul of her mother. For once in her life, Karma obliged to her grandmother's pious beliefs.

Upon her return from the cowshed, she would drink coconut water from the same vendor that Lakshmi used to visit near the temple grounds.

Just a mere thirty rupees for fresh, liquid nourishment. Unimaginable in a city like London, she thought. The daily routine of feeding the revered animal, mooing and pooping dung at random intervals, was strangely soothing to Karma.

It distracted her from reality, albeit briefly.

In those six days of *'shanti'* for her mother's soul, there was hardly any time for her to self-introspect as flocks of relatives, students, and members of the temple and school, where Lakshmi volunteered, flooded the Iyer household to pay their condolences.

During one of the main "havan" ceremonies, Karma observed an aged panditji smoking a cigarette during a break. Anger boiled in her veins.

How could this man live to be so old when her mother died decades younger?

Sadly, one cannot bring God to court to lessen the sentence of a terminal illness like judges do with humans.

A day before Karma and Bharat were due to fly back to Gurgaon, her sister, Sita, prepared their mother's favorite dish - erissery, a pumpkin and lentil stew, with help from Nandini.

All, but Karma, ate it.

On the morning of her departure, Sati finally disclosed her feelings even though Karma refused to open up to anyone since Lakshmi's demise.

"I'm really sorry Chechi. I couldn't fulfill the promise I made to you on your wedding day."

"Don't be sorry Sati. It was foolish of me to make you agree to such a promise. If God couldn't help her, how could have I expected you to do the same?"

Karma hugged everyone, uttered a hurried goodbye, and managed everything without wasting the drop of a single tear.

When Karma was ready to go to London, she thought she had life all figured out. Working hard will lead to optimum results. As long as one was doing good work, the rewards will be observed in this lifetime itself.

But she could not digest the fact that her mother, a woman of the purest intentions at heart, and utmost dedication to her community could have suffered such a fate. Karma could name plenty of criminals absconding their way out of the justice system.

Why didn't God choose them?

"Bharat, why her?"

Bharat put his arms around Karma. He knew it was best to let her vent.

Karma's voice changed to a tone of confused bitterness.

"You know, I spent a goddamn year studying economics! Everything bloody started with the assumption of rationality. But being rational seems like such a foreign concept to me now -- there is nothing to explain this - nothing at all!"

Bharat remained hopelessly silent.

"She spent all her time helping others, couldn't God take care of her once?! Was it too much to ask for?! I don't believe in God anymore. All those prayers did nothing."

"Rama...."

Those were her last words before breaking out of Bharat's embrace. She went to her side of the bed, closed her eyes and feigned sleep. Bharat kissed her on the forehead, turned off the light and quietly moved to his side, while holding on to her hand.

Karma spent many countless nights awake.

One of those nights, she dreamt of her.

Lakshmi was looking down at Karma from heaven, her radiant face peering over the curvature of a floccus cloud. Karma told her that she was sorry, that she couldn't save her. That she would do anything to hear the sweetness of her voice again.

Lakshmi started singing a lullaby to her. Karma was comforted by the fragrance of Lakshmi's hair and the touch of her soft skin.

Karma wanted to tell her that she loved her. And as soon as she opened her lips to say those three words, her mother disappeared.

Forever.

With all her anger directed towards God, Karma would lash out at everyone around her, whether it was a simple vegetable vendor, or even some stranger she would accidentally bump into in her apartment complex.

When Bharat reached home and asked her about her day, she yelled at him for the very first time.

She wanted to tell him to go away for some time, or for good, so that Bharat could find someone else, someone who could give him a child, someone wouldn't cause him all this pain because he didn't deserve it.

Yet his reply demonstrated such maturity that set the foundation for their married life.

"Please, by all means, chuck me out of your life as a husband Rama. But please, don't chuck me out of your life as a friend. I love you."

~

The world around her seemed like a strange nightmare; one that she couldn't awaken from, even if she tried.

There were many reasons Kismat conjured in her mind. Every day, her feelings went from hurt to anger to wanting to talk to him again, in a terrible cycle. But any anger towards him would backfire because those feelings would essentially end up hurting her from the memories she still harbored from the past.

Kismat wanted that Purab dutifully return her heart back in its pristine condition. While he derived good income from his work at the hospital, he had suddenly become too poor to share his love.

Kismat vowed to herself that she would never abandon anyone the way he did.

She hoped one day, she would find the courage in her heart to thank him for his cowardice, for his abandonment would strengthen her beyond a threshold she didn't know even existed.

Frost's road was split into two.

One arrow pointed to Purab and a life spent waiting for him in futile despair.

The other pointed to a life of growth and self-realizations. Kismat made the resolve to set herself free in the same echoing breaths.

And she did just that by taking two major steps.

First, she rallied up all the courage inside her and wrote him a letter, without any expectations of a response, for closure relieves the mind and heart of its tense trance.

Purab,

Our past was wonderful, our future was promising, but our present was neither of those.

The truth is that we do not know how we make another person feel until we feel it ourselves.

You taught me what it means to love, but not what it means to commit. Our souls connected and parted just as well, absorbing plentiful lessons along the way.

I'll still respect your soul because the souls speak a different language, they skip on a different beat, and connect on levels, unfathomable.

I forgive you and I forgive myself.

With this letter, I am free.

Peace,

Kismat

She even wrote a poem, but kept it to herself.

Girte girte hum sambhal jaate hain, aur sambhalte sambhalte kabhi gir,
Zindagi bas ek baar jeene ke liye bani hai,
toh lelo suraj se roshni aur milalo dil se dil.
Hum apne pyaar ke kisse dauhrate rehenge apne hi mann main,
Akhir kab tak, nahi jaanta koi musafir.
Na jaane kab, kin halaat main, mulaqaat hogi phir.

* *Translation: Sometimes we regain our balance just as we are about to fall, and sometimes we fall as we are picking up the pieces of our life to get back up*

again,

We only have one life to live, so let us take in the warmth of the sun and fall in love.

We may narrate our love stories, time and time again, within the depths of our mind, till when, no stranger can tell.

Who knows when, and in what circumstances, we shall meet again.

The next step would be the hardest.

Actually practicing forgiveness.

With each word of forgiveness, tears would roll down her eyes. Another "I forgive you Purab" softly escaped her lips and more tears spilled as, if, directly from her heart.

There were moments of breakdown when her emotions would take precedence. She wanted to relive the old times again but there was nothing to salvage in the present. One can return a piece of merchandise but there are no such refunds in matters of loving another soul.

Their song dedications were now in some forbidden playlist; their meeting spots in some taboo territory, and everything else from her memories with him becoming the misery that is the indefatigable power of the human mind.

She trashed his old letters, donated anything he gifted her, and removed him from all of her profiles.

She did everything she could to relieve herself of the burden of carrying undeserving hurt.

The words of the Gita Saar became even more meaningful to her at that point in her life. These words made all the difference to fight the biggest enemies, the thoughts in her head.

"Whatever happened in the past, happened for the good, whatever is happening in the present is happening for the good and whatever shall happen in the future shall be for the best too.

Do not weep about the past, do not worry about the future, and focus on the present.

What did you bring at the time of your birth that you consider as lost? What did you produce in the present that you consider as having destroyed?"

One cannot hold onto something that isn't theirs to begin with. Everything begins and ends with nature.

A week after sending her last letter to Purab, she penned the following lines in her journal:

"Dear Krishna,

My first love story was a chapter of great bliss followed by great pain. The bliss and pain, though transient, are recurrent experiences of our lives.

I chose to find my balance in this cycle.

Yes, our chemistry was great but our physics sucked.

Like the rays in a combination lens telescope, neither of us could see that our paths converged for a bit, but they were always apart.

Such is the beauty of the Galilean telescope.

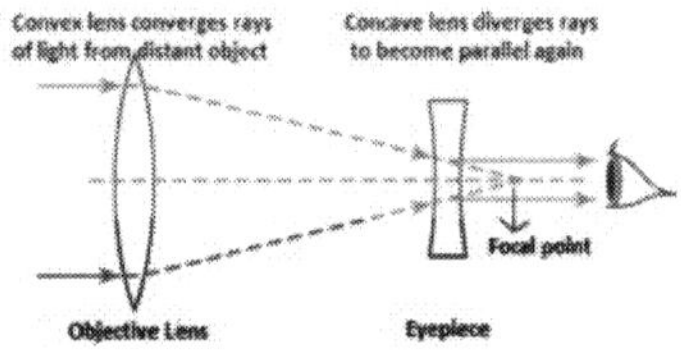

In high school, I was the "moon" or rather the "object" to be seen from his eyes, he was the "moon starer." He would call me the focal point of his being, but in reality, I was much afar at infinity.

His overwhelming expression of love for me in the beginning of our romance was his eyepiece, but if only he could see me objectively, he could see that our paths never intersected at all. Though we became close, we began and ended distinctly parallel, as strangers.

We weren't as tragic as being star-struck lovers, but we were star gazers in the true sense. The image we projected of our future was also at infinity in some space we could not touch or feel, but just believe that it existed.

Two souls never really belong to each other; they just chance to meet. Some stay, some return, and some leave to forge bonds with others in destiny.

I've learned that our hearts are made fragile by burdening it with expectations that we essentially have no control over. When I unbuckled these chains off my heart, and let go, I realized I can breathe from the heart too. It may be true then that the heart can serve many functions.

Perhaps I am confusing the heart with the immaculate, eternally glowing soul located very close to it.

p.s. I often wonder what are the exact coordinates of the soul on the map of the human body. I think it is like the mystery of the Bermuda triangle, where many tired adventurers are said to have disappeared forever, but unlike the myth of the triangle, those that are in tune with their soul aren't lost in misery.

Rather, they have found everlasting peace. I think that will be an interesting entry for another day.

Good night."

For the first time in her life, Kismat had fallen in love and was loved by a man.

God had fulfilled the fourth item on her bucket list.

~

Time ticked on in mending Kismat's broken heart.

The puffiness of her eyes served as an indication to the tears that wouldn't halt their flow.

Every night, Kismat would be alone in her room, shut off the lights, and just dance to her favorite music, as much her lanky legs allowed her to.

This was her secret therapy.

She had been practicing this dance ritual since she was a teenager, serving as an important source of catharsis because there was no one watching, no one to judge her, no one to interrupt her tears.

She was free.

When life would bog her down with deadlines and pressures, she would move her hips to the beats of the music to shake off all her stress; when she would feel low on steam, she would harness the energy from the rhythm of an Enrique or a Shakira hit to feel alive again. The days when she was most beaten down, she listened to the kind of music that would help her reclaim her strength (Stand by You by the Pretenders) and badassery (To the Left by Beyonce).

In the end, no matter how many people or pleasurable things one may seek to stitch their broken hearts, it is ultimately up to the individual to let go.

Kismat didn't know how many days had passed since she had written her last letter to him. She continued her routine at her mother's clinic while occasionally dwelling on gloomy songs; unbeknown to the beginnings that were to come.

It was a regular day at the clinic. Kismat was reviewing the patient profiles and preparing medicines for those who had already finished their consultations. A gentleman introduced himself as Madhav. He was visiting her mother's clinic as a new patient for a skin ailment. Though his eczema was evident in folds of his neck, the first thing she noticed was his efficacious smile.

"I'm sorry to ask out of the blue, but what school do you go to?"

Kismat still hadn't lost the habit of wearing her headbands. Her peach colored jeans and polka dotted shirt didn't help either.

"I graduated from college a few years ago."

"Oh, sorry. Actually I was looking for some volunteers. I

head a non-profit nearby."

"What does your non-profit do?"

He shared a pamphlet about his organization, Bal Bhavishya, with links to a website and online enrollment for volunteers. The organization had even received funding from state and private donors.

Madhav reminded her of her Arabic professor and the wisdom he encapsulated for her in college – that one need not be so pessimistic about the world. There are plenty humdingers around us.

"We teach kids from low income backgrounds, mostly who've been rescued from trafficking, or have been completely abandoned by their families."

"When can I start?"

The man was taken aback from her sudden enthusiasm.

"How many days a week are you free?"

"Three. Is that ok?"

"More than ok."

Within a week, Kismat was teaching English and Math at Bal Bhavishya, just a twenty minute walk from her mother's clinic. She befriended a girl named Rupali, who headed the outreach program for new volunteers, and provided her with a quick orientation.

Every minute she'd spend in Madhav's school passed by with such swiftness, unlike the days of working at her W&W cubicle and staring at the clock that would slowly tick away her life .

The world was still its bittersweet self, but she became more conscious of her present. In those humbling moments of teaching the kids, she never once forgot Sophia and the promise she had made to her at the church.

The Romanian organization continued to update her about her in their monthly newsletters.

Five years had passed since Kismat had last seen her.

Purab or any other man may come, make many promises and part from her life.

But Kismat had vowed to never do the same with anyone that she loved.

Everlasting Friendship

Three months had passed since Lakshmi's passing.

Karma would often find herself sitting at home, thoughts of suicide ravaging her fragile mind. Her scarring, emotionally from Lakshmi's demise, and physically, from her infertility and the blemishes that covered her face, made her recoil in her shell. She had lost intimacy with Bharat on both planes.

Bharat did his best to cheer her up by taking her out for small trips and dates. Karma tried to look happy for him, speaking very little; failing to react to his jokes that would have, otherwise, been rewarded by her distinctive laugh.

Oh, how he missed her hearty laugh. It was terribly loud, as if she was cachinnating straight from her belly. Even the fine lines that formed near her eyes when she smiled seemed to have disappeared.

Bharat took Karma to a family doctor, who referred her to a psychiatrist. The psychiatrist asked her a few questions about the recent events in her life, most of which were answered by Bharat himself.

The psychiatrist diagnosed her with post-traumatic stress disorder and severe depression. His recurring prescriptions of anti-depressants momentarily halted Karma's paralyzing thoughts, but made her numb to the outside world, both in instances of happiness and misery alike. Comedy scenes from movies and sitcoms did not evoke any laughter. News of calamities and suicidal bombings did not shock her. Her grief was like a heavy beast breathing down her neck, suffocating her. Karma was alive and breathing, but it seemed as if the power cord to her amygdala was no longer plugged in.

After weeks of isolating herself inside her apartment, Bharat urged Karma to step outside and get a change of scenery. On his way to work, he dropped her off to the nearest metro station, so she could visit any place to her liking.

As soon as the metro approached the platform, she contemplated jumping in front of it.

A young lady bumped into her by accident, and profusely apologized for it. The lady wished her a good day; her eyes conveying a great deal of strength, as if it was solely directed to Karma to avert her thoughts.

For a moment, Karma felt as if she saw her own reflection in the woman.

The woman, likely in her late twenties, had jet black hair, and eyes, and depressed acne scars on her temples. She entered inside the women's compartment of the train, and engrossed herself in a book. Karma, just as well, boarded the same compartment as her.

A minute later, the doors closed and the train began to move, and now Karma didn't know where she was headed.

After thirty minutes, the young lady deboarded at Connaught Place. Mindlessly, Karma got off too.

Connaught Place had the unique layout of cafes and shops lined around in disjointed concentric circles with open colonnades. A park, with a magnificant flag of India, lay in the middle, with roads connecting to other parts of Delhi. The circular junction reminded Karma of Piccadilly Circus in London. Connaught Place was just one of many ineffaceable marks left by British imperialism but its vibrancy, lent from its famous eateries and fashionable visitors, was homegrown.

Dozens of lovers could be found cozying up behind the bushes of Connaught's Central Park. It reminded her of the time when she and Bharat first met in Kochi, when their love was new and young.

How time had changed their lives!

They used to be like one of those couples, lost in their own world of romance and enamored by the fleeting sense of completeness that love can bring.

The lady from the metro was still in her line of sight.

She took a turn and seemed to have disappeared.

Karma decided to head back home, until she saw the lady again, this time entering a small establishment.

The sign boards outside the building looked freshly painted despite the dust and cobwebs that settled on the corners.

The topmost sign read "*Aarogya Holistic Clinic.*"

The clinic was brimming with patients. There were several rooms inside. The lady from the metro had disappeared into one of those rooms now.

At first, Karma walked past the clinic.

But there was some inextricable pull from the lady that Karma could not ignore. After crossing two avenues, she turned around and entered inside.

The clinic had practitioners who provided a variety of alternative therapies including acupuncture, ayurveda, and homeopathy. Karma was now standing in front of a door that read, "*Dr. Dharma.*"

The young lady had come outside and called the name of the next patient to enter the room.

She saw Karma waiting near the door.

"Can I have your name, please?"

"Karma."

It was clear that this lady did not remember her from the station.

"Okay, do you have an appointment?"

Karma turned silent.

"That's alright, we welcome walk-ins. But you'll have to wait a bit. There are five people ahead of you."

"I was just passing by. I should head home now."

The lady could sense despondency in Karma's voice.

"If you're in a hurry, I can put you in next."

"No, no...I don't want to see the doctor, sorry."

"But we are the CBI!"

"Excuse me?"

"By CBI, I mean a Clinic for the Betterment of Individuals," the young lady added with a chuckle.

Karma, not having further energy to debate, eventually relented to the lady. If the assistant was like that, she wondered how strange the doctor would be. But Sita, who asked her to come in next, was a welcome change.

Sita asked Karma to reveal a bit about herself, before getting to her medical problem.

At first, Karma didn't say anything.

Her mother, Lakshmi, had tried every route, from conventional drugs to holistic therapies, but nothing worked. She, herself, was on an indefinite course of anti-depressants. The last thing she wanted to do was consult another doctor.

Still, destiny had brought her here.

"It's ok dear. Tell me, how are you feeling?"

"Not good," came a strained reply.

"Have you been feeling like this for a while?"

"I just feel this emptiness....like something is eating away inside of me."

"Can you tell me more about yourself? What's bothering you? Anything you'd like to share?"

Karma shook her head. Sita knew it was best to wait till she was ready.

"That's ok. Are you on any medication right now?"

Karma listed the name of her anti-depressants. And added that she had taken a course of estrogen pills that were a temporary fix, but left her with painful blemishes and more irregularities.

"Are you trying to conceive by any chance?"

"Yes, but my body has given up. I don't want to take any

more pills."

Sita assured her that the remedies she prescribed were sourced from nature and stimulated the body's own healing. They had no side-effects and could be safely taken as a complimentary therapy.

Sita calmly explained that any disease is a sign of an imbalance in the body. She also noted that over time, any psychological suppression may become physiological too.

"Take for example acne. Some resort to creams and lotions, or take dangerous medication. While the drug may address the symptoms, the problem persists."

Noting the seriousness of her grief, Sita advised Karma to continue consulting her other doctors and visit a hospital in case of any emergency. And added that while natural remedies were helpful, no therapy could guarantee a cure.

Towards the end of her consultation, Sita gently asked Karma if there was anything else she wanted to tell her.

"I'm just a defective piece."

Karma's eyes were cast down when she said this.

"My dear, your grief is valid. But please know that all of us are defective in some way. I've had a history of depression too."

This time, Karma looked up, meeting Sita's eyes.

"You have?"

"Yes, I suffered silently for months when I was living in the States. Couldn't sleep or eat properly, sometimes for even days at a stretch. Life can bring down even the burliest soul, but remember, there is power even in the tiniest cell of our body to keep us going. In your troubling moments, think of the people who love you and care about you. For me, it was my daughter who helped me get to where I am today."

The ghost of guilt had paralyzed Karma's spirit, much like ALS had paralyzed her mother's movements. But she thought of Bharat, Surya, Sati, Nandini, and even her obstinate grandmother, Jyotimala. They all loved her dearly. Karma knew she had to get better for them.

"Doctor, can you fix me?"

Karma's voice was terribly unsteady from the lump forming in her throat.
Sita held her hand. "I'll try my very best."
Keeping in mind Karma's bottled up grief and her emotional suppression, Sita decided to start with a dose of Ignatia.*

* *Ignatia bean originates from the Loganiceae family tree that is native to Southeast Asia.*

"My daughter, Kismat, will give you the medicine outside. Please call if you have any questions. And come back to me in a week."

"Thank you doctor."

"Karma, you can say thanks to me the day you conceive," Sita added with a beaming smile.

Her heart felt a little less burdened from hearing the possibility that she could become a mother. She was also surprised to learn that the weird assistant was actually Sita's daughter.

Kismat handed Karma a small packet of globules.

"Just follow the instructions on the label. Just take one dose, half hour before you are in REM mode."

"REM? How can I take the medicine when I'm asleep?"

"By REM, I mean Ready (to) Eat Meal."

Karma thought that this girl was the strangest person she had ever met in her life.

"Why must you make weird abbreviations for everything?"

"Because you'll never forget it that way," Kismat added smilingly.

Her words did the trick and Karma remembered to take her medicine half hour before before eating or drinking anything.

Karma returned a week later. Her head felt less heavy on her shoulders and her mind, less foggy.

"How are you feeling now?"

"Still coping but better than before."

"That's good. Would you like to share anything today?"

She didn't make any mention of her past trauma, but added that she had been skipping her menses. At Sita's request, she shared her reports that showed evidence of her imbalance and PCOS.

Noticing her reservations with past trauma and suppressed cycles, Dr. Sita added a dose of a new remedy to help Karma heal further. It was almost lunch time now.

When Karma stepped outside, Kismat asked her if she wanted to grab a bite from a nearby cafe.

"I'm actually not that hungry right now."

The murmuring in Karma's stomach said otherwise.

She hadn't eaten a proper breakfast to reach in time for her appointment.

"Okay, see you later."

Kismat had started walking ahead when Karma exclaimed, "Wait! I changed my mind."

They walked outside to Chotu Ka Dhaba, a hole-in-the wall cafe in the adjoining block that managed to attract a great number of locals and tourists, alike.

"This place is famous for its masala chai and chaat."

Karma inhaled an *aloo tikki* burger even before Kismat could take a bite of her chaat.

"Not hungry, eh?"

"Sorry, I was famished."

"How are you feeling today?"

"Better, but my face still has a lot of blemishes."

"Yeah, I still get zits around my period too. Check out my acne scars from the time I was in college," Kismat added, pointing to the depressed scars on her temples.

"Like my mother always said - if a strawberry isn't afraid to show its scars, why should we?"

Hearing this, Karma showed a hint of a smile, though she quickly abandoned it mid-way.

Both ladies bonded, albeit briefly, on their time abroad. Kismat talked about her nights socializing and working in New York, while Karma mentioned about her days of studying in London; both, ruminating about those moments with a kind of retrospective rosiness when everything in life seemed to be completely sorted.

But there was a difference in the place of privelege they came from. Kismat revealed that she quit her high-paying job to move back to Delhi.

"I don't think I'd have the guts to leave such a good salary," Karma stated, matter-of-factly.

"Well, money isn't my only motivation."

Kismat admitted that though she made less money at her mother's clinic, she was content.

"Try telling that to someone who has seen poverty in their prime. I think you were really lucky to have the choice. I wouldn't have been able to pay my mother's hospital bills or afford London if it weren't for my job and scholarship."

There was merit in Karma's words, and Kismat fully acknowledged this. Karma smiled again, this time from the deep satisfaction of having made her point. Both women agreed on the need to use their spectrum of privelege to help those who didn't have the luxury of choice. And though this was only their first meeting, both Kismat and Karma would find the means to accomplish this, with one woman taking over the legacy of what the other would leave behind.

When Kismat asked about her family in Kochi, Karma didn't say anything about her mother. She gulped down her chai, which was now a cool temperature, and lied that she needed to head back to Gurgaon.

When Karma returned to Sita's clinic several weeks later, she had some good news to share. Though bleeding from any part of the body is typically a distressing issue, Karma was elated that her menses had resumed months after skipping her cycle. She had a renewed sense of confidence about her. Post her appointment with Dr. Sita, she ventured inside a clothing store to purchase some shirts that Bharat could wear to work. Inside, she spotted Kismat in a denim dress, who was trying on an array of headbands in front of a full-length mirror.

"Hey! I didn't see you at the clinic today."

"Hi Karma! I'm here shopping with my friend, Rupali. She needed some retail therapy to fix her bad mood."

Rupali called out from the trial room to help her decide on a new outfit.

"How do I look Kismat? I know it's a size smaller than what I usually wear but I think my boyfriend will like it."

The dress carried a faux animal print and was too body-hugging to look flattering on her waistline.

"Roop, no. Just no."

Rupali was miffed with Kismat's response.

"My tailor can alter the dress, you know? There seems to be a margin on the sides."

"Those extra margins are the reason why you never go running with me on the weekends."

Rupali went back into the trial room to pick a less threatening outfit with Kismat's help.

Karma, too, finished her shopping in the men's section.

The three ladies headed to the register.

"Hey Karma, we were going out for dinner. Why don't you join us?" Kismat invited her.

Even though Karma had been living in her Gurgaon flat for over two years now, she hadn't made any close friends. She spoke to Bharat who encouraged her to tag along with them.

The ladies headed to a pizzeria in a big South Delhi mall. They began chatting about their favorite books and songs, but Karma was relatively quiet. To break the ice, Kismat hinted that she knew a bit about reading palms.

Rupali quickly placed her hands in front of Kismat.

"What do my hands say?! Anything about marrying a handsome man?"

Kismat asked Rupali to make a fist and count the number of creases on her right hand.

"One...two...three....four....FIVE! Is this the number of boyfriends I'm going to have?"

"No, this is the number of kids you're going to have!" Kismat quipped.

Rupali pretended to faint and Karma laughed, this time with abandon. In their chorus of laughter, Karma sensed an old part of herself emerging back.

As their pizza reached the table, Karma observed her hands, as if she could feel them for the very first time. She asked Kismat why her lines were different in both hands.

"Well, I did read somewhere that the lines on our left hand are set by our fate, and the ones on our right are shaped by our actions."

"You see this line here..." Kismat noted, pointing to Karma's right palm.

"It's the lifeline. You have another line running parallel to it. That's a good sign. Almost as if you have some guardian angel looking over you."

Karma didn't pay much heed to all this nonsense, until she noticed that she had a big break in her lifeline.

"Oh, I have one too!" Kismat exclaimed.

Kismat and Karma put their hands side by side and realized that their lines were almost identical.

"I guess we're more similar than we realize," Kismat added with a smile.

"I guess so. But what does this break mean?"

Kismat admitted that she didn't know anything more than what she had already said. Rupali decided to look it up online.

"A break in the lifeline means you have to overcome some major struggle or loss," Rupali calmly added, reading off the text on her smartphone.

Kismat also had a branch on her lifeline, going downward. Rupali consulted her phone again.

"It says here that the branch is a sign of being independent. That makes so much sense! You're always preaching about being detached from everyone and sharing all this spiritual *gyaan* ever since your breakup..."

Rupali realized she had revealed too much.

"Sorry Kismat, I just..."

"That's ok Roop."

"When did you breakup?" Karma asked curiously.

"Recently. Actually, I fell into the trap of wanting love from someone who chose to move away. That breakup made me realize how we all tend to get too attached to those we love."

Karma was surprised to see a sensitive side to Kismat, contrasting to her usual, chirpy self.

"But how can we not be attached to our loved ones? I will go to any length to keep my family happy," Karma stated, matter-of-factly.

"Yes, but detachment doesn't mean leaving the people you care about. Rather, it's quite the opposite. It's letting your love extend to everyone."

Rupali rolled her eyes and added, "The *guru mata* has awakened."

Karma laughed again.

"I hate to break it you Kismat but we live in a capitalist society where many of us love in self-interest. Besides, it's not easy to love everyone when we have so many problems of our own."

Rupali high-fived Karma for the great comeback.

"Yes, it's not easy. Even during my relationship, I felt as if I needed him to complete me somehow. I spent months forgiving him and myself till I could start loving again. The key thing to understand is that we're already complete -- full of love, intellect and strength."

"Huh? How can we already be complete with intellect? We all need an education."

Kismat argued that intellect is the ability to question the world. Everyone is born with it and uses it in their own way to acquire knowledge.

"Education may give us a degree but when we question what we absorb and share our wisdom for the good of others, that's when we become intellectual."

"You should really write in a self-help column, you know," Karma joked.

"Not with my kind of FEE!"

Kismat quickly added that her FEE actually meant - Forgive, Earn and Enjoy.

"Oh, no! Here come the acronyms again! Rupali, is she always like this?"

Rupali smilingly nodded her head.

"Guys, hear me out! This FEE is an easy *mantra* to life – first, we must Forgive ourselves of undeserving self-blame. Next, we must Earn money to be independent, and lastly, Enjoy doing things that make us happy."

"How are you so liberated, oh dear *mata*?" Karma asked jokingly.

Kismat lifted her right palm to bless both ladies, as if she were an idol of a deity.

"My dear disciples, in moments of great pleasure and pain, temptation and torture alike, reclaiming your consciousness is the true means of nourishing your soul. I achieve this by meditating every morning, after I finish a big poop."

Karma and Rupali applauded Kismat's humorous antics.

"And remember ladies - Of the few things that irate us, there are plenty of reasons to celebrate us!"

"I think the wine is really getting to you Kismat!" Rupali quipped.

"Oh, I have one more...while the justice system may fail, karma always prevails!"

"Amen, or should I say – Ah-women!" Rupali cheered.

The three ladies raised a toast with their glasses.

After splitting the bill, the three of them got up and headed towards the main exit of the Vasant Kunj Mall.

Before Rupali could get on the escalator, a couple of teenage boys rudely pushed her out of the way.

One even exclaimed, "Out of my way fatso!"

The boy reminded Kismat of something her dad taught her.

Tongue and *tang* may sound similar, but Ajay said it was important that we use our tongues wisely else it may irritate (*tang*) someone who may not be pleased with what we said.

The boy who made fun of Rupali bumped into a wall, prompting laughter from his friends.

"Like I said ladies, karma always prevails!"

As Karma reached the station to take a connecting Metro train, she looked back towards Kismat. It was the first time in her life that she had met someone who had challenged her rational thinking.

The following week, Karma saw a new assistant working at the clinic. She inquired about Kismat's absence from Sita.

"Kismat teaches at a school on the days that she is free. She should be coming back any time now. Do you want me to send her a message?"

"That's totally fine. I'll see her next time. Thank you so much."

As Karma made her way out the clinic, she was happy to see Kismat parking her car in an adjacent lot.

"Hey! I just wanted to say Hello before leaving," Karma replied, without admitting her happiness.

"Off to Gurgaon?"

"Yeah, I'm about to take the Metro."

"I can drop you to your house, if you want."

"That'll be too far out of your way."

"No no, I have to go to Gurgaon anyway to drop off some important paperwork at my cousin's house. Might as well get it done today."

"Are you sure?"

"Yes. I'll just let my mom know and then we can go."

Once they reached the main flyover that connected Delhi and Haryana, they were welcomed with new signage due to ongoing construction in the area.

In order to avoid congestion on the main road, the traffic police had made several bypass lanes."

"Do you know which road to take from here?"

"Sorry, I don't drive."

It was too late to Google Map the answer, as more cars honked her from behind.

"Ok, einnie meanie miny moe, we are going down this road."

Kismat put an indicator to turn right.

"Kismat, you're really strange."

"Yes, I know. I revel in it."

"But you don't have any false pretenses about you. I like that."

"Gasp! Karma, are you being nice to me?"

"Yes, but I'm done now," she added smilingly.

They reached Karma's apartment complex.

"You can stop here. Thanks again for the ride back."

"Anytime Karma!"

There was a brief pause in the car until Karma posed an interesting question.

"Would you forgive someone if they had hurt you a lot?"

Kismat was taken aback from the seriousness of the question. She took a few seconds to gather her thoughts.

"Yes, I would. Forgiving is one of the hardest things to do, if not, the hardest. But it releases us from our own prisons. Just remember that the person who has hurt us, is not the one who has to heal us."

"But what if that someone abused you? Or killed someone you loved?" Karma asked her again.

Kismat turned silent.

"See, I knew you wouldn't have an answer to that."

"Can I share something with you?" Kismat asked softly.

Karma nodded.

"A boy in fifth grade bullied me to be his girlfriend. When I said 'No', his gang beat up my brother in school. I didn't have the courage to tell anyone. And I can't tell you the number of times I've been groped in public places."

This time, Karma turned silent.

Kismat held her hand.

"Did you go through any such instance in your life? You don't have to tell me if you don't want to."

Karma began having flashbacks of the assault in her hometown.

"I haven't told anyone about this, not even my own family." She finally gathered some strength to speak up.

"When I was in tenth grade, I was assaulted by two men on my way back from my dance class. They had a knife to my throat. They kept putting their fingers inside of me and forced me to get inside their van. I finally managed to bite one of the attackers."

Kismat held her close.

"And then I remembered a prayer that my mother taught me. Those two men ran away but the image of their faces scarred me for life."

"Those bastards!"

"After that incident, I didn't go out for weeks by myself, even in the day time."

The two hugged each other, and Kismat could feel Karma's tears rolling down her back.

Kismat joked that God should just give women the skin of a spiky pineapple, or a hairy rambutan to fend off any lewd men.

"Nah, I think it should be a jackfruit!"

"Why a jackfruit?" Kismat asked curiously.

"You don't know? Jackfruit is like the epitome of self-defense in the fruit world. It's got the thickest skin."

Kismat let out a hearty chuckle.

"You know my mother used to make the best jackfruit jam when I was young. We call it *chakka varatti* down in Kerala."

"Oh, that sounds yum!"

"Why don't you come up and try it with some bread and tea? I have some in the fridge from the market."

"Are you sure? I do need to use the bathroom and then get going...."

"Yes c'mon! Tea will only take two minutes."

Lakshmi would always shower her guests with plates of fried snacks and homemade chutneys. Those traditions of generosity caught up in her daughter as well, who prepared a quick platter of sandwiches with store bought jam, tomato chutney, and banana chips.

Just over the course of a few months, Karma had developed a unique bond with the lady sitting in front of her.

"Kismat, do you remember how we first met?"

"At the clinic, right?"

"No, you bumped into me at the City Center station. I didn't know where I was going...what I was doing...but I saw you and felt like I knew you somehow."

"I had no clue Karma...."

"I was sure to jump that day. I got off at Rajiv Chowk like you did and saw you entering the clinic. You're the reason I'm still alive today."

Kismat hugged her, not being able to fathom the intensity of emotions that her friend had just shared, and how much she had been hurting all this time.

"Karma, I've never been gladder to run into someone in my life."

The two decided to go picknicking at India Gate grounds the following day. They found a sanctuary near the artificial lake, where little children took turns swimming inside, much to the dismay of local cops on duty.

Passing men, some of whom were holding hands, would routinely stare at the two of them, and then move on with their lives, typical of any Delhi girl's experience of simply existing in such a gender skewed part of India.

"You know, one time, I was in the subway in New York, and this man kept staring at me. Made me super uncomfortable. So, I thought of staring right back at him."

"What happened then?" Karma asked inquisitively.

"I was pretending to chew a *paan*. You remember that creepy guy in Devdas who kept ogling at Madhuri and Aishwarya as they swayed to *Dola Re*?"

"Yeah?"

"I approached the guy and pretended to spit that imaginary *paan* near his feet. He immediately ran way!"

The two of them guffawed in unison.

Karma noticed many happy families walking around with their children and clicking pictures with them. Even on the few occasions that Bharat's office friends would come over, they would only talk about their little bundles of joy.

Every time Karma looked at those families, she blamed her own body for not being able to cherish that joy.

"I don't think I'll ever become a mother..." Karma confessed, her voice breaking into tears.

"Have faith....it'll be okay."

"I don't have any faith in God! And we all can't be all as sorted as you. You may think you have life all figured out, but you don't. It will continue to surprise you and pull the rug under your feet."

Before Kismat could say or do anything, she posed her next question.

"Can you explain to me why good people suffer such horrible fates?"

Kismat turned silent again.

"You don't have an answer to everything Kismat. No one does. Just accept it."

Kismat remained calm whereas Karma's voice was elevating with every frustration she was releasing from her spirit.

"You don't understand the pain of losing a parent! How can I forgive God for taking away my mother after so much suffering?"

Kismat held her close.

"I'm really sorry for this outburst," her voice deeply apologetic.

"Ever since my mother passed away, I've always held myself responsible."

Karma opened up about her mother's paralysis, her decades of volunteering efforts, her multiple hospitalizations, and her eventual passing.

"Your mother was a great woman and she's in a better place now. And remember that extra lifeline you have?" Kismat added, pointing to her right palm.

"She's your angel, always looking out for you."

Karma let out a flood of tears that had been held up inside of her.

Kismat decided to cut their afternoon excursion short and asked Karma if she wanted to go to another place that would change her mood. Karma agreed and the two ladies were on their way to a different part of Connaught Place, a part that was far from the affluent markets, with brick walls painted of animal characters from Aesop fables and children book stories.

At the end of the road was a building, housing no more than three floors, with a big board outside that read "*Bal Bhavishya*".

There was a small playground within the school complex, with boys and girls in worn out uniforms, relishing a game of hide and seek, the same game that Karma used to play with her mother when she was young.

Karma had long counted to twenty. But Lakshmi didn't come out of her hiding place to give her a surprise hug like she used to.

"This is where I come to teach a few days of the week. Many of the kids here are without families; some that this organization and a few honest cops saved from being sold in human trafficking, or turning into forced beggars."

Kismat waited for Karma to say something but she remained quiet. A loud bell rang three times and an old man dressed in a gray uniform guided the children back into their classrooms. Some of the kids waved at Kismat and made adorable faces at her, immediately recognizing her as one their teachers, but more so as one of their friends.

Other volunteers, including her friend Rupali, helped the students make their way to the second floor where they had organized their belongings near their makeshift beds.

"They are probably going upstairs to change into regular clothes now."

These sights made Karma reminiscent of Lakshmi and the unique joy her mother derived from teaching her students at the *Kala Kendram* in Kochi.

A lady entered the school gate. A small boy, accompanied by another staff member, immediately raced towards her. The lady waved a hello to Kismat.

"Mrs. Narayan! Good to see you again."

She introduced Karma to her.

"Hello Mrs. Narayan! Do you teach here as well?"

"First of all, I may not be as young as you ladies but please call me Madhu. I used to teach here, but I am moving to a new city. Of all the places I've seen in Delhi, I'm going to miss this place the most. This is where I adopted my son Hriday."

Hriday's attention was focused on a group of pigeons wobbling their way towards a small bowl of water kept near the gate.

"Hriday, say hello."

He became diffident when his name was called out and hid behind his mother's legs.

Karma took out a small key chain from her purse, the one that carried the Taj Mahal floating inside and handed it to him. Hriday moved away from his mother's side and became his playful self again.

"My mommy says that my heart beats at the same time as hers. This means we are always together."

Karma couldn't restrain herself from giving Hriday a tight hug.

"Can your heart do that?" he asked with an innocent grin.

Both ladies shook their heads to keep his wondrous hopes alive.

"I knew it!"

"I love you!" Karma squealed from his adorable charm.

Mrs. Narayan seated Hriday into her car.

Before leaving, she added, "I wanted Hriday to meet all his old friends and teachers today before we move down South. You know, he used to work in a factory and didn't even have a proper name, but he is doing so much better now. He is my gift from God. My closest family and friends love him but unfortunately, not everyone is like that. Thank you for giving him your love."

Karma could only hope that the sparkle in Hriday's eyes would remain intact forever.

Mrs. Narayan had even contributed to the setting up of a meal program at the school, which reduced the dropout rate of the kids.

A young girl was helping her friend open her blue ribbons to redo her braids into a simple ponytail. Their uniforms needed stitching on some torn ends. Still, the children folded them up nicely and preserved them in their reusable jute bags, the few possessions they did have. Karma was inspired by every volunteer working at that school. Seeing those children, she had decided that she most certainly wanted to adopt all of them.

A tall middle-aged man was waiting near his motorbike at the entrance of the school. He was dressed in casual business attire. He called out to Kismat.

The two exchanged a few pleasantries, after which he

waved Kismat goodbye.

"Was that your boyfriend?" Karma enquired smilingly.

"Oh no, that's Madhav. He is the one who started this non-profit. He comes here sometimes, but mostly does consulting for a foreign company."

As they started walking back to the clinic, Karma politely added, "I feel like I have shared so much about my past, but I never got the chance to know more about you."

"Ask away!"

"Well for starters, are you seeing anyone right now?"

"I am in touch with someone."

"Really?! What's his name?" Karma asked excitedly.

Kismat pondered the question and finally said, "Krishna."

"How long have you two been together?"

"I know him from my college days."

"Well, you two should come over for dinner sometime. What does he do?"

"He sort of counsels people in his job -- he does a bunch of other things as well."

"How does he make time for you, being so busy?"

"Let's just say that whenever I feel low, he's always there for me."

"Well, let him know the dinner offer is open anytime."

It was then that Kismat revealed about her days at the Gita Club and how she had created a list of seven goals to complete in her lifetime. Karma was enamored by her motivation, her unique zest for life, but she was more humored by the thought that Kismat had just psyched her into inviting a holy God for dinner.

"Don't worry Karma!" she chuckled.

"I'm positive Krishna and I will drop by your house some-day!"

Karma made her way to what would be her last and final consultation with Dr. Sita. Her face became clearer, her menses were regular, and her libido had improved.

Sita referred Karma to a friend, who was a reputed gynecologist in Greater Kailash, for further consultations on her journey to motherhood.

Karma felt uniquely liberated, even within the small enclosure of their one bedroom flat in Gurgaon. Rather than berating herself for her own fate, and succumbing to the despondent voices that used to reverberate in her ears, Karma made a conscious call to change the narrative of her life.

Bharat was appalled, not by the mention of her troubles in conceiving, but more so at her insecurity that he would leave her because of it. She revealed her childhood trauma with him, and expressed her sincere love, which had dwindled ever since her mother's demise. Even though they had been living under the same roof, Bharat and Karma embraced each other as if they had been separated for months.

"Do you know what true love means to me?" she asked softly, as Bharat lay on her lap.

"Tell me."

"It's caring without suffocating, commitment without deceit, passion without forcing, and everlasting friendship without defeat. No matter how I may try to describe it – our love is all of that and more."

"Yes it is Rama! You are my entire heart." She kissed him on his forehead, followed by a passionate, lingering kiss on the lips.

She guided his hand to her chest and he could feel her heart pounding faster. Sometimes she wondered if his hands were the best part of him, the way they caressed her, protected her, in a masculine, yet gentle sort of way. It was the first thing she noticed in anyone she met, and she had never seen more attractive hands than she had in Bharat.

He moved his hands further down, fully conscious of her pleasure points.

The cadency of her moaning hastened and she let herself sit on top of him; permitting herself to put her pleasure at equal importance with his.

When they woke up next to each other, she calmly said, "I'm sorry for all the pain I caused you earlier."

"You were hurting Rama, but we are stronger now."

"Yes we are. Why don't we say word of thanks to God in the temple tomorrow?"

"But I thought you didn't believe in God and temples."

"I still want to say thanks," and for an instant, an image of her friend, Kismat, surfaced in her mind.

Trinity

Kismat unwrapped a new photo frame in her mother's clinic.

The stock photo depicted an ideal family, flashing their pearly whites in their perfectly ironed clothes. Kismat was humored to think whether such photos should be marketed to all souls who were about to take birth as humans. She replaced the stock with a photo of her mother from an event where she was recognized for her service in charitable clinics. After hanging the frame on a bare wall, Kismat began organizing all the patient reports from the day.

As soon as Kismat got up, she felt unusually dizzy. She opened her bag to look for a bottle of water and felt as if everything became unusually blurry. She rushed to the bathroom; coughing bright, red blood.

Sita heard a loud thud and was horrified to see her daughter lying on the ground with traces of blood on the sink and on the sides of her mouth.

Frantically, she called up the number of a nearby hospital and requested an ambulance for her daughter.

"Please help! My daughter is unconscious. I need an ambulance right away!"

"Sorry madam, we don't have any spare right now. They're out on emergency duty. You can call another hospital or drive the patient to us directly."

Not having the capacity to argue any further, Sita asked for the help of a passing stranger to get Kismat into an auto, knowing fully well that the autowala could navigate through the gaps in between the evening traffic where her sedan would easily get stuck. The autowala did his best to speed his way to the hospital, not bearing any regard for red lights.

Sita phoned Badi ammi about Kismat's condition and awakened Ajay as well, who was still asleep in the States.

Kismat opened her simple, black eyes and slowly regained sensation in the rest of her body. Everything was white, from the walls, to the curtains and to the pills lying in a cup near her. A pink uniformed nurse posed a much needed contrast.

Kismat became conscious of a throbbing pain in her head and asked for her mother. The nurse took a glimpse at the monitor and ran outside to get the doctor. Kismat could faintly hear her mother's voice outside.

A middle-aged woman with short, graying hair, walked in with a stethoscope. The doctor touched her forehead and advised the nurse to inject her with a medicine.

"Hi Kismat, my name is Dr. Neeta Sehgal. I am taking care of you today. Do you know why you're here?"

"I don't remember."

She asked Kismat to focus her eyes on her index finger as she moved it from left to right in a semi-circle.

"You fainted and had weak vitals but you're doing much better now. You had a bit of a fever too but I gave you a paracetemol for that. How are you feeling?"

"I still have a headache. By the way doctor, which hospital am I in?"

Inwardly, she thought, *"Of all the hospitals in Delhi, please don't let it be that one."*

"Gandhimarg Hospital."

The name rang like an alarm. There was a chance he wasn't even here to begin with. He could have easily been shifted to a new location or been out of town.

As much as she tried to forget him in the depths of her memory, she couldn't forget how they enkindled as lovers but parted as strangers. As much as time had healed her heart, she could not open those wounds to see him again. Whatever had transpired between them was now a story not worth retelling.

From the outside, she may appear fragile as she lay covered with blankets in some odd chamber of that hospital; but from the inside, she had a spiritual core of steel.*

**The core that was harnessed from her 'Fe'male fortitude was then put through Bessemer's challenging fires to rid it of the constraining impurities of ire and the onus of hurt, ultimately giving her the strength of the same refined metal.*

"Doctor, I'm completely fine now. When I can go back home?"

"I will try to get you out of here as soon as possible after we finish some tests. I just want an MRI done today."

"Is there any problem?"

"Well, the scan will tell us that. But don't worry, we are here to take care of you," Dr. Sehgal replied, matching Kismat's calmness.

"The nurse will bring you something to eat. I'll send your mother and grandmother in to see you."

"Thank you very much doctor."

Kismat tried getting up to a sitting position but felt too exhausted to do so. After forcing herself to finish her meal of lentils and rice, Sita and Badi ammi helped Kismat onto a wheelchair to take her up to the third floor for the MRI.

The procedure felt like being invited to a North Indian *baraat,* with the most terrible sounds drumming in her ears, as if pots and pans were repeatedly clanking with each other. It was daunting to stay still inside the MRI machine while the cacophony played out at odd intervals.

By evening, the doctor had discharged Kismat to go home.

"Someone will call you once the results come. Here are some medicines that your daughter should take meanwhile.

You can buy them at the pharmacy."

Kismat felt comfortable enough to walk on her own while Sita headed towards the hospital pharmacy.

"Your cousin's driver is waiting outside to take us home. Just call him and wait in the car till I come."

As the driver brought out their car to the hospital entrance, a familiar voice called out.

"Kismat!"

She figured she had mistakenly heard her name until he asked again.

"Kismat, is that you?"

She turned around. Purab emerged from a group of other men in white coats who were taking a drag outside the hospital grounds.

He quickly discarded his cigarette.

"Ammi, I'll just come. Please wait inside the car."

The last line of the poem she had written after her breakup had come eerily true.

Na jaane kab, kin halaat main, mulaqaat hogi phir.

She traced her footsteps back to where he had already walked halfway. They would embrace whenever they would meet after long intervals, but this time, it was different. They spoke to each other as if they had met for the very first time.

"I saw you and couldn't help myself from calling out your name. Why are you here? Nothing serious, I hope?"

She saw his face and realized how much he had changed, not only by his appearance but by his emanating nature. The loving innocence she would cherish from his eyes was gone. Truly, the heart can be torn and the senses can betray but only the soul remains committed till the very end.

"Everything is fine. I just came here for a checkup....for my grandmother."

"Is she ok?"

She responded with a perfunctory nod.

"So, what have you been up to?"

"Just teaching at a school. What about you?"

"Still working crazy shifts."

He abruptly brought attention to the one thing that he noticed when he laid his eyes on her that evening.

"You look a lot thinner. I had to double check to see if it was really you."

"I guess in all that fun of teaching, I forget to eat sometimes."

She did not want to bring forth any discussion about her health.

"Well, it seems like you're doing what makes you really happy."

"Yeah, for the first time in my life...I'm content."

Purab was taken aback by her radiating spirit and genuine contentment in life. It was a rare expression to see in a person.

"And you know what?"

He waited patiently to hear her, not having granted her that patience when he parted ways with her.

"I will never let go of this mindset in my life."

Purab's eyes were cast down.

"I'm sorry Kismat."

She could see a hint of his old innocence emerging.

He blurted out those last three words as if they were resting on the tip of his tongue and were restlessly waiting for their moment to escape his lips.

For many, that moment never materializes and regret settles in like cobwebs instead.

"I made a huge mistake. I ran into one of my exes in Mumbai. We got physical. I didn't have the guts to tell you then. I'm so sorry."

She was looking straight at him, unmoved by his apology.

" I don't even love her. I've always loved you."

Kismat didn't need his apology for she had learned to stitch her wounds herself. She had desperately wanted closure then, but time and spirituality gave her that anyway.

"You know Purab, I wouldn't have become the person I am today if we didn't part ways. Remember all those promises you made?"

He nodded his head.

"We can live without each other."

"You don't hate me for what I did?"

"I did. For months. But not anymore."

His choice to depart from her life made her realize that his love was nothing more than a prolonged infatuation.

"So, will I ever see you again?"

"To be honest Purab, I pray to God we don't."

Sita had returned from the pharmacy, with the bag of medicines in her hand.

"Oh, there is one last thing I wanted to say to you Purab."

"What is it?"

"Thank you."

"For what?"

"Try to recall the last thing you said to me over the phone? Thank you. For that insult."

And just like the high school farewell, she had departed too soon without hearing his last few words, but the timing was just right this time around.

The next day, one of Dr. Sehgal's nurses called up Sita, asking her to meet the doctor for the results of the scan. Sita tried her best to poke out the results on the phone but the nurse did not disclose anything.

Kismat was back to her normal routine at home. Sita thought it best to let Kismat rest and go to the hospital alone. She touched the feet of Lord Ganesha in her clinic and asked her assistant to cancel all her afternoon appointments.

Sita knocked on Dr. Sehgal's room and walked in after hearing a quick, "Come in."

"Please sit down. It is unusually rare for me to see a case like this at her age."

Sita's countenance changed dramatically.

"What happened doctor? Everything is ok, right? Please tell me everything is ok."

"Had Kismat ever been unconscious like this before?

"No...I don't think....."

Sita stopped mid-way.

She recalled the one time when Kismat had lost consciousness earlier that year.

"Yes she has, but the blood reports were all fine – she only had fever but she recovered."

"Has you daughter lost a lot of weight since then?"

"Perhaps she is slimmer..."

"Anyone in the family who has any history of cancer?"

"Well, I can only think of her grandfather."

"Look, I cannot ascertain predisposition for sure. There can be many environmental factors or the cause can be purely idiopathic."

"But the results are normal, right doctor?" hoping that the doctor would change her countenance and afford her some good news.

"I need you to be strong Sita."

Sita realized then that the worst was yet to come.

"Kismat has a tumor in the left side of her brain, in the junction of her temporal and occipital lobes. That's probably why she was having poor vision and trouble remembering what happened before becoming unconscious. I cannot do a biopsy of the growth without performing surgery since it is embedded inside the brain but we can try to determine its malignancy with the help of a tumor marker test."

Sita's mind started racing with memories of her daughter, from the first time she cradled baby Kismat in her arms to the day when she graduated from St. Regents with honors.

"I do not want to alarm you Sita, but I have a feeling that this is an aggressive malignancy. From the scans, it appears that it has reached the last stage. Kismat needs surgery immediately."

A news like that is difficult for anyone to digest, but even more difficult when a mother has to hear that about her own child.

Sita broke out into tears.

"Please understand it is very difficult to predict this kind of a disease early on. Most patients don't find out till it reaches a late stage when they experience major symptoms. I want you to know that there is treatment available for your daughter. Don't lose hope. This is a time when you need to be strong for her."

Dr. Sehgal referred her to a few oncologists and surgeons to help with Kismat's case.

Sita was completely heartbroken when she came home. She handed the report to Kismat.

Kismat looked at the front page summary and didn't change her expression.

"Did the doctor say why I may have gotten this?"

"She couldn't say for sure. But your Dadaji...."

Premchand was the first and only man from his large family of four sisters and four brothers to move from the pristine beauty of their village to the fast paced city life in Delhi.

"Mummy, if there is anything that runs in our family, they are the values of hard work and a fighting spirit."

She put the report back into its folder and saw her mother's despondency hidden in her eyes. "It's ok Mummy, you can cry if you want to.

"No, beta..I......"

Kismat got up and hugged her mother tight.

"Whatever it is, I'll fight it."

Instantly, she could feel her mother's tears slowly rolling down her back.

The next morning, Ajay called in from Jersey. He broke the news to Dhananjay since Sita no longer had the heart to tell him.

Dhananjay refused to believe it. He maintained his composure on the phone.

"How are you doing, sis?"

"Like Ned Flanders would say, I'm okely dokely."

"Dad scared me by saying that you got diagnosed and stuff."

There was pause on the other end.

"Kismat?"

"Don't worry *bhai*. I got this."

"How is this even possible?.....you don't smoke!...you exercise! How could this bloody happen?!"

"Don't worry, I'll fight this disease just like Harrison Ford beat up Gary Oldman in Air Force One."

"Bhai?"

Finally, she heard a strained voice that was on the verge of breaking out into tears.

"I'm proud of you."

"Ok, but if you get any more mushy, I might throw up." And with that last line, their sibling relationship was restored to normalcy.

The Dharmas made the collective decision to get Kismat treated in the States, a decision possible since Ajay had moved his daughter to his company's Family Plan.

When Kismat was employed with W&W in New York City, she had a healthcare plan to envy for. Every doctor was covered and the co-pay was non-existent.

It was almost as if she was walking on a red carpet to every appointment. Once she quit, she was out of insurance. Most out-of-pocket plans in Jersey were expensive and didn't even cover routine blood tests. Kismat could only hope she wouldn't fall sick.

Though India had more affordable healthcare, there were plenty billing scams and reports of negligence. When greed superseded the Hippocratic Oath, the healthcare system was sure to get diseased in any country.

In a few days, everyone in the extended family got to know about Kismat's diagnosis. But Kismat made one thing clear. She didn't want to discuss her health with anyone beyond her closest family members.

Her mother wondered if Kismat was being too hard on herself.

"This disease isn't anyone else's battle, but my own. She told Sita that while many would offer kind words of sympathy, those words eventually felt hollow.

Before leaving India, Kismat had the words of the Gita fully imprinted on her mind.

Do not weep about the past, do not worry about the future, and focus on the present."

Kismat flew to the New York with Sita and Badi ammi by her side. Ajay scheduled her appointment at Adams Cancer Center, a top ranked hospital in Manhattan's midtown.

The City must have loved her so much that it beckoned her a third time, she thought.

In the cab ride to the Outpatient Center, all those old memories resurfaced again; the times spent running in her heels and snow boots to catch the subway; the Friday nights trying out new drinks and dishes, from the risotto to the paella to another rice-based preparation – sake; and the many museums, parks, and familiar faces she could recall in a heartbeat.

The Adams Hospital lobby was abuzz with many visitors. While many patients had at least one family member surrounding them for support, there were also a few patients sitting alone.

The hospital staff could be identified by their white coats, some oversized enough to fit another tiny human inside them. After a few hours wait, the Dharmas met with three specialists -- the oncologist, the neurosurgeon, and the radiologist, to discuss the best palliative route for Kismat.

When Kismat heard the word oncologist, she recalled that '*onkos*' was the Greek word, meaning excess mass. In fact, the word cancer itself was derived from the Greek word '*karkinos*', implying crab, as coined by Hippocrates himself.

The neurosurgeon recommended that surgery would be the first line of treatment. He was the "open file, cut, crop" specialist.

"I can take a sample for biopsy during the surgery itself. Our team will remove the tumor without harming any of the healthy tissue around it."

But he also pointed out the risks of the operation.

"In surgeries of the brain, we have to be especially careful because neurons cannot repair themselves unlike the regenerative capabilities of say, the liver."

He cited that there was a small possibility that Kismat could have some impairment in speech or mobility and even memory loss from surgery because they were dealing with a very delicate and powerful organ. There were also possibilities of the building up of excess fluids within or outside the cellular walls or increased intra-cranial pressure.

"My team and I will do the best to avoid any of those outcomes," he assured her.

Her family tried to maintain their composure. Kismat wondered when the day would come when humans could store a backup of their memory in a chip, remove the parts they didn't like, and replant the chip in the brain when they were ready.

The oncologist started off by mentioning the names of a

few drugs to prolong her survival.

He noted that chemo was partially effective because of the protective blood-brain barrier that prevented the medicine from reaching the malignant tissue, but it was still necessary to control the spread. He added that his team would keep looking out for new immunotherapy agents in clinical trials, as and when Kismat would be eligible.

Upon hearing about this unique blood-brain barrier, Kismat's imagination began running loose again. She wondered how cool it would be if humans could develop a no-nonsense-brain barrier that could preclude any gossip, useless information, hate, disparaging remarks from entering our brain.

Life, then, would become utter bliss.

Finally the radiologist discussed the need for radiation in conjunction with the chemo to prevent the growth from spreading to other parts. The oncologist and radiation specialists were both the "compress, resize, and save file" specialist. Every procedure had its own merits and demerits with the end goal to increase her longevity.

She fully entrusted her life with the team of doctors; their decades of expertise, their surgical knives, state-of-the art machines and blue-gloved hands.

The surgery was scheduled a week later and Kismat was advised that they would need to shave a part of her head for the procedure. Kismat had often received compliments for her long tresses, but she was ready to let go of her locks, most of which would be donated to another survivor.

The night before her surgery, she wrote an entry in her journal that was closest to her heart.

"Dear Krishna,

I am a little nervous about tomorrow.
But I will fight this.

You prepared me for these very moments by giving me the courage to focus on the goals that mattered to me, and spend time with the people I loved dearly.

You are essentially the manifestation of everything good to me.
Everyone I've met and connected with in this lifetime has been, in some forms, a manifestation of that good.
They have been my friends, my family, Sophia, the nurses and doctors at the hospital and even complete strangers I've had the grace to meet.

It is easy to find faults, but it's a greater challenge to find the good. All emotions of anger, hurt, jealously evaporate once you find the good.

At a certain phase in my life, when I thought I had everything, I felt like I had nothing.
And today when it may seem like I have nothing, I realize that I had everything all long: my intellect, my fighting spirit, my love for life.
I can live an unbearably long life, yet be empty without this understanding.
I now know what it means to live.

She was ready.
Because the tumor was on the left side, there was a chance that she could suffer from paralysis in the right side of her body.
To assure that Kismat wouldn't go through such a grave outcome, the surgeon put her on a local anesthesia and asked Kismat to respond to certain questions during the surgery. This allowed the surgeon and his team to remove as much of the tumor and keep the functions of the lobes intact through her responses to sight and sensation.
In the operating room, the surgeon and his team could hear whispers of a hymn playing, filling the room with kind of positive energy.

It was Kismat, softly humming the *Krishna* mantra.

Post surgery, the MRI showed a gaping hole where a big chunk of the tumor used to be. Apart from the pain, Kismat had routine headaches, stiffness, and swelling which were relieved by painkillers and Sita's natural remedies.

To gradually resume her day-to-day activities, occupational and physical therapists at Memorial Hospital attended to her daily. Rest was critical before starting the next regimen of treatment.

The biopsy from the tissue mass confirmed their initial fears.

Kismat was reeling from fourth stage glioblastoma.

The question that came next was from Kismat herself. "What are my chances for beating this disease?"

She opened it up to the floor for anyone to jump in from the three panel team. None of them could accurately say how much time she had left. If they could, psychics and astrologists would run out of a job of playing the same guessing game.

With as much confidence as the many confidence intervals doctors like them had analyzed, they simply said that the statistics weren't very promising in such an advanced stage.

"Most patients achieve a lifespan of about six months to a year after starting treatment. The success rate depends on how well you can tolerate the medication and how you respond to all the treatments in particular."

The message was clear — **Live your life, at least what remains of it, to the best you can.**

To avoid battering and bruising the veins from constant pricking, the oncologist inserted a chemo port near the nape of her neck. The port made her appear as if she was some form of a humanoid; the kind that Hollywood so fancies in their dystopian, apocalyptic fantasies.

Every day, she would carry a lingering fragrance of alcohol swabs and her skin was accustomed to the touch of cold, latex gloves.

On the first day of her chemo session, the oncologist provided her with two options that specifically worked on her tumor type. Kismat wasn't sure which option to take: the heightened chance of seizures, or one with the debilitating muscle pain and bleeding.

Nausea, constipation, rashes, spasms, hair loss, vomiting, and loss of appetite were common to both and therefore ruled out as any factor.

There was also another list of side-effects that was provided in a separate piece of paper which stated, "This is not an exhaustive list. In case of an emergency, please contact the national helpline and reach your nearest hospital."

The doctors prescribed such dangerous medication, in the hope that the benefits would hopefully outweigh the risks.

Finally, Kismat went ahead with the second option.

Before the oncologist left to attend to another patient, Kismat posed a very pertinent question.

"Just one last question doctor..."

"Yes, go ahead Kismat."

"About the hair loss – is that permanent?"

"Don't worry, your hair will be back once your treatment is over."

As Kismat was due to receive her first dosage through the port, she whispered to Sita, "Mummy, I really wish...."

A nurse interrupted them by asking if they needed any water and blankets.

Sita had a feeling her daughter was going to wish that she would be able to escape the fate of being stuck inside a hospital.

"Beta, you were saying something?" Sita asked, worry swept across her face.

"Oh yeah, I was saying that I wish this medicine would make me lose all the hair on my body too – I wouldn't have to wax my legs ever again!"

Her lively laugh caught on to her mother as well. Sita gave her daughter a tight hug even though there were multiple tubes pumping the medicine into her arm. Kismat was the truly bravest little soul that her mother had ever seen.

Nausea was a persistent complaint after every chemo sitting. Sita was alarmed to see Kismat vomiting after the second cycle. When Kismat came out of the bathroom, she yelled, "Mummy, I think I'm pregnant!"

Sita's face looked like a deer caught in the headlights.

Panicking, her mother yelled, "What?!"

Kismat was poor at making a serious face in emotional situations. One time, she even cracked a joke at her Fufa's (uncle) funeral to lighten her cousin's mood.

"Just kidding Mummy! Isn't this what they show in all the Bollywood movies? That vomiting equals pregnancy. Don't worry – you're not a grandma just yet, but you will be someday."

Kismat wasn't certain how her fertility would cope with the chemo, but she was certain that of all the things chemo could take away from her, her sense of humor would never be one of them.

Twice a week, she would make a trip to the local library because the thought of sitting at home and having her family members ogle at her every move out of concern would drive even the holiest saint insane.

She found a space in a quiet corner, where no one could judge the cancer that had marked its territory on her appearance; her balding head, or the blotches on her face that failed to respond to the corticosteroid cream.

Kismat explored new authors on bookshelves that would take her mind off her prognosis. Still, some words like 'terminal' or 'death' managed to trigger her disease again.

She avoided crying in public, say from the sight of a couple embracing each other, or a mother playing with her granddaughter at a park because she didn't know if she would ever be able to experience motherhood or marriage in her lifetime.

Her tear glands had to work on overdrive. She knew she wasn't alone in this; no one was immune to tragedy; tears being the anguish relieving mechanism that is so symptomatic of humanity.

The mind is an amazing apparatus because the moment Kismat forced herself to not think about something, say her untimely passing, and the immense grief that would cause a weeping Ajay or Sita, it repeatedly showed her those images. Thoughts were still not entirely in her control; they being an invention of the subconscious. Yet, meditation emboldened her to let them come and go with ease, and focus on getting better.

At the pharmacy counter at Adams Hospital, Ajay purchased a course of chemo pills that Kismat could take orally at home. The co-payment was close to a hundred dollars for a month's supply, still expensive, but a fraction of what the actual cost was.

He noticed a big sign next to the pharmacist's window which stated the following–

"If you are taking oral chemo at home and have any excess medicine left over, please do NOT discard it in your trash cans or flush them down the toilets. Please bring them to the hospital so we can discard them safely."

When the medicine was fully administered via her chemo port, the nurse disposed her gloves and the unused medicine into a yellow trash bin marked with a hazardous substance warning.

"Nurse, why did you throw the medicine in there?" Ajay asked nervously.

"Oh, we can't let such strong medicine lying around. It has to be collected and put away separately. We can't let it mix with our water supply, or seep into our soil else it can affect other people with its side-effects."

"But that same medicine is going into her body!" he exclaimed.

"I understand your concern. We always check her blood and vitals and administer the dosage accordingly so that it can be tolerated by her body.

The nurse proceeded to attach the next batch of chemo bags to her port line. Ajay was unable to hide his despair as he met his daughter's eyes.

Since Ajay was a devotee of Lord Shiva, Kismat decided to enlighten him in the words he was most familiar with – Hindu mythology.

"Papa, do you know why Shiva is called Neelkanth?"

"Of course. I used to narrate these stories to you when you were little."

"Can you tell me the story again?" Kismat asked with beaming eyes.

"You want to hear the story right now?"

She nodded with a smile. He smiled in turn for having the chance to relive a storytelling tradition with her.

"The legend goes that the Hindu Gods once joined hands with their enemies, the Asuras, to restore immortality to the Gods who had been cursed by a powerful sage," narrating every word with excitement.

"Based on the recommendation of Lord Vishnu, the Gods and the Enemies had to put aside their differences and work together to produce *amrit*, the nectar of strength and immortality. They did this by churning a vast ocean which could not be done alone by either party."

Though she knew the ending, she listened on intently.

"During the course of the churning, poison was released from the ocean which had the potential to spread everywhere and destroy all of Earth. That is when Shiva intervened and drank the entire poison himself, to save humanity, thereby giving him the name of "*Neel Kanth*" or the Blue Throated One."

"You see papa, if Shiva had to endure something like that in his body in the hour of need, then so can I. I will take strength from his strength."

Lord Brahma, Lord Vishnu and Lord Shiva are collectively known as the holy Trinity in Hindu mythology where Brahma is the creator, Vishnu is the preserver and Shiva is the destroyer of the cosmos.

Ajay gently put his hand on his daughter's head.

"I hope he blesses you as his dearest devotee and makes everything alright soon."

"Papa, one of Shiva's dearest followers was the evil Ravan. I don't want to be a follower of any God to get something in return. I'd rather be a follower of you."

Every three months, the doctors would take a new scan of her brain and conduct a tumor marker test from her blood sample. Since the bio-marker* was naturally occurring, Kismat wondered if everyone had cancer cells floating around in their blood.

**Bio-substance that is naturally found in the body and can be detected through a blood or urine test. An elevated marker is a preliminary indication of cancer, but not entirely reliable as it can be false positive in some cases.*

She discovered that cancer originated from the cell damage caused by free radicals in our body. Our bodies relied on the strength of our immune system to fight these radicals and prevent bad cells from multiplying further.

Kismat thought of the mighty Ganga. The holy river could only take in so many toxins from the industrial wastes dumped into her for decades before becoming polluted, the same way, a human body could only take in so many toxins from a synthetic lifestyle before it started to get sick.

Many of the chemo drugs were approved and brought into

the market by testing on one particular type of animal species - mice. These tests often caused irreparable damage to the animal's molecular and biological compositions. Sita always placed a framed photo of Lord Ganesha, known as God of prosperity, in the family prayer room. In that photo, Kismat recalled seeing a few mice sitting in close vicinity to Lord Ganesha's feet as his proud devotees. She wondered how Ganesha must have felt with mankind performing all kinds of tests on his favorite animal species that were as fond of *ladoos* as he was.

The Dharmas became worried to see Kismat losing pounds with every chemo session. Her clavicle seemed to be poking through more than before. The chemo killed the cancer cells as well as her healthy cells and that it didn't help that those medicines played havoc with her appetite too.

Whenever Kismat felt nauseous, Sita would rush to make her Homeopathic pills, while Ammi would prepare her cumin and ginger *paani* and place a cardamom in her mouth till the nausea subsided. When Kismat declined to eat, Sita and Ammi would argue on what type of meal to make for her, and how to give it. From the hyperactive mother who would worry about the freshness of every morsel going into Kismat's system, to strong-headed Badi ammi who used the age-old principle that eating more equates to more health, it was Ajay who ultimately played the balancing act to resolve the conflicting views of both women.

When a family member is struck with a terminal illness, it is not just an individual battle, but a team rally. The combined effort of the team helps to win the race, or at least make it easier to cover the distance. All three of Kismat's bodyguards were emotionally weak in some respects and mentally strong in others but together, they formed a spectacular team.

In the midst of all of crazy moods revolving around Kismat's needs, a new bodyguard showed up and he was dearly needed.

Dhananjay had taken a month off from his job to be with Kismat.

Badi ammi and Sita would get too emotionally attached with the kind of food they wanted to give to Kismat, so Dhananjay took the lead. He revamped her diet in accordance with the nutritionist who advised Kismat to add adequate fats and protein and minimize sugar.

Dhananjay, who used to be the junk food enthusiast in his teens, stressed on eliminating any foods with preservatives and chemicals and made sure every item was freshly cooked, while maintaining a healthy gut.

Kismat still obliged all her bodyguards by eating their favorite foods - Badi's white butter parantha and *rajma chawal* (rice and beans), Sita's peas and cottage cheese curry, and Dhananjay's spicy egg curry.

Kismat began to approach every food with a renewed sense of consideration before consuming it. In the midst of eating quick meals, Kismat had lost track of what it meant to nourish herself.

Dhananjay took Kismat on an enlightening, sibling trip to the supermarket. A quick glance at the nutrition labels of her favorite snacks made her realize that she had been eating a concoction of synthetic oils, preservatives, and unpronounceable ingredients that she did not want rotting in her small, or large intestine.

She couldn't believe that her favorite on-the-go smoothie that she once considered to be a healthy snack, contained a whopping 53 grams of sugar per bottle serving.

"Bhai, take a look at how much sugar this thing has."

"And it still tastes like crap!"

A week's worth of organic eating cost them over $300. This came as no surprise to Dhananjay who cited that the government provided millions in subsidies for corn, but none for organic produce. This helped explain why unhealthy fries and burgers (with additives like corn starch, high fructose corn syrup) were a regular feature on dollar menus.

Once they got back home, Kismat opened a container of organic strawberries, labeled "*Fresh from the Farm.*" One rather odd looking strawberry dropped on the floor. The rest of the batch had a gorgeous color and perfect shape, but this strawberry looked mutant, as if it had an extra arm growing from its torso.

Kismat picked up the piece and held it near her face. A measles like rash had developed all over her back and cheeks from the last chemo.

Her mother's wisdom about the fruit was valid more than ever.

At the supermarket, there were many stares at her shaved head and blotchy skin. Of the many things her immunity had fought, tears were the one thing she couldn't.

Back when they were teenagers, Dhananjay used to make fun of her zits and acne all the time and Sita had to intervene between them.

But this time around, he simply wrapped his arms around Kismat and let her cry.

The Balance Beam of Destiny and Actions

Karma resumed her love for reading and Bharatanatyam and began researching companies that met her profile. Bharat and Karma even managed to squeeze in a long holiday at a cozy rental in Mussorie to celebrate her birthday. The following week, a slight implantation bleeding prompted Karma to phone her gynecologist who advised her to get a pregnancy test.

The test was negative on the first go. A minute later, Bharat walked into the room with more gay abandon than Mary Poppins on poppy seeds. He was holding the test with a faint line forming to the first one.

She shared the good news with her family in Kochi who were just as ecstatic as she was. But she also wanted to share her news with two other people who had made this wonderful day possible.

Karma had messaged Kismat a few times in between, but didn't hear back from her. She assumed she was holidaying abroad.

When she finally paid a visit to Connaught Place clinic, Sita's room was occupied by another physician.

She inquired about Sita from another attendant.

"Dr. Dharma and Kismat left two months ago, madam."

Karma had had her last appointment close to that timeframe.

"Do you know where they might have gone?"

He shook his head in the negative.

Karma could not understand why Kismat and her family would disappear this way.

There was only one other place where she could go in order to find her. She drove her car and visited the school that Kismat had once introduced to her. That school was the last place the two of them had interacted before they lost touch.

She opened the gate and went straight into Madhav's office.

"Hi Madhav. Sorry to barge in so abruptly. I am Kismat's friend. Do you know where she is right now?"

"Kismat left a while ago."

"How long has it been?"

"Two months, maybe," Madhav added in a monotone.

The timeframe seemed about the same as the man at the clinic had told her.

"Did she give you a reason why?"

"Well, she told me that she had to move somewhere. But when I asked her why and where, she said she couldn't tell me. It was very unlike her."

"But why would she leave without telling anyone?!"

"All her students asked me the same question but I have no answer to give to them. What is your name, by the way?"

"Karma Naidu – but why does it matter...."

"Oh! Actually, wait here one second."

Madhav looked inside his drawer and found the neatly preserved envelope.

"Before leaving, she did ask me for one last favor."

"What is it?"

"She said that in case any woman named Karma came asking about her, I should give her this letter."

He handed it to Karma.

"Thank you."

Kismat tore the top and found a one page letter enclosed inside.

She started reading it immediately.

"Dear Karma,

I had to leave India to finish another goal on my list. I'm sorry I couldn't meet you before leaving but I have written this letter to compensate. I hope you read this letter in full because it relates to us both.

Think of a balance beam and you are standing right in the middle of it. One side represents our destiny and the other side is our actions.

As we grow up and self-introspect, we try and attribute what is happening in our life to either side of the beam. We can only gauge at our past and our present for evidence, since the future will always be unknown and it is better left that way.

If we are going through a rough patch, we tilt towards the side of fate, knowing fully well that it is out of our control and thereby relieving us of accountability. If we are doing well, we tilt towards our actions that merited such well-deserving outcome for us, tainted by our ego. Of course, there may be exceptions, but this is what I have commonly seen.

The disgruntled worker may blame his boss for the bad work day, the student may blame the teacher for the poor exam results, the child may blame his parents for not becoming what he or she wanted to be.

On the flip side, the same worker gets a promotion and reasons that it was on accord of his own efforts, the student does extremely well in school and inherently feels smarter than the rest, a child grows up to make a lot of money and attributes his success to solely to his own hard work.

Some of us may also factor luck and God in the good times, or blame our stars/planetary systems for not being properly aligned in our favor in the bad. But if we actually listened to our thoughts, we will realize that we are always titled to one side of the beam.

Either tilt is an avenue to become in sync with our conscious-

ness, or in other words, true 'yoga' with the divine.

The good we experience is a gift of the divine, just as much as the bad humbles us to invoke the divine and relinquish us from our suffering.

You are free to accept or reject what I said. At the end of the day, everyone is free to think whatever they want. The mind is, what I believe, the most wonderful and terrifying gift of God that remains an elusive mystery.

Our organs, our body, our biological functions are restricted to the extent of their functioning warranty. They can't do more than what they are assigned to do; the liver has to excrete the bile for digestion and the aorta has to pump the blood but they can't switch responsibilities.

The mind, however, is open to whatever we like for it to conjure.

In one instant, we are happy.

In another, we are angry or sad.

These feelings do not come from anywhere else but from the way we think.

Reasoning about an experience is an invention of our mind. It doesn't matter which side we side with, blaming destiny or glowing in adulation for our actions.

That is irrelevant.

What is relevant is the intention behind our actions that accumulates as our karma. Our thoughts decide our actions, which in turn decide the way we mold our destiny. When we think without tilting to either side, treating happiness and sorrow equally, we can achieve true peace, like the equilibrium of a beam.

When we met in Delhi, your approach to life was rationality and my, faith. Yet, we connected on our own plane, balancing each other's tilted view of the world.

I guess what I'm trying to say is that we may not be able to change what's destined for us, but we can certainly change the way we live it, through our spirited actions.

I hope we meet again soon but till then, you have this letter to remember me by.

I will always remember you.

Kismat"

Kismat had spoken to Karma like her own conscience would. When Karma was awarded a full scholarship to study abroad, she attributed that success to her own hard work. When her mother passed away, she squarely blamed her marred fate. When she cleared her job interviews, she thought she was deserving of it on her own accord, yet when she couldn't bear a child, she felt slighted by God again.

Karma was always titled to one side of the beam.

Somehow, she had always been in contradiction with her own thoughts.

But not anymore.

"Well, what does the letter say?" Madhav inquired after he saw Karma smiling after reading it.

The real answer would have been that Kismat encouraged all of us to do good, and not fret about the rewards; to balance our inherited conventions with pure common sense; and to take ownership for our thoughts and actions in order to achieve harmony, within us and around us.

"Nothing more than what she told you. She had to leave for some personal reasons."

"She didn't say anything else about when she will be back?"

"No, she didn't specify. I have a question for you though."

"Yes?"

"Have you found any replacement for her spot?"

"Not yet."

"I would like to volunteer. I can start as early as tomorrow."

“That would be amazing! The kids would be very happy to have you.”

He handed her a one page document on a clipboard.
“Here is a form you can complete to get started.”
She borrowed a pen and started filling in her details.
In all the enlightenment of reading Kismat's letter, Karma forgot about the biggest news of that day.
“Madhav, I need to tell you one more thing."
"Yes?"
"I’m going to have a baby bump in the coming months and I will need to take leave after my delivery. I apologize that my stay is only temporary for now.”
“Oh, many congratulations to you! Please don't worry about it. We keep recruiting new volunteers. Any time you spend here is valuable to us and more importantly, to you.”

~

At any public place, Kismat would put up a brave front. Much like the lioness spirit she was born with, Kismat roared with humor and courage on the outside, but was vulnerable on the inside.
In the calmness of her room, there were no stares or commentary at her bald head. In the privacy of her room, there were no remarks about the scars and eruptions that formed post chemo. She continued her favorite therapy of turning the lights off and dancing to soulful music. In the serenity of her room, she could be herself again.

At Adams Cancer Center, Kismat would see many children in wheelchairs with a movable drip machine that was dispensing the chemo into their bodies. They children would be running and goofing around with their siblings and parents standing close by.

These children were too innocent to understand the nature of their disease. Though Kismat was in a similar predicament, seeing those cancer-striken kids, with a look of wonder and curiousity still intact for the world around them, made her heart want to cry in pain. It made her think of the kids at Bal Bhavishya. And of little Sophia.

All of a sudden, the first few lines of the Gita Saar didn't make sense to her anymore.

Whatever happened in the past, happened for the good, whatever is happening in the present is happening for the good and whatever shall happen in the future shall be for the best too.

Do not weep about the past, do not worry about the future and focus on the present.

How could such little souls braving such a bold affliction be happening for the good?

How could one not weep about the future and worry about the present of these children?

How could they deserve such a fate at an age when they hadn't had the chance to enjoy a childhood of good health?

The question of deserving a destiny that was not in line with the goodness of one's actions reminded Kismat of her friend, Karma. Karma had posed the same question -- why do some good people end up suffering such undeserving fates?

Kismat did not have an answer. No one did.

Karma was right when she said that life would continue to surprise Kismat and pull the rug under her feet.

But it was also clear to Kismat that the good people, from the nurses who took care of her, to her town's librarian who would hand deliver all the books she needed without judging her appearance; all of these souls were committed to helping others. And though they did their work without expectations, Kismat would send them a handwritten note or flowers every now or then.

In the end, the Gita served as an eternal guide to be mentally prepared for any outcome, good or bad.

Its universal principles needed to be continually absorbed and applied at every instance of despondency or delight.

As evidenced by Krishna and Arjuna, in the toughest of battles, in the most bereaving of crises, it was necessary to uphold our duties without any expectations.

We must do good, and fight to live, but live to do good all the must.

After completing her third cycle of chemo, the nurse noticed Kismat looking less than her cheery self. She handed Kismat a pamphlet about a wonderful peer group program and encouraged her to attend one at the hospital.

On the first day of her group therapy, Kismat found herself in a group of diverse faces, united by their chemo ports, varied catheters, and shaved heads. In subsequent meetings, Kismat saw that every member was comfortable enough to be naked with their thoughts, even amidst complete strangers.

"Ever since my diagnosis, I've become closer to God than ever in my life. I don't know if he's real or if it's even a He or a She. I got no family. God is all I got today," said one man, with third stage lung cancer.

"My husband left me a month after I got diagnosed. In the end, you have to be strong for yourself," added another lady, holding onto a cane because of second stage bone cancer.

The last testimony was shared by a man who was diagnosed with last stage pancreatic cancer, "the kind that Steve Jobs had," he added later.

He opened up about his wife passing away at a time when he needed her the most. In a few minutes, he broke down in front of the entire group. No one said anything further, but it was acknowledged that sensitivity was just as natural and integral to a man as it was to a woman.

Every now and then, the therapy staff organized painting and dancing activities and even celebrated birthday parties of its cancer-striken members.

In another peer group meeting, some members expressed their biggest regrets.

"I have a five year old daughter. Passive smoking ruined her lungs. And the worst part is that I was the smoker. God please, I want to see her grow up," a lady with advanced stage esophageal cancer bemoaned.

"I wish I hadn't been such a heavy drinker in my marriage."

"I regret that I didn't take care of my parents. A few pals just sent texts but didn't bother to ask again. Today, when I see my mother's teary eyes, I can see my guilt reflecting back at me like a blinding mirror. I hope my mother forgives me."

These sessions also provided avenues for members to cherish what they had left in their lives.

That evening, Kismat finally expressed her sorrow to the people who gave her life meaning since the day she was born.

The bond yield curve she had once postulated for them was showing signs of decline with the onset of Kismat's treatment.

"I'm sorry that you guys have to take care of me at an age when I should be taking care of you."

Ajay held her hands.

"Kismat, you've always made us proud."

Sita chimed in as well.

"You will be the same little Minni to us no matter how old you get. Now will you please let us fulfill our duties as parents?"

Even the basic task of using the bathroom was not without its set of grievances. The chemo had a tendency to cause constipation and cramping and Kismat would rejoice the day she managed to poop. The chemo would often produce fevers in her body that would persist for days.

Badi ammi employed her "*nazar utarna*" (casting off evil eye) ritual by preparing a mixture of mustard seeds, rock salt, and red chilies, placing them tightly inside her fist, and rotating her hand seven times around Kismat. Ammi burned this mixture on the stove. Typically, such a mixture would emit a strong odor but with Kismat, there was none. Badi ammi cited this as a sign that Kismat was deeply affected by evil energy.

Sita, on the other hand, would employ her Homeopathic pills to manage the side-effects. When Kismat would feel better, both ladies would feel appeased with their own philosophies.

Badi ammi seldom accompanied Kismat to her chemo sessions. Instead, she would keep herself busy by praying for her granddaughter at their home mandir, and preparing Kismat's favorite meals including khatti dal, saag, *kultha* dal, and parathas. In between this schedule of praying and cooking, Ammi would feed crows and pigeons with pieces of leftover roti as she would always do in the balcony of their Delhi home. If there were any cows lurking around in Jersey, she would have fed them too.

Of course, there were times when Badi ammi brought in more culture than what America could handle. At one particular dinner outing at their local Olive Garden, the waitress was pouring water in her glass when Ammi, in her native Himachali dialect, calmly added "Payede horr bich."

Translation: Please give me more.
The American couple seated nearby, mouth agape, kept staring at this sweet, elderly woman who sounded like she'd just cursed the server in public.

Humor played an important role in a journey laden with umpteen battles. In January, Kismat stepped outside to see all the snow that had piled up in her backyard. She was excited to make a full snowman, but the exhaustion from her last radiation caught the better of her. The following morning, Badi ammi and Sita rushed inside Kismat's room and told her that a miracle had occurred. Bemused by their words, she got out of bed to see what they were referring to.

"See that *shivaling* out there! Lord Shiva has graced our home! Now our Kismat will be okay!"

Sita and Badi ammi had placed a small garland on the partially melted snowman that Kismat had left incomplete the previous evening. Kismat whispered about her incomplete snow-making activity to her father. The two didn't say any word to the happy ladies who continued to pay reverence to the melting snow structure. Only when they left the room did both father and daughter laugh to their heart's contentment.

Every other worry in the Dharma household seemed insignificant in front of Kismat's health. Her recovery after cumulative effects of chemo was like the addition of a shining star in the dark sky; the starry night continually reminding them of hope, and of a new day to come.

Every day, Kismat fought the darkness.

One evening in particular, the sun seemed to set earlier than ever before. Kismat began shivering uncontrollably the same night she had completed her fifth cycle of chemo. Sita, Ajay, and Ammi did their best to cover her with layers of blankets and hot water pads but the relief was temporary.Adams Hospital advised the family to bring her to the Emergency Room.

It was snowing outside and slush had piled up on the roads. Dialing the emergency helpline was futile as the ambulance would have taken them to a hospital within the closest proximity which was not equipped to handle cancer patients.

In a span of three minutes, Ajay aided his daughter to get seated in the car, and drove the family to the Emergency Center which was housed in a different location from Adam's

Outpatient center.

Quickly, he wheeled her inside.

There was already a long queue of other patients to be observed before her.

Kismat, her bald head tilted to one side, was completely passed out from exhaustion and high fever. Ajay, exasperated from waiting for half hour, persuaded one of doctors to check her.

The doctors did thorough examinations of her blood samples and urine and moved her to the ICU. Kismat had a serious septic infection which was further exacerbated by her weakened immunity.

And this was after completing only one course of the chemo drug. They put her on broad-range antibiotics to fight the infection.

Sita and Ammi's eyes remained fixed on the blood pressure monitor. Every fifteen minutes, the blood pressure machine would pump air and recalculate the disconcerting statistics about her sub-normal blood pressure and weak pulse.

As the antibiotics fought the infection, she was simultaneously receiving three bags of electrolytes that were slowly dripping into her body.

Kismat opened her black eyes on the night of the second day. She had no memory of being asleep for so long.

Her family's biggest concern was that Kismat hadn't eaten any food for over a day. The doctors changed her liquid diet to one that had more nutrition and recommended that she slowly start walking to prevent any blood clots.

There was a huge snow storm that had rattled the East coast only a week ago, and it seemed as if the outside chaos was mirroring the mental chaos of Dharma family. Even as Ajay went to work in between, Sita never left Kismat's side and she slept on a makeshift bed to keep her company.

By the morning of the fourth day, Kismat's health had improved to the point where she could walk with the help of a cane and consume more food than just vegetable broth and soups.

Each day, a nurse would come and draw her blood into a syringe for testing. Neupogen injections were administered to boost her low WBC count. In those seven days of her stay, her veins were flooded with fluids for nutrition and her arm was punctured with tens of injections.

The hospital was routinely filled with patients of varied ages and backgrounds; some on wheelchairs, some still lying on stretchers to await scans or treatment.

It was an overwhelming sight.

No one would expect such a sight to become ordinary but it eventually did for the Dharmas. It was akin to becoming immune to pain.

There were a total of six floors in the hospital and each floor was dedicated to a specific organ or a group of related organ functions. A panel of specialists came each morning to check on Kismat in their daily rounds.

After five nights in the hospital, Kismat was itching to get back home and enjoy the comfort of her own bed but the doctor had different news.

"I'm sorry but we will have to keep you here for some more time. Your platelet count is about 11k right now. It should average between 160-400k. Your body will produce more platelets on its own but we'll need to monitor it for the next few days. If we're happy with the count, we can let you go. Do you have any questions for us?"

"Can I please have a look at my blood reports?"

The hematologist handed her the copies. Kismat recalled that *haimatos* was the Greek word for blood.

Kismat took a minute comparing the readings and flipping back and forth between the pages.

"Doctor, I see here that the platelet count was completely normal the first day, then it dropped a little bit on the second, and then it dropped dramatically on the third and fourth day. What's the reason for this?"

"It could be because of the cumulative effects of the chemo," the hematologist replied.

But the oncologist responded with a completely different answer.

"Actually, we have never seen such massive drop in platelets on account of that particular chemo drug. I believe it might be because of the broad-range antibiotics, which is why we stopped administering them to you on the fourth day."

Both doctors arrived at the conclusion that it might have been because of a combination of both drugs.

"But how can you let my daughter take such medicines without knowing what they do for sure?" Sita added in a tone of hurt.

"Sometimes the medicines can have very adverse effects. We try our best to monitor the vitals."

The nurse later confided that the antibiotics had saved her life. There was another wing of antibiotic resistant patients, who had to remain in isolated rooms for treatment, with very little hope for recovery.

Only when her platelet level reached a safe 75k, Kismat was finally discharged.

After the prolonged hospital stay, Kismat decided to return to the remaining goals on her bucket list with renewed vigor.

She had survived six long months with chemo and survived a near fatal septic infection at the hospital.

Though she appeared weak from the outside, inherently now, she was fearless.

Time, as a human invention, may appear to be in our control, when in reality, it is far from it. A judge can announce how much time you must serve for a sentence; a doctor can estimate how much time your wounds will take to heal; a pessimist may approach every passing day with squandered time, and an unscrupulous capitalist may think of all the money he can make with every second of his time. Impatience disrespects the teachings of time and materialism prints it into a currency to expense our youth, and at times, our morals. On the contrary, patience teaches us to value the moments in which time resides.

And Kismat knew nothing more than to befriend time, whatever little bit of it she had left.

Three of her goals were remaining.

Goal #5: Go Scuba Diving

Goal #6: Sky Diving

Goal #7: Adopt Sophia

She added a final goal -- something that stemmed from her passion to dance in the privacy of her room since she was a little girl

Goal #8: Learn ballet.

Somewhere in the depths of her mind, she wondered the futility of this exercise. But all her life, she had learned that it is best to try anyway.

Before embarking on these remaining items, she had to consult her team of doctors.

Her most recent reports were in a safe range, but she was still advised to avoid the adventure sports and minimize exertion and exposure to crowded places to avoid catching any infection.

Of the four goals left, Kismat chose ballet first.

She reviewed a few dancing institutes in the City and picked one that offered an elementary ballet course during the early spring. Even though her family apprehensive of her health, Kismat had shown great resilience ever since she had been discharged from the hospital.

Within a week, Kismat got herself enrolled at the Broadway Academy; her class was due to start in a few weeks. On the morning of her first class, she wore a beautiful scarf to wrap her bare head, followed by a black leotard, leggings, and ballet slippers.

Each class began with a warm-up session to avoid straining the muscles followed by an overview of the five basic positions that would become the foundation of the extremely demanding dance form. The instructor, a red-haired lady in her fifties with the agility of a twenty year old, walked around to help her students with their movements. She aided Kismat in the correct positioning of her feet. She did the same to the arm and calves of another student so it would flow naturally with her body.

But what inspired Kismat even more was the presence of immensely flexible members of the opposite sex in her group. Their robust physique and fluid movements surely defied any societal concepts of what defined masculinity for a male artiste.

Kismat always assumed that the main requirement for excelling in ballet was having a lithe, flexible figure but she soon realized that it required far more demanding attributes. To become a professional, it was imperative to have an impeccable core and strong arms, calves, shoulders, feet and back. Pretty much every muscle of the body had to be employed in order to maintain the positions at a stretch of time. Over the six week course, Kismat also became familiar with some ballet parlance. She quickly grasped the ones that started with a "p"; the *plié* -- bending of the knees, the *porte de bras* related to the movement of the arms and the upper body, and finally, attempting (but actually falling on) the rare *pirouette*.

The most memorable moment of learning a new dance

form was when the instructor asked the entire group to place their hands near their thighs and feel the tension of the muscles when they would flex their toes to attempt en pointe. Sitting for hours during her days at W&W and now, her three hour long chemo sessions, Kismat would have never valued the amazing range of muscles that supported her relentlessly. Kismat may have learnt about the names of some important muscle groups in a high school biology class, but to experience the intricacy of these muscular movements through an expressive dance form was a humbling feeling altogether.

On the last week of her session, she received an email from a man she thought she would never hear from again.

"Hi Kismat,

Hope you are well.
Actually, I wanted to know more about the human rights project you were a part of in your college trip.
Can we meet?

Looking forward to hearing from you soon.
p.s. I promise I never forgot you.

Kindly,
Jason"

Kismat was simultaneously surprised and overjoyed
to hear back from him.
She replied soon after.

"Jason,
It's great to hear from you!
Please let me know what you need you to know.
I will try my best to answer them or direct you to the people who can.

Keep in touch,

Kismat"

To her surprise, Jason's reply popped up in her inbox the very same day.

"Hey! Actually, I will be coming down to Manhattan next month to participate at a conference for my alma mater. Are you in the City?
Let me know."

Then it struck her that Jason didn't know about her diagnosis. She responded back to him in full honesty, wondering if Jason would still be interested in meeting up.

"Jason,

Just to let you know, I'm diagnosed with cancer and
still undergoing treatment in the City.
If you want, you can directly connect with the Dean of
my college program. She can assist you better.
deanlagone@douglass.edu

All the best."

Jason didn't reply that day and Kismat was sure that he must have decided on an alternative course of action. But to her surprise, his email came in the wee hours of the morning.

"Ok, forget next month.
I'm coming down to New York City this weekend.
I really hope you make some time to meet me.

Here's my number.
723-654-XXXX
Jason"

She wondered why he was so adamant on seeing her after so many years. Kismat messaged him to confirm a time and place that would be convenient after finishing up her last ballet class. They both agreed to a grab lunch at a small cafe in the Lower East side.

On the day of her final class, Kismat thanked the instructor who wished her a quick recovery. Kismat quickly rushed to the women's bathroom and changed her attire to something more suitable for meeting a man she hadn't met in years.

She kept on the same headscarf and wore a button down dress as the weather was considerably warm and breezy. She hadn't used any makeup in years but something within her wanted to put some on for Jason.

First, she applied a line of black kohl that brought focus to the courageous optimism in her eyes. Then, she smeared a dab of rose colored lip balm on her cheeks and lips and used a tinted sunscreen that concealed most of the blotchiness on her face.

When she looked at herself in the mirror, she saw an old part of herself emerging once again, a part she thought she had long forgotten to play since the recent turn of events. Her dress and makeup added to her youthful self-esteem. As she headed off to the cafe, she wondered what Jason may think of her after seeing her in her new avatar.

When she entered the cafe, she saw him looking as handsome as he did before. It was as if he hadn't aged a single day. Jason didn't notice her right away as he was busy talking to a beautiful lady seated beside him.

How silly of me! He must be having kids by now, she thought.

She took a deep breath to overcome any pre-meeting jitters before walking over. Some people stared at her scarf as she made her way to his table.

He got up and gave her a warm hug.

She felt the same spark she once felt when he inadvertently touched her arm on the plane.

"Kismat! Thank you so much for coming."

The lady got up as well and extended her hand.

Kismat noticed that her smile was even more beautiful up close.

"Hi Kismat, I'm Clara Waugh."

"Nice to meet you Clara."

She had even adopted his last name, after marriage.

"I'm Jason's sister, by the way."

Kismat breathed a sigh of relief.

Good genes were not only running in that family, but they were going way past their designated speed limit.

"So, how are you keeping Kismat?" Clara asked her, realizing that Jason must have intimated his sister about her diagnosis. Kismat responded without bringing up the obvious subject of her treatment.

"I'm well. Just been fulfilling some bucket list items. Today itself, I finished a ballet course at the Broadway Academy."

"Oh, that's wonderful! I've been living in the City for a decade now and I take for granted all the opportunities this place has to offer. I might look into some courses now that you've mentioned it."

"How's your treatment going?" Jason asked politely soon after.

"The doctors do a scan every three months to check on the progress. I still need to continue on the chemo and radiation. Anyway, forget all that. How've you been? You must be an Assistant Professor by now, right?"

"You remembered! Yes, I teach some of undergrad classes in the Physics department. I didn't tell you before but I was so moved by my experiences in India that I wrote a whole bunch of blogs on it when I came back. I'll share them with you sometime."

"I would love to read them. India can inspire people in the most unexpected ways."

"Yes, she sure does have this unique charm about her," and

he smiled a little longer at Kismat.

"So, what was your most favorite place?"

"That's a tough one but I'll go with Benaras."

After ordering their coffees, Jason calmly added, "I know you must be wondering why I wanted to meet you in person and why I brought my sister along."

Hearing her name called out, Clara started speaking where Jason left off.

"Actually, Jason remembered how you told him about the wonderful kids you interacted with in Romania. In your email, you also mentioned an organization by the name of Meritas."

Kismat felt that perhaps Clara wanted to volunteer her time there.

"Actually, I lost my husband a few years ago. We didn't have any kids." Her mouth turned dry and she quickly sipped from a glass of water in front of her.

"I've always wanted to adopt. I'll be super grateful if you can connect me with the Romanian organization. I saw their website and loved their work! I trust your guidance since you have volunteered your time there."

There was genuine affection in Clara's voice. Kismat couldn't believe it.

It was as if her prayers were being answered for Sophia.

"Kismat, I know this isn't the best time to ask for your help. I won't mind if you refuse. And please let us know if we can help you with anything at all."

"Clara, you have no idea what your words mean to me! I'd love to help you."

Clara almost jumped in joy.

"I know of one girl who doesn't have any family yet. I can contact the teacher of the school and we can start the process from there."

"You're a godsend. Let us know what we need to do."

In the next few days, Kismat got in touch with Ms. Rosanna

and initiated the conversation between Clara and Sophia's school principal. Clara, who served as Senior Director with a repute Arts Institute in the City, had a round of video interviews with several administrators from Meritas.

The process for adoption was tedious but the Romanian organization was happy with Clara's financial stability and educational background.

A month after submitting her paperwork with the help of her lawyer, Clara was notified that they could start their formal adoption process for Sophia. Even though getting appropriate authorizations from the state could take up to a year for an international adoption, Kismat's volunteering connects and the recommendation of her University Dean helped to expedite the process. In three months, Clara could go meet their new daughter in Romania and bring her to their home in Jersey.

Clara and Jason were elated.

But Kismat was in a different realm altogether.

After all these years, she would get a chance to see Sophia again.

~

Jason would shuttle between his University and the City every weekend to meet Kismat and check up on her health.

Kismat was overwhelmed by his kind gestures.

Inwardly, she felt blessed to have him in her life again.

He made her an offer. He requested that she share whatever inkling of yoga she knew, in return for him to teach her how to improve her Cricket batting skills.

She agreed.

At their outing in Tomkins Park, he showed her the correct

posture of holding the bat and angling it according to the type of delivery.

She tried to match his stance.

He threw a few soft balls at her, but she kept missing them.

"Wait, let me show you."

He inched closer and moved his hands around her waist to correct her stance. She only hoped he couldn't tell how much she was attracted to him.

After a few rounds of bat and ball, she taught him about *pranayam*.

She explained how *Pranayam* gathers its roots from Sanskrit; *pran* meaning 'the life force' which comes from the breaths we take, and the other being *ayama*, meaning 'to extend.' Essentially, *Pranayam* was a way to cherish every breath we took. Next, she taught him a simplified version of the *surya namaskar.* Last but not least, she showed him the art of meditating in peace by sitting in a cross-legged position.

"Kismat, you seem like an expert."

"Honestly, I don't know any more elaborate poses. My best yoga move is simply to laugh my heart out."

"I never knew laughing was a part of yoga. What do you laugh about?"

"Nothing in particular. One doesn't always need always a reason to laugh."

"But how do you manage to start laughing out of the blue?"

"You don't need anyone to make you laugh. Just fake it."

"Fake it?" he asked, with a look of confusion swept across his face.

"Try it."

Jason started doing a fake chuckle and after hearing his own awkward laugh, he couldn't help but laugh out louder. Kismat started laughing by hearing him laugh and the whole exercise became a contagious activity.

The two of them headed to Saravana Bhavan on Lexington

Ave for a dosa lunch. At the restaurant, Jason noticed an eyelash on her cheek. He gently picked it up from her face; unsure of where the sudden courage of his latent affection for Kismat was coming from.

"Make a wish," he added gently, placing her eyelash on the back of her hand.

She gently blowed the little lash away, secretly wishing that she would get to meet Sophia while she still had the chance.

“Kismat?"

She looked up, hoping Jason wouldn't be able to tell her genuine liking for him from her eyes.

"Yes Jason?"

"I really want to make it up to you for all that you are doing for my sister. You have no idea how much it means to her. Is there anything I can do?”

“Yes, you can stop asking me that question.”

“Ok, how about you go on a trip with me? It might take your mind off things,” he asked, as he dipped his dosa in his sambhar bowl.

“I already am. Every time I meet you, I feel like I'm on a holiday.”

But Jason didn’t give up.

“I remember you mentioned something about a bucket list when we met at the café with my sister. What else is left on that list?”

“I have two things but they're just adventure sports.”

“What are they?”

“Scuba diving and sky-diving.”

“Ok, great. Let’s do them together.”

“Look Jason, please don't be compelled to return a favor. I don't know how much time I have left and that is why I want to try those experiences.”

“No one knows how much time they have left Kismat! Besides, I can use some adventure in my life.”

Kismat decided to consult her team of doctors. They had ruled out any pulmonary or cardiac toxicity from the chemo. Though her implanted chemo port would pose no issue underwater, her oncologist advised her that her immunity could be compromised from the dive. For the time being, she had to rule out scuba-diving.

However, her blood work showed that her biomarker was at its lowest level since the onset of the disease. And the side-effects from chemo were at their minimal best.Her next appointment was scheduled a month later. It seemed as if God had given her an open window to soar in the sky.

Jason upheld his promise to her.

He picked her up from her home in North Jersey.

She introduced him to her family as an old friend, even though they shared a connection that transcended the concept of old and new.

Though Sita and Ammi were not happy about her risky endeavor to jump from a plane, Ajay convinced them to let her go. These goals were Kismat's means to get some control in penning the narrative her life and Ajay had sensed this too.

Jason and Kismat arrived at the skydiving facility in Long Island, an hour before their scheduled jump. The facility was located in a vast green expanse in the vicinity of Westhampton Beach. It was equipped with two small aircrafts, a landing strip, and tons of open space flanked by the Atlantic Ocean; miles away from the skyscrapers of Manhattan.

Kismat was about to cross of the eighth item on her list. Patiently, they waited their turn amongst three groups; all keen to jump for their own unique reasons. The crew made sure the weather was acceptable for tandem jumping since the wind thrusts could disrupt their safe landing. Everyone was made to sign off their lives in necessary waivers. Finally when their names were called out, Kismat and Jason suited up with the harness and gear before making their way to board the plane.

One of the tandem jumpers made an attempt to test the full extent of Kismat's courage.

"You know, sometimes the parachutes don't work."

"I am already getting a dose of karma every month with my chemo. Worst case scenario, I'll get a dose of reincarnation too," she joked back.

As the plane gained some more altitude, Kismat glanced at her window seat and started to become more aware of the craziness she was about to embark on.

Jason, who seated beside her, had a similar countenance of nervousness. She smiled at him which helped to ease some of his impending fears.

There were five other passengers aboard the flight, including an older age couple. Kismat was impressed by the mere fact that they were so venturesome at their age. The lady's eyes met with Kismat.

"Is this your first time jumping, dear?" she asked Kismat.

"Yes. How about you?"

"Every year, my husband and I skydive on the day of our wedding anniversary. We got married just out of school and we are celebrating our fiftieth today! Can you believe it? We must have spent more money jumping off a plane than traveling on one."

The couple did not appear to be so old as to be celebrating their golden jubilee. Perhaps their childlike spirits did well to keep their hearts ticking young.

"What? That's amazing! Where do you get the courage?"

"Let's just put it this way -- I've had more exhilarating experiences getting French-kissed by this man than I have had from jumping off a plane," and she simultaneously winked at her husband.

As Kismat continued her banter with couple, Jason was asked to move up to the front of the plane as he was due to jump next.

"Kismat, I wanted to tell you something."

She paused her conversation with the adventurous lady.

Her eyes met his.

"Kismat, I was scared before but there's no point now when I'm about to jump from 13,000 feet up in the air."

"What is it Jason?"

The next words he uttered seemed to have taken some inspiration from the daredevil couple.

"I love you."

Jason proved to her that when it comes to duality of two beings in love, nothing else '*matter*'s.

The physicist in him framed his next question.

"Kismat, will you be a part(icle) of my un(wave)ring love?"

Because of the queue of other jumpers, the instructor who was linked to Jason's harness prodded him to hurry up. The bird's-eye view of the forest, clouds, and ocean below was breathtaking enough, but Jason's question left her completely breathless.

Before she could respond, he had already jumped.

A few minutes later, Kismat jumped off as well.

For a full thirty seconds, she was in complete free fall and could not comprehend the grandness of the view below her. Time had come to a complete standstill and each second seemed like a breathless eternity.

Her instructor let open the first parachute. Her movement became steady and she was now floating against the push of gravity. She was captivated by the sights of the cotton balled clouds and wondered how close she might be to that much elusive heaven.

There was just sublime bliss of realizing her minuteness in the world below; just a speck, a drop, a little particle finding her place amidst the air, land, and ocean waves below.

Finally, her instructor opened the second parachute and navigated their descent to the safe landing zone.

Kismat was now steadily gliding downward.

In those precious moments, she only had one person in mind - Jason.

The instructor high-fived her for being such a good sport during the landing.

When she turned around, she saw Jason standing only a few feet away.

"Kismat, we did it! Can you believe it?"

Tears started moistening her eyes.

He reciprocated by hugging her and bringing her even closer to him.

"Thank you Jason."

"For what?"

"For being here with me. For being who you are. For everything."

Their tight embrace conveyed everything.

Jason was present in all of her remaining treatments. His persistent endeavors to make her heart smile made her realize that the strength of true love doesn't lie in the grandest of words, or the most elaborate of gifts.

True love is being there for the ones we love, even if they are at their worst, and we, at our best.

Universality of Love

Clara had finally received her Romanian visa and necessary clearance to meet the newest addition to the Waugh family, who had turned ten only a week ago. She flew down to Sighisoara and brought Sophia to her home in the City, located just a few blocks from Central Park.

Clara had invited Kismat to Sophia's homecoming at their apartment, but she was scheduled to receive radiation that day. At Kismat's insistence, Jason drove Kismat to her apartment as soon as her treatment was over.

She would be seeing her again after nearly a gap of seven years.Jason and Kismat took the elevator to Clara's apartment floor.

The thirty storey building had striking views of the Hudson and it was equipped with a swimming pool, a kids and fitness center. Kismat was thankful that Sophia had found a loving home with Clara and after all the emotional hardships she'd been through, she'd never have to worry about comfort again.

Suddenly, Kismat became a bit apprehensive about entering inside the apartment.

Would Sophia remember me? Would she even want to see me?

Would she be angry at me for not seeing her after so many years?

Kismat tightly held onto Jason's hand, those very thoughts racing her mind.

Jason gently whispered, "There's a part of you waiting over there. After all this time, you deserve to see her as much as she deserves to see you again."

Dressed in a simple yellow dress and white shoes, Sophia looked just as endearing as Kismat remembered except she had grown a bit taller. Her hair had grown several more inches as well, which was neatly clasped with the help of a matching hairpin.

When Kismat had just turned twelve, she had playfully asked her mother, Sita, "Why did God only make women have babies? Do I need to make one too? It seems like so much work."

Sita assured her that the reward of bringing up one's own child surely surpasses any pain or work.

"*Minni*" as Sita would lovingly call her, "a mother's nurturing roots have the power to develop any small sapling into a sapient tree."

"But what if I put all that effort and my kid is not nice to me?"

Sita chuckled. "We still kept you, didn't we?"

Kismat walked towards Sophia and embraced her immediately. Her arms had been aching to hug her since the day she left Romania. Little Sophia hugged back with even more warmth.

"I missed you so much. Do you remember me?" Kismat asked hopefully.

"Sophia, this wonderful lady is the reason we are so lucky to have you with us today," Clara added.

"Da, I showed you my mama's photograph at the church!"

She showed Kismat the pink beaded bracelet on her right wrist.

"Look, I still kept your bracelet."

Sophia gently touched the grey scarf that covered Kismat's head.

"Where is all your long hair?"

Kismat held little Sophia's hands.

"I gave it away to someone special."

"All of it?"

"Yes."

Sophia took a look at the length of her own hair.

"Can I give away mine too? Then we will both look the same."

Kismat kissed her cheek and handed her a decorated doll and a box of chocolates, the few things she could purchase at the last minute. Sophia kissed her back to convey her liking for her presents.

"Jason, I think you and Kismat should spend some time with Sophia this weekend. She would love to explore the City with you. Would you like that dear?"

Sophia's face lit up.

Before leaving, Kismat passed Clara a countenance of deep gratitude for giving her that opportunity.

On a clear Sunday morning, the trio made their way to the subway to take the 'A' train to Broadway.

There were a couple of minutes before the next train was due to arrive. An old man was leisurely stringing along on his violin, as the rest of the commuters waited for the train to approach. The man had the cover of his violin resting in front of him. A few dollar bills were scattered here and there from donations of passersby.

Sophia continued staring at the senior artist.

"I would listen to music like this on the radio, but I never had enough money to see a live performance at the opera -- today, I could."

She opened her small white purse that she had lovingly strapped onto her chest. She found some coins and a few dollar bills that Clara had provided to her. Sophia walked over to the few square inches of area occupied by the struggling artist and smilingly said, "Thank you for playing."

She set all her coins and the bills into his box.

The old man put his hand on his heart to express his sincere thanks to the humble little soul standing before him.

Their first stop was a 'Toys R Us' store. Sophia enjoyed going on the free rides inside the store but to the Jason and Kismat's surprise, she didn't make any demands for toys. Even after much insistence from Kismat, Sophia refused to pick out a new doll from the store and expressed her contentment with the doll she was already gifted.

Kismat's maternal instincts to love, teach, and protect Sophia grew with each passing moment she spent with her. They made a pit stop for lunch. Kismat ordered a kid meal box for Sophia, a salad bowl for herself and a veggie quesadilla for Jason.

Post lunch, they headed to Central Park.

At the entrance to the park, a young man with a backpack and a baseball cap started haggling Jason to buy tickets for a comedy show later than evening.

"Hey sir! Yes you! Do you and your wife want to see a comedy show tonight? Your daughter can come in for free."

Kismat turned pink.

"My wife makes me laugh all the time. Maybe next time," Jason humored him back.

After more futile attempts at persuasion, the man found another couple to attend to.

"Jason, it was very sweet of you to say that. Thank you."

"But, I was just saying the truth."

"What do you mean?"

"Wait, I'll show you."

Jason guided Kismat and Sophia to Belvedere Castle housed inside the park premises.

"This place reminds me of Bran Castle!" little Sophia exclaimed. The Castle, though small, was a mix of Romanesque and Gothic style of architecture, giving both Kismat and Sophia the feeling that they had landed up in famed Bran Castle in Brasov.

The three of them further climbed to a quiet space on the observation deck of the Castle, with a captivating view of the sunset overlooking the Turtle Pond. In between these two souls, all of Kismat's uneasiness about her future seemed to evaporate.

Moments later, Jason held her hand, and asked with the most earnest eyes she'd seen in a man –

"Kismat, can I be your husband? It would make me the happiest man."

It was the second time that day that her heart was struck with such intensity of emotions; nothing but pure love bursting at its seams.

Yet, she felt Jason's kind spirit deserved more.

"But Jason....my diagnosis..."

"Kismat, you have made me feel more alive than I have ever felt before. You are magic, you know that?! Can we share this life together?"

She couldn't hold back from kissing him on the cheek and finally saying those three precious words to him.

"I love you."

"Kismat, can I kiss you? On your lips? I don't want to risk you having an infection..."

She kissed him immediately and neither of them could end the tenderness of their love for each other. Their first kiss was extraordinary, so much so that they became completely oblivious to everything around them; to the world of tourists and rushed City natives; the chaos of people's voices colliding with the big city noises.

It was only when Sophia lightly tugged Jason's shirt that they finally ended their brief moments of romance on the deck.

Contrary to the definitions of what an ideal lover may be, Kismat's heart rarely raced in his presence; her mind seldom flustered. She was always at ease from his gentle embraces and the ways he intertwined his hand with hers. The definition of a soulmate is personal to those that invent it; yet she knew Jason had manifested as one.

Finally, they landed up near the streets of Times Square to show Sophia how amazing that junction can look all lit up under the starry, night sky.

Sophia took a look around. All that her innocent eyes saw were big adverts of beautiful people in lingerie, nightclubs, movie trailers with extravagant clothing and cars.

Kismat recalled her own days of working in Manhattan and passing by the signage. The Vogue covers and electronic billboards did nothing more than paint images of ideal human figurines. Kismat herself hailed from a country that prided itself on beauty pageant winners and if ranking women on physical attractiveness had affected her in her youth, she wondered how a little soul like Sophia would be impacted by these sights?

But Sophia's eyes did not bother with the aforementioned impressions of *maya* – these illusions of happiness. Rather, she told Kismat that she was tired and wanted to go home.

When they finally got back to Clara's apartment, Sophia embraced Clara immediately.

"Did you have fun today?"

Sophia nodded, but as Kismat made her move to leave, Sophia held onto her hand.

In the presence of Clara and Jason, she said something with such heartfelt maturity that it gave Kismat so much more than what she could ever ask for.

"I didn't like God when he took away my mama."

Kismat and Clara were now standing on either side of her.

"But today, I really love him because he gave me two new ones."

~

Karma was resting inside one of the rooms within the maternity wing of a hospital in Gurgaon. When she opened her eyes, she saw a smiling Bharat sitting close by, holding their baby girl in his arms. Two years ago, she could have only dreamed of such a sight.

"How are you feeling?"

"Exhausted. How's our baby?"

"Rama, she's the most amazing and beautiful thing I have ever seen in my life. Her little fingers and her precious eyes and her cute little nose. I think she's got all my good looks."

Karma's heart smiled in joy.

"Let me hold her."

Bharat gently placed their daughter in Karma's arms.

Karma planted a light kiss on her baby's forehead. The baby woke up from the few tears gently flowing down from her mother's eyes.

Both Bharat and Karma's lives were now eternally connected to her.

"Bharat! Can you believe it? This is OUR daughter."

Bharat needed some moments to let that feeling sink in.

"Rama, thank you for giving me the best gift of my life."

Karma was fully conscious of how her body had changed and the stretch marks that the delivery left behind on her breasts and tummy. But Bharat had already apprised her of the value of such scars in their first meeting.

Karma was exhausted and was ready to take a nap when a nurse popped in to check on the health of the baby and the mother.

She began marking some items off her list.

"Ma'am, have you thought of a name for your daughter?"

Karma and Bharat debated on the names and eventually

settled on *Sanjana,* if it were a girl, or *Sanjay,* if it were a boy. But when she held the miracle that is her daughter in her arms for the first time, she chose a new name altogether.

When a person realizes their purpose and follows through on it without expectations, by virtue of their noble actions, they achieve true self-fulfillment, which is a key pursuit of all beings.

Krishna represents that divine unity of our destiny and actions.

She shared the name with Bharat, who gave his wife the exceptional authority to name their child.

"Krishna," she told the nurse.

"Ok, I'll get some papers ready and you can all go home with Krishna shortly. Congratulations once again!"

Little Krishna beamed when she heard the nurse say her name. The baby had inherited the soft cocoa complexion of her mother and father, much like her namesake God.

In Sanskrit, 'Krishna' means dark, and even translates as one who is 'all attractive.'

Karma recalled the day when Kismat had told her that Krishna would drop by at her house some day. She finally understood the meaning behind her friend's words.
Kismat had indeed lived up to her promise.

~

So many remarkable changes had happened over the course of the last year.

Kismat had been reunited with Jason.

Sophia found a loving home with Clara.

And Kismat had completed all, but one, goal on her list.

Her next MRI was coming up in a week's time.

The last scan had shown no major improvement.

In fact, the oncologist suggested that more cycles were necessary, possibly even for the rest of her life or till the time her body could stomach it, whichever came first.

This time, Jason, Clara and Sophia were also present on the day of her MRI result.

The doctors were shocked to see her final report.

All her scans were clear.

They called her an outlier from the bell curve; her family called it a miracle, sounding the curved bells of their North Jersey temple.

Doctors attributed her survival due to her young age, lack of other risk factors, tumor typing and the fact that this was the first occurrence of the disease and so her tumor did not develop any major resistance to the medication and radiation.

Her family attributed it to the strength of her positive spirit. Both views weren't detracting each other's merit. Rather, they complemented each other.

Kismat made sure to give individual hugs to her bevy of nurses at the Cancer Center. The doctors recommended that she come back for periodic scans as this was just a remission and not a complete cure.

Jason and Kismat decided to have an intimate wedding in Florida, post which they would complete Kismat's last and final goal of scuba diving in Key West.

After all this time, Kismat finally reached out to Karma to share the news of her recovery and invite her to her wedding.

"I was really worried that you left without meeting me. Madhav had given me your letter."

"I'm really sorry Karma. You were right."

"About what?"

"That I don't have an answer for everything..."

"But you did....you told me to have faith...regardless of what happens. And the most important thing is that you're okay now. I'm so happy for you and Jason!"

"Honestly, I really didn't think this day would come. How are you and Bharat?"

"You'll be happy to know we are parents to a beautiful girl."

"Really? I'm a Masi (aunt) now! This is the best news!

"Actually, you are her cheriyamma!"

Karma admitted that she would not be able to attend her wedding with baby Krishna in tow but she would be present virtually through a video call.

Six months later, Jason and Kismat tied the knot in the island of Key West according to Hindu Christian customs with their closest family in attendance.

Kismat's hair had grown to a short length by the time of her wedding day. She was dressed in a light crimson sari and kept her jewelry to a minimum. Jason matched her traditional Indian attire with a beige *kurta pajama*.

Everyone came up to the couple, one by one, wishing them the best in their newly married life. The only gift they requested was to make a donation to a cancer fighting charity of their choice.

Clara had a surprise gift, which she revealed during her toast to the newlyweds.

"Jason, I couldn't have asked for a more wonderful brother than you. You have always been a constant source of strength for me. When Mum and Dad left us for heaven, you became my best friend. And Kismat, you have been an angel to us in so many ways. There are very few people who are as kind and brave as you. Words are not enough to express my gratitude to the both of you. On this special day, I feel blessed to name you both as Sophia's godparents."

Sophia was dressed in a soft pink colored Indian suit with matching bangles. When she heard her name out loud, she started blushing, matching the color of her attire.

After some interlude of musical performances put together by Kismat's cousins, the time came for the couple to recite their vows.

Jason went first.

He didn't make use of any paper or other form of writing to read them aloud. He just started speaking directly from his heart.

"In school, I learned that two particles can be entangled if they are close together and their properties are linked. Even if you send those particles away from each other, they remain inextricably connected. But Einstein was apprehensive of this whole 'spooky' quantum entanglement because it lent to uncertainty in the classical understanding of particle behavior. Instead, he proposed that everything related to the properties of those two particles is already decided well beforehand. Bohrs, on the other hand, was the first to indicate that there is some inexplicable connection between the two. Clauser and Freedman's novel experiment proved that this particle connection is indeed relevant and true."

The folks in the audience listened on intently but their countenances were marked by confusion in grasping all the scientific references.

"My dear Kismat, this is exactly how I feel about my connection with you. When I traveled to India, I received the biggest awakening of my life. Einstein's argument had given me the impression that the uncertain outcomes we experience cannot be changed as they have already been decided by our destiny. On the other hand, Bohr's view made me feel that we have the ability to change what we experience because at some deeper, conscious, subatomic level, we are all connected to each other through our thoughts and actions. I met many people and restlessly moved like a pendulum between those two ideas. But when I saw you again, with all your zest for life, regardless of what you were going through, that's when I stopped looking outside for an answer and started to look within. I can no

longer separate my scientific knowledge with my spirituality. They, too, are connected more than I could have ever imagined."

The audience's confusion dissipated with Jason's last line.

"Honey, the point I'm trying to make is that there are still many things I don't know and they continue to ignite my curiosity about the world but there is one thing I'm definitely sure about, and that is -- I want to spend the rest of my life with you."

Kismat kissed him on his cheek before commencing with her vows.

"It's often a challenge to try and define true love with just a single word. In my life thus far, that word has changed several times from commitment to sacrifice to honesty but today, that one word, for me, is peace. In peace, you discover that you had everything all along. This concept of peace is not easy to grasp and may only be realized when we have experienced love and its lessons from being brokenhearted. Of course, it is an absolutely brilliant feeling to love another person and even better, if it is reciprocated. However, we often rush ourselves into love, when in reality, peace only comes with time. As for me, I've come to learn that we may find many who touch our hearts but only a few who can really awaken our soul. Jason, I have experienced such a rare form of awakening and unconditional love with you."

She took a moment to wipe the tears that had slowly moved down her cheeks.

"Jason, I always believed that anytime I have bared my soul to someone, they have been some form of a soulmate to me, whether it was the kids at my school, my closest friends, my family, or you.

As my fate was decided by my diagnosis, I felt fortunate enough to continue fulfilling my goals. In that pursuit of my bucket list, I asked for eight goals, but you and Clara gave me even more than what I anticipated.

You fulfilled a ninth wish.

You gave me the love of a new family -- as your wife and as a godmother to Sophia."

The bride and the groom culminated the beautiful ceremony with a tender kiss. The whole audience erupted in cheery applause for the newlyweds.

The same kiss was beautifully captured by the photographer who later framed it and found its way on Kismat and Jason's side table in their new home, along with the photo of their skydiving adventure.

But there was a final adventure awaiting them.

Two days after their nuptials, the newlyweds got ready for their early morning scuba dive.

Their instructor, Santiago, was a burly man with multiple tattoos on his arms and legs. His skin was showing signs of sagging owing to repeated sun exposure.

Santiago told them that they would be diving in a special, reserved area westward of the Keys, which had less depth than other sites, keeping Kismat's recent recovery in mind. Santiago began his training with a simulation of scuba diving procedures inside a shallow pool so Jason and Kismat could get a feel of the equipment and effectively communicate underwater. He stressed that they needed to be careful as the slightest touch could infect the delicate reefs.

Santiago taught some preliminary hand signals so that they could safely navigate their boat in an orderly fashion behind his to reach the diving spot, which was a twenty minute boat ride from the pier.

The first signal was like drawing an imaginary halo with the index finger. This was a signal to press the acceleration pedal and increase their speed. The second one, making a fist, indicated that they needed to slow down and the last one signalled whether they needed to move left or right.

Jason and Kismat proceeded to their designated boats that were neatly docked to the pier. A question arrived as to who would sit in the driver's seat. Jason did his best to mask his nervous sweat by citing it as an after-effect of the heat and Kismat happily obliged to be their driver.

"You can drive on the way back so we both get a chance," she added as they seated themselves on the boat.

"No, that's okay. I want you to enjoy. Besides, I'm happy being a passenger."

"Are you sure?"

He nodded profusely.

Each time Santiago would make a halo and signal them to drive faster behind him, the world around them seemed like an action packed blockbuster. It was as if Jason was Bourne personified and Kismat was his *femme fatale* accomplice to nab the bad guys who were trying to escape by sea.

Of course, the stunts were nowhere near as cool as the movie but Kismat had no trouble letting her imagination soar. Jason often caught himself holding onto the sides of the boat as Kismat sped their boat to get ahead.

"Don't worry Jason. I won't capsize our boat."

He didn't do much of sightseeing of the daunting sea around them. His eyes were fixed on Kismat; joy radiating from every cell of her being that no radiation could touch. She was soaking in every minute of the exhilarating drive, as the cold water from the ocean splashed onto their bodies under the benevolent sun.

When they finally arrived at their destination, Kismat lightly stepped on the brake pedal to bring them to a comfortable halt.

There was nothing but a large expanse of water surrounding them, inspiring them with its serene calmness, and yet challenging them with its innate strength. There was no land, no civilization till as far as their eyes could see.

"Do you guys see that small expanse of purple in the ocean?"

Santiago pointed in its location.

That's where you have to swim to see the beauty of the coral reefs below."

Kismat encouraged Jason to jump in first.

When he didn't budge for a minute, Kismat softly asked, "Is everything ok?"

"Oh, nothing. I don't know how to swim," he said, matter-of-factly.

"What?! Why didn't you tell me before?"

"Because I didn't want to miss this experience with you."

Kismat's heart completed a cartwheel in joy.

"I'll stay here in the boat with you."

"No Kismat, you've come so far. Don't stop because of me."

In the midst of their back and forth politeness, Santiago noticed they hadn't jumped in yet.

"What's the problem amigos?"

Kismat told Santiago about Jason's reservations. Though Jason pretended to be fine during the training, he became very apprehensive to breathe from the scuba mask in the sea. Santiago assured him that he would not let anything happen to him.

"Our first instinct is to breathe out of our nose. Our mouth only comes into the picture when we are gasping for air after an energizing activity like running or swimming or....sex."

Santiago gave out a loud chuckle, but the humor did little to mollify Jason's nerves.

"Try covering your nose with your thumb and index finger. This will force you to breathe through your mouth and through the mask."

After repeated attempts, Jason finally got the hang of it. The instructor stayed close and helped Jason paddle his feet with the fins. Slowly and steadily, the three of them made their way to the coral reef patch within the large expanse of the sea.

They saw a kind of civilization they had hitherto seen before. It was like seeing a rainforest submerged underwater.

There were a host of mollusks, crustaceans and other marine species floating in and around the colorful corals. Sea anemones and cnidarians tried to run past them as they paddled to get a closer look of some of the other splendid aquatic life. They even spotted a baby shark that sped away just as quickly as its sighting. It was startling to see the extent of biodiversity compacted in such a small space.

Kismat noticed that his right leg was very close to a coral structure. She pulled him close. As their eyes met through the scuba goggles, she could see that his happiness surpassed hers, for he had seen a world that he would've never encountered because of his fear of being underwater.

Santiago took a photo of the two of them with his waterproof camera, though Kismat and Jason had already captured that precious moment through the lens of their eyes.

~

Three years later, Kismat faced a major relapse as the cancer resurfaced; this time in her right breast.

In a span of five months, it spread to her lungs and liver, despite aggressive chemo and immunotherapy trials. The cancer cells kept outsmarting whatever chemo was thrown at her.

The doctors at Adams Hospital intimated the Waugh family that they had run out of options.

An unperturbed Kismat conveyed her love for her family and her friend Karma before her passing, but not before penning a letter for Sophia, just like the one she had written for Karma when she left for the States.

~

Karma started working as a Senior Analyst at a bank and continued to volunteer at Madhav's school on the weekends.

Bharat finally got around to setting up his own software investment firm with two of his closest friends. Both Karma and Bharat setup a fund to support the higher education of all the students at Bal Bhavishya.

Little Krishna developed a strong inclination to dance, following in her mother's footsteps.

By the time she turned five, Karma enrolled her in Bharatnatyam classes.

The Naidus decided to spend Krishna's sixth birthday in Kochi with the rest of Karma's and Bharat's extended family. Though Karma had taken her daughter to Kerala before, this trip would be unlike any of her previous family trips.

Karma held her daughter's hand as they climbed the flight of stairs to the temple. Karma hadn't set foot in that temple ever since her mother had passed away.
First, they paid their respects to an idol of Goddess Lakshmi.

A line of devotees waited in a chaotic line to pour milk on a *shivaling*. Krishna was amused by a lady who was fervently whispering into the ears of the *Nandi* idol.

"Can I go say something into the cow's ears too Ma?"

Karma used to queue in such lines and whisper in a similar accord when she was at that tender age.

She nodded and little Krishna made her way to the decorated Nandi.

"Well, what did you ask Nandi?"

"Oh, I didn't ask for anything. I just said thank you... for everything."

Karma was shaken from the wisdom that Krishna shared and embraced her daughter immediately.

"Do you know why we are here, dear?"

Krishna shook her head.

"I want to share something with you that your *Amma* taught me when I was your age."

"What is it?"

"A prayer."

They were now facing two idols.

One of Krishna and the other of Radha, standing close by him.

Karma used to stand in that very spot with Lakshmi when she first taught her the sixteen-word chant of the Krishna mantra.

"Whenever I've been in trouble and I needed help, this mantra helped me to stay strong. It carries our names and connects you to me. I just want you to know that, no matter what, I'll always be there with you."

Ha-re Krishna, Ha-re Krishna,
Krishna, Krishna, Ha-re Ha-re
Ha-re Rama, Ha-re Rama
Rama Rama, Ha-re Ha-re

The words of the mantra connected three generations of women - Lakshmi, Karma, and Krishna.

But it was more significant than that.
It symbolized the means of doing good and finding the good in everyone.

Pieces to Ponder On/ Epilogue

Is our life wholly fated to destiny, or is it a sum of our actions, or a combination of both?

A scientist by the name of Lemaitre first sowed the seed that the Universe started out as a "primeval atom."

Further pursuit of this idea led to acceptance of the Big Bang theory which suggests that the Universe originated as a hot and dense mass full of energy that expanded rapidly close to 13 billion years ago. Through various forces, that energy transformed over time and led to the formation of the galaxies and stars which are made up of elements which are made of atoms which are made of subatomic particles, namely electrons, protons and neutrons and which all boil down to the same energy it once started out with.

Quantum mechanics postulates that the sub-atomic particles carry a unique wave-particle duality as demonstrated by the double-slit experiment. The most notable fact that maintains the validity of the Big Bang theory is that the present day components of our universe still seem to be moving farther away due to the expanding space between them and even that space carries vacuum energy.

Since everything came from one big energy source, then wouldn't everything in the universe be related to each other? Or would the continuous expansion hinder our shared inter-connectivity?

That is where the theory of quantum entanglement comes in to shed some light and raise some more interesting questions. From the galaxies, to planets, to humans and all life-forms, they are all made up of the same set of elements and molecules at macro level and subatomic particles and energy at the micro level. Since everything is essentially made up of the building blocks of matter, can this idea evolve into human experiences and how we experience relationships in reality?

As different materials that transition from one quantum phase to another and large number of subatomic particles get entangled, can it be true for how we perceive our entangled connection with each another?

~

Uncertainity of Life

The whole world is, in and of itself, a game of chance and all matter is ruled by probability.

Classical Newtonian laws of physics originally suggested that the properties of momentum and position of all matter can be predicted at a definite time, with certainty. But quantum mechanics changed our thinking and added more depth to our understanding of the duality of particle-wave behavior using Schrodinger's equation and uncertainty of prediction using Heinsenberg's uncertainty principle.

Today, every microchip, laser, and electronic gadget runs on the validity of this quantum theory.

Balance Beam of Destiny and Actions

The body is a complicated piece of machinery with cell regenerations, secretions, neural transmissions etc. taking place every second to keep everything under equilibrium on the physical plane. But it's interesting to think how equilibrium works on the mental plane. The balance beam is a representation of that.

Kismat and Karma

As for the story of Kismat and Karma, one of the key themes is how our interactions with those who are similar to us, or have had similar experiences as us, can make us better.

Can 'like cure like'?

A Note about Homeopathy

Homeopathy originates from the Greek words, hómoios, "like" and páthos, "suffering." Hahneman, the founder of the field, postulated "similia similibus curentur" (like cures like) or simply put, what makes us ill is also what makes us better (or the aphorism – what doesn't kill you, makes you stronger).

Homeopathy is based on using diluted preparations of natural remedies to stimulate the body's own healing mechanism to bring it back to equilibrium. The practice focuses on treating the person, as a whole.
The body consists of millions of energetic subatomic particles that create their own vibrations and can be affected by the vibrations around us. Every system of the body, whether it be reproductive, circulatory, nervous, immune, endocrine etc. work in harmonious conjunction with each other. Any disease is an imbalance in the body's energetic plane.
This is is vastly different from pharmacology which works on creating synthetic/chemical preparations (e.g. pain killer oxycodone mimics real-life opium) to treat the symptoms.
The two practices cannot be conflated.
While Homeopathy, like any other system, can't guarantee a cure, it is worth a try to alleviate symptoms without the harsh side-effects of pharma drugs.
However, in matters of any serious illness, it is better to depend on life-saving pharma drugs as the first line of treatment.

Efficacy of Homeopathy

The Prasanta Banerji Foundation in Kolkata has been treating cancer patients from low-income backgrounds for decades. One noted remedy in the Foundation's protocol for brain cancer is Ruta graveolens, a native herb of southeastern Europe that was cultivated for its medicinal properties.
Ruta's effectiveness in naturally inducing the death of brain cancer cells and promoting the growth of lymphocytes to strengthen immunity was even published in a report by MD Anderson, the highest ranking cancer hospital in the States.
Personally, Homeopathy has worked wonders to remove my warts, regularize my menses, manage my post-traumatic stress after my

father's demise, recuperate after surgery and even helped my baby's gas, coughs, and any digestive complaints.

ABOUT THE AUTHOR

Sakshi Sharma

Born in Delhi, Sakshi has spent nearly as many years living in Delhi as she has in the United States.
She has worked in finance teams at Johnson and Johnson, Penguin Random House, Helen Keller International and also interned at Columbia University Press.
Sakshi formally started writing on her blog (kismatandkarma.wordpress.com) when her father got diagnosed with last stage cancer in New Jersey.
Till date, she has published poems in Hindustan Times and Rutgers University magazine.
When she is not blogging, she does funny dance videos with her two year old at her Insta handle @mere_meer.

Printed in Great Britain
by Amazon

32290694R00178